NEWS OF THE AIR

NEWS OF
THE AIR

JILL STUKENBERG

BLACK LAWRENCE PRESS

Black
Lawrence
Press

www.blacklawrence.com
Executive Editor: Diane Goettel

Cover Design: Zoe Norvell
Interior Design: www.ineedabookinterior.com
Cover Art: "autumn forest in the mist" by Igor Vitomirov

Published 2022 by Black Lawrence Press | Printed in the United States

*for Yvonne and Keith,
and for Travis and Julian*

Our daughters stroll together in the garden,
Chatting of news we've chosen to ignore

—from "Parent's Pantoum" by Carolyn Kizer

TABLE OF CONTENTS

PROLOGUE

THE FIRST TIME the borders closed, Allie Krane, thirty-six and pregnant, had just passed into the city. Her basketball-sized belly inconvenienced a shoulder check, so she pulled without looking to the far lane of the exit ramp, leaving behind the knot of slowing traffic. There were no barricades here, not like by O'Hare. She followed the curlicue of the ramp to the museum's underground garage, the same route she funneled every day.

Allie left the noise of it behind—the vague reverberation of sirens always a part of city life. In the cool damp of the empty basement, in her lone ride up the elevator, she didn't trouble to wonder what it was this time: protest, or one of the things the protestors variously protested against. None of it—city life or office life—was weirder than being pregnant, living inside her own wobbling, expanding orb. Nor that yesterday she and her husband Bud had woken in a musty cabin in distant northern Wisconsin to the calling of loons. The smell of lake water lingered in Allie's hair.

Behind her desk in the museum's front entryway, she slipped her feet from her shoes and soon began to think of eating her lunch. She'd been the only one coming in since the grant had run out, about the same time as the start of the summer's turmoil. On her way to the breakroom, she paused at each of the office doors vacated by "the museum kids," as she'd thought of them. But her younger co-workers had taken their odd degrees and their odder haircuts and cleared their stuff weeks ago. Gavin was not in his office, the last one on the right.

At the cabin this past weekend, Allie and Bud had brewed morning tea in an electric kettle, and Allie had waded into a lily-padded lake to swim, her pregnant-lady suit billowing around her. She'd gone three days without thinking of this place, office or city. While Bud had first introduced her to the Northwoods, Allie was the one most recently in love, the one who'd insisted last Friday that they hop in the car last minute. It was so hot in the city, and since becoming pregnant, she'd craved silence and cold the way women were supposed to want peanut butter and pickles, peaches and dirt.

She was standing with the workroom's refrigerator door open when she heard the noise—a blare or burst, a buzz of static. Allie froze, not unlike the number of deer they'd caught in their head-lights last night, those they'd seen and those others watching from the dark fields. City sounds didn't normally rise to this floor, but following the tinny warbling, a sound that turned into a human voice, frantic, backed by sirens but relayed electronically, she found Gavin. He was in his office after all, on the floor, under his desk with a laptop.

The bits of metal in his ears and above his lip glinted.

"Allie."

"It is I," she said in the light, teasing tone he and the other museum kids used, ten years her juniors and possessed of their own way of talking, of taking in and assessing the world. His eyes flick-ered over her belly. But that brief moment with Gavin had been more than a year ago, before Bud, when Allie's first marriage was breaking up and she'd first found herself in the city.

There was something about his hand that was odd, a mitten or a glove wrapped around it.

"You the only one here?"

Allie shrugged. What was he watching? She leaned for a glimpse at his laptop.

"They closed the airports," Gavin said, the fear in his voice a contrast to his sprawled body. All the museum kids had lounged that way, perching places Allie hadn't thought of as chairs.

"They're still permitting business travel," Allie said. People with the approved-in-advance documentation. And all day yesterday they'd been warning people about the airports, though maybe only she and Bud had heard it, Allie's new husband the last man on earth who listened to public radio. Allie herself did her best to avoid the news.

Gavin shook his head and sighed. He rubbed his eyes. That her politics were different than his—than everyone's in the office—had perhaps been what attracted him to her for that minute. She was a puzzle to solve, code to crack. But Allie wouldn't say she held a set of politics, of any kind.

They caught sight of the smoke outside the window at the same time. Allie registered its jellyfish motion, a ballooning upward, before she took in the muffled sounds, sudden cracks, its successive partners elsewhere in the city below. It all seemed very far away except for the shiver in the building beneath her bare feet. Soon the whole sweep of sky had turned the same swirling gray as in the scene on Gavin's laptop.

"Oh, Gavin," Allie said, as if he were her errant child. She rose, smoothing her palm over the heft of her belly. And then, looking down at him hiding under his desk with his little worried face, she thought of what in the office was hers, what she needed to leave this place. Not much. A mug, a plant.

Gavin followed her to the parking garage. He asked, cradling his arm, if he could get a ride. Oh all right, Allie said. She'd returned to thinking about the Northwoods resort where she and Bud had stayed, Eagle's Nest. The one they had come to think of as their cabin was one of eleven ramshackle structures perched along the north rim of a small lake—all of it perennially for sale, or so they'd joked last night, returning again and again to the idea.

An hour later, Bud exclaimed at her return—why hadn't she turned back sooner? It was all over the news! But he didn't notice, not immediately, the box of her things in hand, her work shoes dangling, and she didn't tell him who'd ridden out in the trunk of her car, a former lover with a bleeding hand. Nor about the time she'd spent stopped at a checkpoint drilling her nails against the leather steering wheel while the baby kicked, as if it too had caught sight of the tanks. The car, a Benz, was all she'd taken with her from her first marriage, a thing that had vanished beneath her like a blown-out bridge. So far the baby was all she had from the second—but was a baby ever really your own? Allie didn't tell Bud that while she'd waited a military police vehicle upended in a flooded ditch nearby had sparked and smoldered, and then begun to drift in the muddy water, as if this were just what cars in the city did now—float away.

Bud had not even tried to go into the library, his job. He'd spent the morning on personal research at home. Did she know that many small resorts practically ran themselves, the same guests returning year after year like extended family members? He'd looked up the property taxes—wait until she heard.

For Allie and Bud, buying the Northwoods resort, moving

there, became a plan that survived the joking stage, the dream stage. It remained reasonable, possible, do-able even the next day with the downtown rubble cleared, the expressways and airports re-opened. Travel was to be permitted again; the protestors had been dispersed. On the whole if the world were changing—its weather patterns and disasters, the sheer number of people and how and where they lived, worked, moved, and what there was to feed them—it was only changing as it had always been, in increments, with time enough for response if things got serious. The day's confusion had been temporary, some kind of glitch.

Still, it wasn't a bad time to invest in a vacation destination, Bud mused. A domestic one—for the avoidance of future border hassles. No matter what was going on in the world, people would always need their little getaways.

PART I

CHAPTER 1

PENCIL! SCISSORS! CAN opener!

At first the children's cries were only vaguely alarming. Allie heard the shrieks from inside Pines, where the late summer breeze ferried their voices, isolated and individual, like lost birds or straggling summer tourists.

The old cabin's wooden floor was strewn with the detritus of the project she'd begun at the start of the summer, more like a flood had washed through than a remodel was underway. A pulled cabinet perched atop the debris like a glacial sheaf ready to slide. Allie bent to extract one wooden handle from the rubble. Could this be the good hammer, subject these last months of a near manhunt in her household?

Jack knife! Screwdriver! Another gust brought the children's voices as if offering guesses.

Now, Allie was in her fifties. She'd lived long enough—eighteen years—in a northern, rural county that she'd learned to guard her energy. Still, *such* screaming. She followed the cabin path to the resort's small beach, tapping the tool. She only frowned a little noting a place at the path's edge where alternating rains and drought had nibbled. Thin strands of swaying grasses and the rash of spike rush that Allie was encouraging held everything—the one small clearing of their lawn with its swing set, horseshoe pits, bonfire circle—from ruin.

Reaching Maples cabin, Allie understood what had been nagging her in the children's cries: they weren't followed by splashes.

"Corkscrew!" The girl called, twisting as she dropped, not into the water—glittering in the near distance with the inviting sheen of a Leinenkugel's commercial—but from the top bar of the swing set.

"You supervising this?" Allie turned to her daughter Cassie. The woman she was becoming flickered like a strobe light beneath the girl she'd always been—the one who could track deer, wriggle a hook from a fish belly. Allie tapped the heavy tool she still carried against her thigh. Its mysterious end terminated in short stubby spikes, each like a teenager's lip stud.

"Not well," Cassie answered, shrugging.

"Who are these children?" Allie asked.

Little Eagle wasn't a large lake—in fact, Eagle's Nest was the only resort on it, unless you counted the very first place Old Ferdy, original proprietor, had attempted to build, the remnants of which lay directly across the water from their lawn and beach. Thousands of interconnected lakes pockmarked the Northwoods of Wisconsin. At its far narrow end, Little Eagle connected to Big Eagle Lake, though by low water in August even kayaks in the narrow passage would tangle in the swirling weeds and knock against submerged rocks—especially these past Augusts.

Allie and her family had grown accustomed to meeting strangers in their yard—people who found their own way from the parking lot to their assigned cabin or walked out on the dock before ambling up to Maples for official check-in. They didn't usually arrive by canoe, nor did children appear without adults. Allie scanned the water, but it lay flat and empty.

Her daughter stretched her long legs and stood from the chair. Cassie often earned tips entertaining people's kids, more if they never discovered she was homeschooled. Then they thought she'd be impressed by twenty.

"Are you visiting someone on Big Eagle?" Cassie addressed the boy.

"We *saw* the eagle." The boy avoided her eyes.

Clearly siblings, the children had similar dark hair and eyes. Both wore swimming suits, the boy's the baggy style that fell past his knees, the girl's a one-piece with straps that crossed at the back like the X-shaped bars that ordered marionette strings. For it being the end of the summer, they seemed particularly pale. Video games, Allie figured.

"Can we go swimming?" the boy asked.

"Kate always makes us wear our life jackets," said the girl. "Like if we're *near* water."

"Could we play with that paddleboat?" The boy was already in motion, calling over his shoulder. The paddleboat had spent the summer tipped against the grass bank, its white belly a beached sea creature's, the flap of rudder in the crotch of its back nook the comic completion.

"It has a leak," Allie said.

But Cassie grinned. "It's okay. I'll help them." Despite the money she made off their parents, just as often Cassie "helped" new kids by getting them soaking wet, tripped up in lake weeds or turned around in the woods, shaking from stories of what might have been a bear or crazy ex-lumberjack with a chainsaw. It was something Allie used to admire in her girl—she was fearless and reckless and playful—if lately the trait had come to seem like something other kids would have grown out of by now, by eighteen.

Allie paused by the canoe, its seats of frayed lawn chair netting. Two pairs of battered high tops comingled in a puddle of water at the bottom. No life jackets. Still no sign of any adult in a second canoe out on the lake.

She turned her back on the scene, taking her new tool up to the house.

When they'd first come up here, Cassie only a heartbeat (*already* a heartbeat, highway billboards insisted), Allie had imagined a child who'd know which berries to eat in the woods, who would ski with her through the back country, all that snow falling with no notion as to border. Friends thought they were overreacting to leave the city, despite its heat waves and brown outs, water contamination and shootings. In response, Allie began saying she wanted to live *less* deliberately. In the story of her and Bud leaving the city, she became the one who wanted it most, pregnant and drawn to the woods and the wild.

And it was true the city hadn't imploded behind them. People still lived and worked and shopped there, more or less as they always had. If masked from time to time. If required to carry documents.

Two decades later, instead of a child who could navigate the El, Allie had a Northwoods girl. Give Cassie a wheezing car engine or outboard motor and she'd get in there with her bare hands and a screwdriver and nurse a sputtering turbine back to health. She baited hooks for thick-fingered tourists, for herself in winter for lines dropped through holes in the ice. She used to be as good too with scaling and filleting. More often these days, with catch and release, guests were as satisfied anyway with the selfie as with the hors d'oeuvre.

In Maples, Allie set the odd tool near the laptop. It had hiccupped all morning with incoming messages from guests trying to find their way, or who were just now as they were leaving wondering what to pack. Should they bring their own towels? There *was* air conditioning, right? How were the cabins sanitized?

She picked up the business cell to call Bud. Her husband had chosen this week of all weeks for a trip to Minneapolis.

"Need anything?" Bud's voice tunneled through space. Allie didn't share what had become his nostalgia for city life, his occasional jones for a hip microbrew or new cannabis strain. He found traffic patterns interesting. So too drone surveillance and evacuation routes.

"Thought you were going to be home by four."

Bud said he *should* be back by then.

"Should? Where are you?"

A familiar silence interrupted her question. "Hello?" Allie spoke into the blankness. It wasn't their end, she knew, not since last year when Cassie had ordered the new satellite system, set up the fancy modem. Now guests stalked about the front lawn of Maples with their phones outstretched like water witching dowels. Some believed the signal to be governed by the old horseshoe pit stakes, half-hidden in the tall grass where the mower circled.

"What's going on?" Bud asked when the signal resumed.

Allie drew the curtain of the small window that looked toward the lake.

"Cassie and some new kids are playing with that old paddleboat."

"That's got a hole in it."

"Cassie knows. She's been the one saying she'll fix the thing." Allie peered through the window.

"That's what I should have picked up. Some fiber glass repair."

Ostensibly Bud had gone to the city for a gauge, something someone was selling online but for some reason couldn't ship, and which he needed for his latest project, home brewing—not beer but biodiesel. In the past he'd involved Cassie in undertakings like these, her home-based education folded in with his lifelong one. But for half the summer he'd been at work in the garage, tinkering, before Allie and Cassie knew what he was up to, or how it was connected to the pretty lime slime that occasionally formed on their lake, floating from one end to the other. In Cassie and Allie's view, though even they didn't swim in the mass directly, the algae separated the real swimmers from the sissified.

"Isn't today the day you give Cassie her phone back?"

Allie had been about to accuse him of having forgotten the orchestra regrouped tonight, thus signaling the end of summer, and end of the Northwoods Girls Orchestra mothers' confiscations of their daughters' phones. It had turned out that even girls who sported shit-kickers and badly cut Fleet Farm jeans could get up to trouble on social media. But Allie wondered if Cassie were ready to have hers back. She thought of the way she had greeted the new kids, something hard in her grin.

"Should have given it back weeks ago." Bud had been against the whole thing—a communal punishment like from the time of Salem. "I don't think Christina ever had hers taken," he mumbled.

Allie put the phone against the flesh of her arm, muffling it. She'd heard Christina—closest they had to a neighbor girl, Cassie's childhood best friend—had taken over her mother's job as bartender at Tiki's, a half mile away on their same side of Little

Eagle Lake. Allie didn't know what Bud thought he was doing bringing up either Christina or her mother, Shara.

"Did I lose you again?"

"I think we should build a little porch off Pines."

Bud sighed. "You should see the porches on the new houses already going up along the river."

"Is that only as far you are?" There'd been mudslides along the St. Croix all spring, Minnesota and Wisconsin crumbling away from one another like the eroding grass banks lining the cabin trail.

"I'm farther than that," he said. "I'll be home soon."

"Guess we won't retire on a houseboat though." Bud had a knack for circling back to his own subject. Did Allie know there'd been one washed all the way to Missouri? *One what? A houseboat.* From the point of view of the people in it, looking out their curtained window as they floated downstream, it must have looked like the rest of the world was leaving them behind, rushing north.

Little Eagle still froze solidly in winter, a phenomenon guests weren't around to observe but nonetheless wanted to hear about. Yes, each fall they had to bring in the dock, Cassie, Allie, and Bud donning waders and, their fingers clogged with cold, fumbling a J-hook or two to the deep. The raft came in too, the dislodging of the anchor a trickier affair, sometimes requiring Allie or Cassie to dive, to dig with their hands in the weeds and silt beneath. They swam the freed platform to shore, Bud with the dripping anchor their Triton.

Crossing to the beach, despite the wave of heat that greeted her on the lawn, Allie thought of winter again. It settled not long after the dock came in—absorbing them into its long white shock and breathlessness. After all these years, it had become the season

Allie longed for. On its other end, she'd be ready for people again, to greet them as fellow survivors.

She opened her eyes to the sight of small figures on the end of the dock, black outlines against the bright. "Hey," Allie called, "That water's too shallow for diving!"

But the new visiting girl departed from the top of the dock's bench before Allie's words reached her, tightening her legs and then flipping effortlessly, as if some great invisible hand had brushed her from her perch. The height and direction were alarming, incongruous, like a fall leaf jetting upward in wind.

She surfaced far out in the lake, her pale face bobbing over the dark water.

Allie strode along the wet dock. She'd brought her daughter's rhinestone-encased phone from the cupboard where she'd stashed it last June and gestured wildly with it now. "Hey!" She addressed Cassie, shaking the phone, her stomach folding over itself like a wave slapping the beach. Cassie knew their lake levels better than anyone, their fluctuation with the season, time of day.

She knew how easily girls could die.

It was the boy who responded, extending his hand. He was Marius, he said, small and officious. His sister was Miranda. "She's an experienced diver," he continued. "Don't worry. *I* know not to try the stuff *she* can do."

Cassie's eyes had tracked to the phone in Allie's hand. Allie could imagine its satisfying plop into the lake. Instead, she blew out a breath and made herself recall the day Cassie had saved the dog, a hot busy weekend like this one was going to be, with kids and parents and new and old guests in and out of inner tubes and kayaks and lawn chairs. Through the confusion of the crowd, of margarita pitchers and a freewheeling Frisbee game, Cassie had come bolting. She'd hammered the length of the dock at full sprint and dove, resurfacing with a small quivering dog in her arms, someone's pet that had been quietly struggling in the water, drowning in the midst of the party.

Quintessentially Cassie, the story almost always worked to calm Allie, to remind her of just who her daughter was—not a person who followed crowds, not a girl who'd only learned to toss her hair and wheedle and not how to do or act. She was not her teenaged trouble, that recent snag.

Allie held out her daughter's phone—gleaming prize that marked the end of a three-month punishment. Cassie began thumbing immediately, just as a second strange canoe nosed from behind the tangled top of an elm fallen over the shoreline.

The paddler sported a spiked silvery hair do, a fisherman's life vest, and a visor. She took in immediate sight of the kids in the water and Allie and Cassie on the dock, their attention trained to the small square of the screen.

"Where are your life jackets?"

Marius spit a fountain of lake water. "Kate! You found us!"

His sister had quietly submerged. Then, in a blink, she disappeared.

* * *

Bud, Allie's husband, observer of houseboats, was not dawdling along the St. Croix on his return home from the Cities. He'd woken early to beat the weekend's exit traffic, and now, within miles of Eagle's Nest Resort, he pulled to a stop in front of the Wild Fire Post Office. The two dropped calls might have given away how close he was to home. Only here in Vilas County did the old copper cable lines and sparse cell towers knit together for such a perfectly leaky, totally inadequate telecommunications net.

Across from the Post Office loomed the new watercraft dealership. It had sprung from nowhere last May, blossoming like any newly transported thing, seed on the wind, pod on the bottom of a boot. The only other business to attempt recent root in Wild Fire had been a coffee roasters run out of a converted ice shanty. Looking at the two today—the giant lot of the dealership, its kayaks and lifejackets and jet skis pulled into a fire sale—Bud saw a shared fate.

He let the sleigh bells on the P.O. door jolt Tammy awake. The postmistress thought they were cheery, though Bud, at least his inner, former librarian, objected to the public alert of a government official when he was checking his own United States mail.

Even Allie hardly remembered it, but when they'd first moved here, there'd been a job for him at the tiny branch in Wild Fire, now long closed.

"Hey Tammy."

"Now did I call you? Thought I hadn't gotten to that yet."

In their box waited a dozen college brochures addressed to Cassie, even one from Wyoming. Bud flipped through, taking in long-haired girls leaning against oak trees, the hint of male legs in soccer shorts behind them. Cassie's ACT test last spring, despite a few dismal sub scores, had opened the door to this—and what bright luck. Bud had begun to worry that, for all the years they'd put into Cassie's early education—Bud and Allie divvying subjects, each choosing those that mattered to them—they'd too long ignored the question of her future. They'd raised a girl who could knock around here but had never been on an airplane, had hardly set foot out of the county, and didn't know enough of the world there for her taking. Not that Allie's reaction to the first brochures was the same as Bud's. Were people still going to college? She'd asked as if amused.

But Allie had a way of turning from the future as if it were a place one could choose not to travel. At least she'd finally agreed Cassie could attend a senior year at Satuit High School, a decision committed to, thankfully, before the trouble of last spring.

"What was that you said, Tam?" Bud called to the postmistress.

"You got packages out back."

Bud followed Tammy to the loading dock. They received everything at the post office, mail and deliveries, their decision a decade ago to re-do the resort's long driveway, to reconnect to a different spot on the highway a mile further down, having lost them entirely to the satellite map-making service on which everything relied. *You don't exist*, Bud had been told by online sellers, guests, even utilities providers. *Tell me about it*, he thought.

The mounded packages sat off to the side of the dock.

"You unload these Tammy? If you did, you don't have to do your Zumba this week."

"Some are for Tiki's," she said. "Could you run those out, you think?"

Bud squinted, deciding if he was going to take the implication: that he was such a familiar at Tiki's bar, such a close friend of Shara's, the bartender there.

"You don't have anything for Kent or Kendra do you?"

Everyone knew Shara had left town.

"Oh, you're the snoopy one. You'd be first on my case if I gave your mail to Kent."

Guests regularly confused Kent and Kendra's Eagle's Edge with Bud and Allie's Eagle's Nest, the two resorts separated by just fifteen miles. For his part, Bud tried to direct people properly.

Most recently, though, an entire bachelor party with reservations at Kent's had announced themselves too exhausted from the long winding drive through the trees to care where they stayed. Bud had put in a call to Kent, a courtesy, but hadn't heard back.

Tammy looked over her shoulder. "We're back here," she hollered, just as a kid—a twenty-something—stepped into the sunlight. B.J. Spring.

Bud grunted a hello of recognition.

B.J. was a scrawny kid with a bobbing Adam's apple and today he wore a red polo with a name tag. He came up with a new business every few months, more or less while the last was still in midst of failing. The coffee roasters had been his. Bud had heard he was working the floor at the new watercraft dealership, which confirmed it was owned by outsiders. No one local would have put B.J. in charge.

"Day off?" Bud could never resist teasing him. With the coffee shop, B.J. had made a big deal about roasting his own beans and "going green." He had purchased recycled to-go cups and announced alignment of Wild Fire Roasters with the organic grocery delivery out of Minocqua and the wood pellet manufacturer in St. Germain that used only local scrap. But where do you *get* your beans? Bud had asked on his first and only trip in, sliding over his well-worn plastic gas station coffee mug.

B.J. defended himself now. He was between shifts at the coffee shop and dealership, and he had a third job now too. He picked up a stack of telephone books.

"You got a fire to build?" Tammy cracked.

"For my backpackers. I've got to pick up my trailer at Kent and Kendra's and run another group out to Sylvania."

"What's your trailer doing out at Kent and Kendra's?" Bud

asked. B.J. was eager to fill him in. Now he was ferrying kayakers and canoers to put-ins and take-outs. Kent and Kendra let him use their ramp since they'd sold.

Here he'd got Bud. Kent and Kendra had sold? For years he'd wondered how he and Allie would ever retire, a seeming impossibility with guests at check-out lining up "their" weeks for the coming summer. And with the slew of for sale signs lining the back roads and highways—so much that when you remembered to notice, to see what you were seeing, it was like living in a Walmart aisle.

"Now who'd buy Kent and Kendra's place?"

B.J. dropped his voice. "You know their lake hooks up with the Wolf's Tail."

Bud didn't know if he'd known that. The Wolf's Tail stretched over the state line into Upper Michigan, disappearing into the Sylvania wilderness.

"Well it didn't hook up before," B.J. allowed, "but Kent saw what the water level did last spring—connected it for a time—and then had some dredging done to make it stick."

Bud nodded. It was just the kind of overinvestment Kent would make. What weekenders these days had the skills to picnic at the edge of the Sylvania, much less to kayak into it, to set off on journeys involving portages and compasses, the cell service and even rescue-copter view over the Sylvania notoriously bad, blocked by the canopy of ancient trees?

"State fine him for dredging?"

"Nah," said B.J., "that's why the state *bought* it."

Bud's face must have betrayed his surprise, his jealousy.

"They want to be able to get their boats in better. Rescue boats, patrollers. You want to ask him about it, you can give me a ride out there."

The large guest lodge Kent and Kendra had built only five years ago rose three stories into the trees. A single car with North Dakota plates occupied the empty lot—the adult daughter, Bud thought, the geologist. Locals took turns reminding each other of her salary, Kendra's story of the Canadian oil company headhunting her.

Before B.J. hopped out to reclaim his truck and trailer, Bud had a question for him. "If Kent closed on the Fourth, what did he do with his existing reservations?"

B.J. smiled. "Hasn't he been sending people to you?"

Bud thought about that as he sponged his way over Kent's newly re-sodded lawn. Eagle's Nest had been booked these last two months, such that Allie believed all kinds of fantastical things, from the economy taking an upward tick to her new yellow flag at the top of their driveway drawing in more highway traffic. But if their nearest competitor had closed up shop mid-season with no warning, and that was the increase they'd seen, they were in more trouble than they knew.

Kent sat on his lake-facing porch watching two children— grandchildren—dart across the green lawn.

"I gave our young B.J. a ride," Bud said. B.J. had made his way down to the truck and trailer parked by the boat ramp. It would take him a few tries to back that thing out.

"You been getting our people?" Kent asked.

"Think so."

An empty chair sat next to Kent, but Bud stayed on his feet, near-enough level with Kent for talking. He leaned an arm on the rail and took in the wool blanket spread over Kent's lap. It occurred to him that Kent might be sick, which wasn't something he'd thought on hearing of their sale, imagining their retirement. Italy, he'd thought. France. Kent and Kendra the kind of people who might have managed to squirrel away that kind of money—even the kind of money such trips required now.

His wife came from the house, screen door sighing before a final bang. Kendra marched past Kent and Bud toward the lake, only pulling up in her stride at its edge to holler across it. "This is private property, you hear?" Her shout reverberated over the dappled water. Her grandchildren kicked their soccer ball, unfazed.

In the distance, Bud could make out people in a small boat.

"We're getting them all the time these days," Kent said.

Bud shaded his eyes. He hoped it wasn't anybody from one of the reservations that Kendra had just shouted at. "B.J. said all his canoers were okay with you?"

"Folks B.J. brings are one thing. It's these others we get." Kent waved in a northern direction, toward the passageway B.J. said he'd had cut through to the Wolf Tail.

"Who else is coming through?"

"They come and go from both ways." Kent wasn't directly admitting he'd had the passage dredged. Poachers, Bud figured. Deer hunters who didn't see the need, herd sizes what they were and their families' freezers empty, to wait for a special season. He had met those families during the year he'd been a librarian in Wild Fire, before that little place had closed.

"The ones who know what they're doing—the one's B.J. brings—*they're* fine. Too many others just hike on in without the right gear. We've seen them come out half-starved, soaked through. Wearing tennis shoes full of holes. Or out with *kids* like that for weeks." Kent stopped, likely recalling that Bud had homeschooled his daughter and was maybe into that kind of hippie shit. "You should see what they leave. Crap floats up on the beach—clothes, plastic trash, diapers."

B.J. had the truck and trailer turned around and came over to join them. He dusted his hands together, as if that had amounted to work. "You should let me bring people in through your place," he said to Bud. "You still got that ramp?"

Bud could hear Allie's opinion on that—cars and people on the old road she was trying to grow over in habitat for pollinators, his wife another one who believed the flapping butterfly wings of her own actions could have effect on the world, as little as she otherwise wanted to venture into it or take part in it. "Sure," Bud drawled, "Kent makes it sound fun."

"Oh, B.J.'s backpackers are different," Kent said. "Doctors, lawyers, CEO types. They compete in these outdoor adventure races. Sometimes they're out for days running and canoeing, carrying their bicycles on their backs."

"They try to carry as little as possible," B.J. said. "One girl I picked up, I thought they should bring her to the hospital." He'd missed Kent's earlier complaints.

Kendra crossed to join them. She wore a pink tank top, white shorts, and no shoes, trailing her toes in the grass as if she were a young girl enjoying summer break. Not as if she'd just hollered at someone—possibly native someones—to get off her lake.

"You tell him the good news yet?" she said to her husband.

"B.J. told me most of it," Bud said. "Congratulations."

"Sometimes you're in the right place at the right time," Kent said.

Bud thought about the houseboat he'd seen on the river, the one he'd tried to explain to Allie on the phone. What would it be like to live in a house that floated? You could move so that you were always in the right place at the right time. You could move fast enough, which was how people had to move these days.

"We'll send over some new brochures and maps." Bud gave a slap to the railing post. He didn't have any more stomach for hearing about Kent's deal, whatever it was the state was going to do with this place and how much they'd paid.

Kent chuckled. "You want to talk to the people I talked to, you let me know."

"We're not there yet," Bud said. "Allie still loves it." Then he added something else, the truth. "She can't see how it's changed."

"But sometimes you can't have what you love now can you." Kendra crossed her arms as if to hug herself for the victory.

Bud gave no acknowledgment that the dig had landed. Everyone in town thought they knew the story of Bud's affair with Shara, bartender at Tiki's and mother of his daughter's best friend, just as they thought they knew what had happened with Cassie and the orchestra girls, with the girl who had died.

* * *

They found the girl, Miranda, though she surfaced in a different direction than any of them had been looking, back in the direction of the shoreline, almost as far as where the big willow trailed the water's surface near the west dock.

She'd come up on her back, just her nose poking above the surface. A hard thing to do after having swum that distance under water, Allie thought.

"Very funny," Kate called, clapping. Allie helped the new silver-haired woman pull her canoe near the one the children had arrived in. She'd introduced herself, sized Allie quickly, and produced her own phone.

"You get a signal here?"

"It's better by the main cabin."

"It's all those people on Big Eagle with their game cameras," she grumbled. "Taking up the bandwidth."

Allie nodded. She too had little use for excess electronic devices, or Big Lakers.

Kate stood with hands on hips surveying the front lawn and fire pit, the little trails that led off to the other cabins, the hammocks and lawn chairs—all as if returning to a place she knew.

"Well, we'll take one, I guess," Kate said.

"Huh?"

"A cabin? If you *have* a vacancy on Labor Day weekend."

Red Oaks was their largest cabin, normally held for large groups. Allie and Bud had spent a good part of one winter working on the loft railing, installing the spiral staircase. Now Allie stared upward toward the sloped ceiling, realizing with astonishment how long ago that had been.

"Surprised you have *any* availabilities," Kate murmured.

"You're lucky." People didn't usually show up on a holiday weekend without reservations, Allie might have added. Nor by canoe.

Kate squinted around the room one more time and then produced a packet of bills from her vest pocket. "That should cover the week." Allie nodded, taking it. It had been so long since anyone had handed her cash that she didn't know if she should count it. Kate wandered over to the kitchen table, running a finger as if checking for dust. Then she pointed to the ugly wallpaper runner rimming the kitchen, star fish and seashells in a pastel peach.

"Murphys hang that, you think?"

"You knew the Murphy brothers?" Allie herself had never met

the previous owners of Eagle's Nest, though she'd now spent nearly half her lifetime repairing what they'd neglected or slapped together badly: crooked porches and poorly fitted pipes, a giant half-buried propane tank slowly leaching into the garden soil.

"Lord did I." Kate crossed to the staircase, still behaving as if, were she to spy a crack in the plaster or loose banister rail, she'd ask Allie to log it: she and her grandkids hadn't done that.

Had she said she was the children's grandmother? Allie thought that was right. Then something annoying occurred to her: she couldn't rent Kate the cabin for a whole week. For years she'd been the one defending Labor Day as their end-of-season date, despite the dollar signs Bud saw in fall weekends.

She pulled the money from her shorts pocket.

Kate sighed. "You can't make an exception for a former Hodag?" She had wandered into a bedroom where she sat on one twin mattress and then the other, giving each a bounce.

Allie startled. The Hodag was the mythological mascot of the public high school Cassie was set to attend, starting up on Tuesday. But had she said that yet?

Perhaps that had been what Allie was avoiding, in forgetting the season was about to end.

"Satuit's the only high school left now isn't it?" Kate pulled her phone from her fisherman's vest pocket.

"There were more?"

"Three when I was a teenager. One in Wild Fire."

Allie hadn't known that. Where had the building been?

"I don't blame you for wanting to keep her close. Keep an eye on her." Kate had moved to the window. She was looking down to the beach.

Allie had been about to drop to the other twin bed, to give in to this random moment of pseudo-slumber party with the new guest to whom she'd rented past the end of their season. Now she cocked an eyebrow, wary. Kate thought she knew a lot about her family.

Kate gave a tap to the window glass. "Teenagers these days, right?"

Allie stilled.

"I had to get rid of our TV, our internet, just to keep my kids from watching it."

Allie bristled. She and Bud had seen one of the videos of the orchestra girls from last spring, a thing that had racked views on local social media like a captive ball pinging through an arcade game. But what did the video show other than kids drinking at a party, trying to act tougher than they were? The flutist lay passed out in a recliner chair. Someone had markered across her forehead. And then, unfortunately, the shot panned to Cassie, smirking.

"I don't believe everything I see on video," Allie said.

"Don't know how you couldn't believe it. You could tell each of those kids filmed themselves, some with bad angles, and some who hadn't poured enough fuel to do the job quick, only half their bodies catching."

Allie flushed. This was not Cassie, not the orchestra girls. No one had been able to look away from those other videos last spring, made one-by-one copycat style by teenagers in cities like Seattle, Boston, and Denver, all in the run-up to Earth Day. The videos started automatically in social media feeds, in pop-up windows, replayed later in your own memory.

"That your girl out there? She's got quite the sense of humor." Kate tapped on the glass.

Allie sat up for the view—not her usual angle on her own lawn. On the beach the paddleboat had been flipped upside down.

Abandoned and partially submerged, it banged against the shoreline in small rushes, tossed on the little waves that had come up. And face down in the sand lay Kate's grandson, Marius. Not a muscle twitched in his small body, the waves and the boat knocking at his feet.

Cassie and the girl lay three feet to the west, all of them as still as shipwreck victims. How long had they lain there waiting for Kate or Allie to return, to catch sight of them? How thrilling it must have been to imagine their fear.

Allie didn't know where it came from, the anger that propelled her down the stairs and across the lawn to the edge of the dock where her daughter's phone rested. Cassie looked up just as Allie raised her arm. "Mom! No!" she called, her voice breaking like it hadn't in years, like it hadn't since she was a girl—when she was a child and she had *had* to listen to Allie, *obey* her. And that was so satisfying to Allie, so clarifying, she nearly yelped with joy as the arc of her arm continued and her fingers released, as the phone sailed over the lake and Little Eagle snapped shut again over the hole.

Allie's heart rung like a bell, clattering and discordant. She didn't know what she'd been feeling all morning—dread, some quiet voice whispering *ruin*—until she'd found the release.

The look on daughter's face had been one of horror, and something else Allie hadn't seen yet this summer but had been waiting for: remorse.

And *good*.

A shimmer in the air above the water, maybe where the phone had gone in, caught Allie's eye. Evaporation—the actual, visible absorption of their lake on this hot day, in this hot dry week, at the end of this long dry month.

Bud said you couldn't see that when it was happening, but Allie could. She knew.

CHAPTER 2

NO, ALLIE SAID. *No*, they were *not* going to take Cassie's truck. Her daughter had started marching in that direction. Her battered Ford, dented and muddy on most days, parked perennially under a damaged, pitch-dripping maple at the far end of the lot, appeared in the afternoon light even more rusted and out of square than usual.

They only had an hour to get to the orchestra meeting in Satuit. Allie grabbed the handle of the garage door where her car, an ancient Benz, was housed, and gave it a heave, dust and debris falling. A bat colony lived above—an important species, one Allie wouldn't dream of running off. Reluctantly, Cassie lifted one corner of the tarp Allie kept over the car, just enough for her to slide into the passenger side.

Allie supposed she deserved this: wrangling the rest of the bat-shit covered tarp alone. Cassie adjusted her seatbelt, water still glistening on her bare arm. As far as Allie could tell, her daughter had simply pulled her shorts over her wet suit and shoved her feet into her torn flip-flops. She hadn't even grabbed a wallet or ID.

"You're *soaking*," Allie said.

"People dry."

That was true. People also developed yeast infections.

Allie navigated the turns of their driveway. Arriving guests complained about the zigging curves that further slowed the agonizing end of their long drives. Amid the lush green of summer they couldn't think of snow—and the necessity of creating places to push it.

She regretted throwing the phone. Already. "They call her Kate, huh?" Allie asked. She'd noticed the new kids calling their grandmother by her first name.

"What, you think they should call her *Mom*?" Cassie laughed meanly.

"Very funny." People regularly mistook Cassie for Allie's granddaughter—to Allie's embarrassment every time. It was true she'd been an older first-time mother—and in comparison most of the girls in the orchestra had already reached half their mother's ages. In the mistake, Allie heard judgment—as if there was something so off in the way Allie and Cassie interacted that people didn't think see them and think *mother and daughter*.

She turned to Cassie, to her large bare feet and too-long toenails pressed against the dash. All summer she'd squeezed against cabinets to get by her daughter in their kitchen, offered a goodnight wave instead of squeeze, left rooms where they both had reason to be.

Too often this summer—like what had just happened out on the dock—a knot rose in Allie's throat to look at her daughter, to wonder just who she'd become.

They arrived in Satuit for a view of its Friday afternoon, high-summer-weekend activity. Slowed-down tourists peered from car windows to read the Happy Hours of the restaurants and even putt-putt course. Location of an old train hub, Satuit was home to several thousand people in summer—larger than Wild Fire, where Allie would run for milk from the gas station—and on this warm summer evening people were out on the sidewalks and jaywalking in clumps. Allie gripped the wheel.

She parked in the large lot in front of the converted church where the Northwoods Girls Orchestra rented their space. Cassie's truck would have fit in better with the other vehicles in this lot, and Allie wondered if that had been what her daughter had been thinking. During her own childhood, in a Chicago suburb, her mother's luxury cars with their buttery interior upholsteries and iconic hood ornaments had embarrassed her, though the older she became the more she appreciated such cars. Despite what Allie's cars probably made her Northwoods neighbors think of her, nothing else felt as solid to her, as safe.

Cassie swung her door open to a wave of heat radiating from the blacktop.

"Ugh." She leaned back inside where she began pulling off her shirt, her legs hanging out with the door open.

"What are you doing?"

"Just a sec." Cassie rolled down the top of the tank suit. Allie couldn't look away in time and caught a glimpse of her daughter's nipples.

"Take a picture. It will last longer."

Dutifully, Allie circled around to the opened passenger door and attempted to shield her daughter. She could only be in one place, though, at one angle, and now Cassie was laughing at her for this prudishness as she stood to yank down her jeans. "These are *still* going to be wet from where I sat," she complained. She emerged with the flannel only loosely buttoned, braless, her jeans no doubt rough on her bare butt. She began working a rubber band—not a hair tie but a regular rubber band—through the wet mop.

Allie did not say *I told you so. I told you you'd be uncomfortable.* It was probably what Cassie had in mind, this entrance in dishevelment.

"You'll look like you've been having a fine time," Allie said. "Such a *nice* tan."

Cassie's face fell.

A blue vein ran from her daughter's neck down to her heart like an errant necklace chain, something confused about whether it belonged on the inside or out. She'd had that vein, so visible, since she was a baby, throughout girlhood.

But she was also a girl who, with only her own mouth and a hose, could transfer fuel from a jet ski to a snowmobile, and back again for the next change in season.

They filed into the orchestra room.

"I forgot to tell you," Cassie said, "we're going to the Freeze after this. On Nina's parents."

Nina Taylor's parents owned the Dairy Freeze. While most of Cassie's peers, like their parents, worked in tourist service jobs—cleaning hotel rooms or bussing buffets—Nina was another who might have been teased about the relative cushiness of her job, her summer tan.

"I don't see her." Now Cassie was craning around the orchestra room.

"Who?" Allie's eyes had drifted to the flute row. It was hard not to travel in that direction, the empty chair.

"*Nina*, Mom. I don't see Nina."

"Well, maybe she's not doing orchestra anymore."

"She's first chair. It's her senior year."

Allie looked at her daughter. Without her phone, how had she known about the plan to go to the Freeze after this meeting? She hadn't yet *talked* to anyone. Nina Taylor was one of her daughter's most forgettable friends, in Allie's view. She reminded Allie of too many of the girls she'd grown up with, their please and thank you's as tidily clipped as their swinging hair. Moving here, she'd hoped her daughter would escape girls like that, and the fate of becoming a girl like that, one like Allie had been for too many years back in one of her other lives.

"Oh? And what are the *other* girls saying about her?"

Cassie stared blankly. "I hope she didn't quit," she finally muttered.

Allie sighed.

Just the other day, Cassie had come on her own to Satuit, begging to make the sixty-mile drive for an important thing she needed before her first day of high school—of any school. When she'd returned, Allie looked for sign of a notebook or set of pens, a clean t-shirt or even something fun, a new jean jacket. But Cassie had driven all that way for a parking pass. No, there wasn't anything else she needed, she said, in her old jeans and bare face. Later, passing her daughter's truck in its spot in their lot beneath the dripping maple, Allie caught sight of the thin laminated card dangling from the rearview mirror. Why anyone needed a pass for the giant lot at the half-deserted school she had no idea, at the same time as she understood, without a doubt, that somehow Cassie had intuited the right thing, the only thing, necessary for fitting in at a Northwoods high school. It hadn't mattered that she'd spent the last eighteen winters in a cabin with her aging parents, her summers with the same smattering of tourists' children, that she'd been permitted to join the orchestra just last year.

She was such a quick learner. That was her troubling power.

For the most part the girls had taken their seats in their usual sec-tions, though because of the parents with them the lines between woodwind and string sections began to blur. A man in a ball cap wedged into the aluminum chair next to Allie—father of a viola player, Allie thought, one whose mother was a hostess at one of the nicer restaurants in town. Allie had heard they were transplants too—even that she'd been a dentist, or hygienist?, a decade ago in Texas. Ms. Tomas, the orchestra director, was from further south, Ecuador, and from a time when that had been possible.

"If I had a phone, I'd look up those kids," Cassie said.

"Huh?" The meeting was late getting started, the parents shift-ing uneasily on their chairs. Like it had been in the suburb where she'd grown up—Allie had groaned to discover it here—some orchestra parents sought their daughters' membership in the sole, sad hope of future college scholarships, and so the chance to leave. Allie wondered at these people, the old rules they still believed.

"Kate kidnapped them," Cassie said.

Allie laughed. Strangely, it reminded her of what someone had once said of what she and Bud had done to Cassie, absconding with her to the woods.

"You don't think Kate's their grandmother?"

"No," Cassie said. "She is."

"Well then."

"Didn't you see Miranda was trying to swim away yesterday?"

Well Allie could have said a lot about that—daughters who wouldn't listen. Just then, Ms. Tomas ascended the podium, raising her arms to command the attention of the room.

Behind her, Allie caught sight of Julia—the ragged shadow and wild hair of this infamous orchestra mother. She leaned against a wall of instrument cases.

"Look," Allie said to Cassie.

"*Mom!*" Cassie hissed. The girls did not talk when Ms. Tomas was about to speak. Allie wondered if she could learn that stern, already-annoyed look of the orchestra leader. Or what it would be like to have Julia lurk behind her looking so tragic and also, as she often did, bored.

Like a teenager herself, Julia slouched in too-short jean shorts and a too-low tank top. She was thin and wiry from a lifetime of work scrubbing bar floors and cleaning rooms. Her tan came from her third job at a beauty salon; it balanced her witchy black hair and makeup-darkened eyes. That Julia had to work hard was long understood—who didn't? Plus she was a single mother. Though when she'd started dating and then moved in with a VP with a mining interest looking at the Gogebic, this need for her to keep working became unclear.

Similarly, that she'd signed on again to work for Ms. Tomas, to lug equipment and photocopy sheet music, seemed bizarre. Her daughter, Hattie, had been the flutist who'd died.

Allie had been angry at Julia in the aftermath. How had she been responsible? But seeing her now, Allie's distaste melted. It shifted for the distaste she felt for everyone else in the room, staring at the woman. How had they figured out parenting today?

"Maybe she'll know what's up with Nina," Allie said to her daughter, and stood.

If no one talked while Ms. Tomas was talking, no one got up and moved across the room either. Behind the back of the still-speaking orchestra leader, Allie met Julia's outstretched arms and allowed herself to be pulled in for air kisses.

For those who'd wanted to single out Cassie, or any of the orchestra girls for last spring's trouble, for Hattie's death, let them find Allie's behavior here as odd as midnight flashes of heat lighting in September, as the booms people had been hearing near Crandon, events of sound though they had something to do with the earth.

Julia's scents dizzied—lotion and gum. Allie hadn't air kissed since the country club outside Chicago. As she pulled away, she felt Julia's warm arm trail her neck. Was her arm hairless? Was that the source of its smoothness?

Julia's grin revealed the lipstick smudged on her side teeth. "Girl," she said, punching Allie on the arm. "That's the way the European ladies do it. Don't look so scared." Her gold bracelet jingled.

"I'm not scared," Allie said.

"Hey, I've been trying to get a hold of Cassie all summer."

They both turned to Cassie, and to meet the eyes of everyone staring back at them, except Ms. Tomas, her flat rear shielding them as poorly as Allie had shielded her daughter stripping down in the car.

"That makes two of us," Allie said.

"You having trouble keeping track of that girl?" When Julia crossed her arms, the long pink nails of each hand dug into the bare upper arm of the other.

"No—she's been with us. Working all summer. I just meant, I guess, teenagers."

Julia cracked her gum. Now Allie was telling the mother of a dead girl what teenagers were like.

"Spent my summer on the boat," Julia said, brushing at her arm.

"I can hardly stand." She said it like it was a joke, though Allie was at a loss to follow. Was it innuendo? There were sea legs, which had to do with walking.

"Spent some time on a boat myself. Covered in fish guts."

"Aw, you guys are doing all right though, aren't you?" Julia was scanning the room. Without moving, she'd pulled her attention from Allie and Allie flushed, aware of the cold, of being left to stand here in the open. Julia had chosen this place to park herself.

"Julia?" Ms. Tomas turned to ask Julia for help. She had a stack of papers for her to hand around. There would be a release form this year.

And she had something for Allie, back in her office. Allie followed Ms. Tomas as the crowd of girls and their parents banged down from the carpeted risers. There Ms. Tomas presented a check, reimbursement for gas Allie had bought as a driver for a competition trip last spring. Allie pocketed it, knowing as she did so that Ms. Tomas hoped she'd refuse it. The belief among locals— because Allie and Bud had come from a city, lived tucked away on a resort—was that they were doing well.

"Don't worry," Ms. Tomas said. "I'll twist someone else's arm this year."

Allie understood she was being fired as a chaperone.

"It's good to get the younger girls' parents involved."

"I can see that," said Allie.

She returned to the main room for sight of Cassie at the far door, with Julia in the last crush of people leaving. Cassie managed to gesture, rocking an imaginary car wheel like a child pretending to drive. She was going to catch a ride with Julia. The two slipped out.

Allie had hoped she could talk Cassie out of the Dairy Freeze.

Allie followed the line of cars from the parking lot along the three streets that led to the Dairy Freeze, the late August air through her window like a salon's hair dryer—another old memory.

Last spring she'd been talked into chaperoning when Ms. Tomas had pleaded that she needed a mother unafraid to drive a van in a city. That life had been years ago for Allie. Nevertheless, she'd found herself accepting a set of keys in the early-morning dark of the Taco Bell parking lot where the orchestra girls were to meet. Ms. Tomas, circling with a clipboard and flashlight, announced another chaperone and her daughter, Shara and Christina, would ride with Allie and Cassie in the equipment van.

In the half-light, girls in sweatpants hauled pillows back and forth between cars, rearranging themselves. The back of the van weighted with cellos and basses, there would only be room for the four of them. Cassie scooted on the bench seat to make room for Christina, her old friend who'd introduced her to orchestra in the first place, who'd driven her to rehearsals last year—the first year Allie and Bud had let her do something like that. Now each girl settled against the opposite glass, earbuds in. Allie hadn't known yet about Bud and Shara, Christina's mother, and not knowing that, sensed nothing between the girls—who, apparently, did know.

Shara knew too—obviously. But if she'd thought at the time that Ms. Tomas had assigned them to carpool as some kind of joke, something for the other mothers to laugh about, she hadn't said, hadn't acted any differently.

Allie had always liked Shara, even before their daughters had met and become friends. Shara—who tended Tiki's bar just through the trees from Eagle's Nest—was sturdy and strong, most comfortable in jeans and hockey jerseys. She wore her long blonde-gray hair straight, no frills or fuss—though she did attend to her nails, painting tiny designs that she rotated with the season. On that trip, not long after St. Patrick's Day, Shara's nails featured shamrocks and stars. Her middle finger was tattooed with a purplish circle— a Minnesota Vikings helmet, she said, holding it up and grinning.

Her husband, Allie would think later, had an affair with a woman with a *middle* finger tattoo.

But unlike other people Allie had met, even in eighteen years of living in the Northwoods, Shara was easy to talk to, and that day she and Allie had flipped radio stations and chatted all the way to Madison, the snowbanks shrinking along the way. Their daughters in the back seat listened to their separate music and stared out their separate windows, but they were teenagers who'd been woken before dawn. Nothing seemed wrong until, in northern Madison, they'd pulled into the wrong high school. The large lot was covered over in such a layer of snow that Allie had to stop in the entrance. Clearly, no one else was here.

"When did it last snow in Madison?" Shara asked.

It must have been a while. The roads had been clear and dry. This high school lot looked like it hadn't been plowed all winter.

Cassie had an answer pulled up on her phone, though not to their question. You heard of high schools closing in smaller towns all the time—where one flood or utility-destroying ice storm, or one employer or grocery store pulling up roots in the night, affected everyone all at once, dominoes falling in a line—but Madison was one of the places everyone still wanted to go, supposedly.

Cassie texted Nina for the correct directions. The orchestra competition had been moved.

"We going to be late?" Christina pulled out an earbud, but Cassie didn't answer her long-time best friend—a thing at the time that had nagged Allie but didn't stay in her memory.

Shortly thereafter, on the same trip, Allie had her first real introduction to Hattie, the flutist.

Finally finding the high school, rushing in, they were assigned to change in a boys' locker room. The girls made no small show of trying not to touch anything. A smaller girl who had arrived that morning with her hair done in curlers—like Allie hadn't seen since her mother's generation—crafted a wadded mitten of toilet paper to open a locker. This was Hattie.

"Afraid you're going to get pregnant?" another girl said, just low enough. This was Nina—a tall girl with straight brown hair and eyeliner she must have applied in the car. She was Allie's daughter's newest bestie, Christina's replacement, though Allie was just picking up on the switch.

A few of the other girls laughed but Hattie only responded by laying more toilet paper across the bench seat, strip by strip, before sitting down to pull on her nylons.

Some of the girls had packed their black concert dresses within their giant instrument cases so these had to be lugged into the locker room, the cases opened, and the dresses shaken out. Cassie turned on the hot taps in the showers to get some heat and steam going "for the strings"—for the hopelessly wrinkled dresses too, Allie hoped. The girls swapped their boots for high heels (borrowed, ill-fitting) and began tottering around the tiling; they took turns with the sandpaper that had been laid at the entrance to the showers to scuff the scuffed toe bottoms further.

Only Hattie didn't dress quickly. She complained that the steam was making her sweat and stalked about the room in her nylons and small white bra. The curls she'd loosened from the rollers bounced in uneven ringlets. She'd yet to run her fingers through them.

She stopped circling to stand in front of a mirror, tilting her head to inspect the springing coils of her hair, the frizz that had escaped. She began to shake a mascara wand.

"We don't have time for that," Ms. Tomas said, breezing through the locker room. "Let's go, girls." Not only had they driven to a school that no longer existed, but they'd missed their rehearsal spot.

"But I only did one eye," Hattie wailed, still staring at herself in the mirror. She made a sad face. Then a sadder one.

"Just do the other quickly," Allie said, the mother standing closest.

"But how can I go out there with just one *eye* done. I'll look *ridiculous*." Hattie pouted.

"Come on," Allie said, "let me." Hattie handed her the tiny brush.

"Here you go. Now your dress."

"Are they *even*?" Hattie was still peering forward, eyes widened.

"No one's going to look at your eyes!" Did Allie only think that, or had she blurted it at a girl who'd be dead in a month?

The heat rose in waves from the blacktop of the Dairy Freeze. It was a wonder that the entire shack didn't melt against it like an upended cone. Thick cables snaked from the back, electric lines to generators. At the front, the line of orchestra girls and their parents wobbled in the heat.

Cassie and Julia had claimed a paint-flecked picnic table under an evergreen. Allie didn't care about joining the line either— realizing all at once its similarity to the viewing line at Hattie's funeral. It was all the same people. She wondered if Julia could be thinking that same thing.

"Not so many this year huh?" Allie said and then bit her lip. She would continue to say—accidentally, terribly—the worst thing. "So many graduated, I think. Last spring. A big group of seniors." Allie took a seat on the picnic table, feeling it tilt toward her weight.

"Only three graduated," Julia said. "But yeah. We're gonna have chair challenges."

So Julia was going to continue to work for Ms. Tomas, Allie thought, mystified—Ms. Tomas who'd made Julia pass out this year's new indemnification forms.

The complicated thing (among so many complicated things) was how unlikable Julia's daughter Hattie had been. She'd been tiny and snide, with her mother's compact gymnast's body and toughness but not her vulnerability; without the poorly done and cheap tattoos that invited sympathy, or her way of touching your arm, greeting you as *girl*.

At the funeral, Allie hadn't been able to think of anything to say to the grieving mother and felt the same loss now. What could you say to cover over the thing everyone was thinking—*at least it wasn't my girl?*

"What size shoe are you?" Julia said to Cassie.

"Nine," Cassie said. "Too big."

"I got this great pair of green heels. I'm dying to find the right Cinderella for 'em. I can't wear heels anymore, my doctor said."

Allie noted Julia's two-inch wedge sandals. Not heels in her book.

"Maybe your big friend," Julia said. "That girl with all the ink. She could probably use some shoes."

"Mom?" Cassie said, turning to Allie. "Can we go now?" This like she hadn't been the one who'd come here with Julia, jumped in her car so Allie had to follow.

"You get ice cream?" Allie asked.

"She's still around, isn't she?" Julia said to Allie. "Shara's girl. She didn't go to California after all. I heard you check in on her."

Now Cassie turned to look at her mother.

"It's not easy without her mom around," Allie said.

"That's pretty big of you," Julia said, though her head was cocked, tilted to the side.

It was uncomfortable that Julia knew the story too—Shara and Bud—though of course she did. When Christina had been accepted to Stanford last spring, a school most Northwoods kids would have had to google, it had highlighted the affair even more painfully for Allie. After all, who must have helped the bartender's daughter, even smart as she was, navigate that application to begin with, the financial aid? Someone like Bud, with a college degree. A former librarian. And Allie imagined the worse rumors that surely sprung up—maybe Bud and the daughter, not the mother. Maybe Bud and both. People didn't know the hours Christina had spent at their kitchen table throughout her childhood, how she and Cassie and Bud had trellised tomatoes and measured snowmelt in rain barrels, how with Allie the girls had studied Roman architecture, built a coliseum of cardboard. All of it made his affair with Shara, whatever had happened between them, more painful. Like there'd been something sinister, unwieldy and wrong, in the close alliance of their two families, living on their remote properties on Little Eagle Lake.

Allie looked to Cassie. Her shirt was misbuttoned. Two pimples near her hairline had scabbed.

"Did you see Nina yet?" The line had finally dwindled, and Allie could make out a pale arm slung from the serving window.

"No," Cassie said. "She's gone."

Julia popped her gum. "The Taylors moved. That's just Jorie

Jenkins in there, scooping out the last of the inventory. They already ran out of vanilla."

The Taylors had given away free ice cream a few times last spring, too, after the PTA and school board meetings, after Hattie. And after those freebie days Nina Taylor's name had stopped coming up in the tongue wagging, the online commentators shifting to vent against "those orchestra girls" as a collective.

"No," Allie said, scoffing, "they wouldn't move before Labor Day weekend." The Taylors owned the only ice cream shop in town. Labor Day weekend was the busiest tourist weekend of the year.

Julia shrugged, used to being disbelieved. "You can't have dinner?" she said to Cassie when Allie said it was time to go.

On the ride home, her daughter's big feet on the dash, the two lines of darkening trees enveloping them again, Allie reflected that her daughter hadn't known her friend Nina was gone, that her family had moved out of town.

Perhaps she'd not been cheating the phone punishment after all, as Allie had long suspected of her daughter who'd learned to code at eight, who'd built their business webpage and set up the internet satellite system. All summer Allie assumed that Cassie kept a burner phone stashed somewhere. Now she had to admit her surprise.

Perhaps Cassie was also unaware that Christina hadn't left for Stanford, had instead taken over her mother's vacated position at the bar and her one-bedroom apartment behind it, just half a mile through the trees. Allie had brought the girl food a few times, an extra jar of jam when she made it, dinner leftovers.

Allie still remembered Christina as a nine-year-old, lost and alone and stumbling through their woods. That day Allie had been hammering new shingles onto the roof of Hemlocks, their westernmost cabin nearly reclaimed by the undergrowth. First catching sight of the flapping flannel in the trees, she'd thought they had a poacher, some man trespassing on their property. Then Christina had come into focus—a girl, only a child her daughter's age.

Allie brought her home, fed her snacks and a tall glass of water, and was just pulling brambles from her hair as Cassie came thumping down the stairs.

Taking in the scene, Cassie had said, "We do *not* want any more eagles, thanks."

"Cassie!" Allie had admonished her. Cassie certainly knew the girl sitting in their kitchen was not the woman from the DNR who placed eagles every year—the large woman with an unfortunate skin condition and distinctive smell. It was true that both nine-year-old Christina and the DNR woman wore similar glasses—red-rimmed and crooked, a decade out of style.

How had her daughter, an only child, homeschooled, raised as far outside the known world as Allie could bring her, known so instinctively how to hurt another girl?

Christina was no pushover and had replied that day without missing a beat—leaning into the joke and telling Cassie she'd come to collect the eagle eyeballs, that they were delicious roasted. That had won Cassie: the new girl at the kitchen table was one of her own kind, fellow member of her own species. The two had trooped off together, friends by the time Christina's mother arrived to get her—and Allie had hardly remembered her daughter's dig, until now. Until what had happened this last spring.

Maybe if Cassie had been abiding by the phone punishment, it meant she felt she deserved it.

In line at Hattie's visitation last spring, Allie had ended up next to one of the youngest girls, a viola player. They all wore their ill-fitting and ragged-hemmed black concert dresses, but the viola player had paired hers with a pair of boys' blue moon boots and left her ski jacket over the top.

At least she hadn't been texting like more than a few of the others, fidgeting with their phones as they waited (and who were they texting? Each other?) though then at the casket the young viola player did pull her phone from her jacket pocket to snap a picture.

Allie had sucked in her breath. Photographs of the dead were as old as photography, but did people take casket photos now?

They would cover a dead girl's page with heart emojis and photos of fun times, *good byes* and *good lucks*, even *safe journey*—as if the afterlife were another virtual reality from which she might yet be checking her messages.

After snapping the picture, the viola player had turned to Allie. *Her hair was almost as long as Cassie's too*, she'd said, sighing.

Back at Eagle's Nest they found Bud had built a bonfire and their small lot had filled in. This was Labor Day weekend, last hurrah of the season. Cabin lights winked through the trees, the sun dipped below the canopy so that night had fallen sooner in some parts of the yard, on the property. The lake waited black, ink-stained and still. Children's laughter shook the grove of aspens near the end of the parking lot—aspens the type of trees that grew well where soil had been disturbed, the land wounded—and Cassie ran to join them.

Watching her go, Allie felt a stir of a memory from another of her distant lives, from college, where she'd pursued an art history degree. At one time she'd studied how to pay attention, how to *see*—if the details and signs she'd learned to recognize were of different places, different times; within the world of representation and not of reality.

CHAPTER 3

A SNOW SHOVEL stood permanently in the front vestibule off Tiki's, winter never that far in retreat.

Bud raised a hand to knock on the inner door. He doubted Shara had returned to the bar, but he'd been by the Post Office again and indeed Tammy had a stack of packages for delivery to Tiki's.

It didn't hurt to check.

When no one answered, Bud set the boxes on the front step. Then instead of leaving he wandered onto Tiki's crumbling lake-edge landing. Here a rusted gas tank threatened to topple into the water below. An old wooden totem pole towered from the beach, something a guy who did chainsaw art had done decades ago and the woodpeckers had added to, interspecies collaboration. In the small electrical box, Bud found half a joint. He'd sat out here often enough with Jeff, Shara's old boyfriend, and later, after Jeff left for Wyoming, with Shara.

A lot of people were starting to talk about Wyoming, Eastern Montana too. Years ago Bud had agreed with Allie that getting out of the city made sense, and it had seemed both logical and liberating to buy property in the quaint Northwoods, run their own business. Now Bud felt the property like a weight, the least wise investment of the times. The people who were doing well, who were keeping ahead of the game, were those who could move quickly, try new ideas, relocate on short notice. But this ran directly counter to the way Allie wanted to live—increasingly like a burrowing, hibernating animal. Look how she'd responded to the trouble Cassie and the orchestra girls had gotten into: take away her phone, cut her off, and then wait as if time could take care of it.

Bud had been the one who'd urged Shara to leave, who'd ended their short affair by not going with her. (Was "affair" even the word for it? A good friendship that turned into a confused fling, mutual aid and comfort, not something meant to hurt anyone else.) He'd sent Shara after Jeff, with whom she had been on-and-off for decades, that relationship with a life and beauty of its own kind—though also, like all relationships, merely occupying its blip of time in the scheme of things.

He closed his eyes to the wind, to the distant honking of a single goose and the splash of some small creature leaping from the shore. When he opened them, Shara's place looked as it always had, wooden cabin with neon beer signs obscured by overgrowth, now with shingles curling upward and a downed branch slid into an eave. It wasn't just the outer property Shara hadn't maintained in the last years. She'd been having trouble with vendors before she left and then let other things go, first the bar's landline and then its liquor license.

In fact the cut landline, the flat dial tone when he'd called her one day after a storm, had been the thing that brought Bud over the first time they'd got together, when the friendship had morphed.

It was late April and had been raining for days, which worked to melt the heaped banks of snow, except the ground was not thawed enough yet to absorb any of it. He wondered if she lost power, and then what she was doing for heat. Because of the rain and high water, and the last small bergs of ice floating on the lake, he found his way over by kayak through the boggy wetland that usually separated their properties.

It was the strangest way to travel the distance between their places, the swamp now a legitimate inlet of the melting lake. He'd paddled around islands of bramble, under the spooky archways of tree limbs, the glinting surface of the dark water crisscrossed by the shadows of the trees above. Though that winter he'd trooped over in snowshoes for company and beer (snowmobilers met regularly at Tiki's) it had felt like discovering a new place, a new shore, to find the nose of his kayak meeting the soggy lip of grass at the edge of Shara's backyard, the small clearing where she sat in a lawn chair behind the bar's back apartment, occupying the one slant of sunlight that crept through the hole in the canopy. She wore shorts and sunglasses. A can of beer stuck from the lopsided snowbank beside her.

"I was worried what you were doing for heat."

"I make my own." She smiled, indicating the ring of yellow, winter-exposed grass in which she'd perched the lawn chair. Squirrel and bird tracks skirted, and stray pine needles dotted the dirt-flecked banks melting around her.

But she also held a piece of mail in her hands, bad news. Bud pulled up his kayak, found a stump to drag over. Shara passed her beer.

She had been managing Tiki's for over twenty years. A decade ago, Tiki's owner had moved to Florida, first as a snowbird and then he'd stayed. She waved around the piece of mail, on which Bud recognized Shara's handwriting, a letter returned. "You want to know what I think happened?" she said. "I think he's dead." She spoke in the same matter-of-fact voice Bud had heard her use to recount the time she'd been robbed.

Though she'd heard from him less and less over the years, Shara had communicated with the owner of Tiki's every few months. She made the bank deposits. While he'd let her write her own paychecks, he filed the taxes and signed off on big orders online or by fax. But it had been months now since she'd heard from him and her most recent letter had been returned. It had been since September, she added, emphasizing the month. Even Bud had seen the pictures of those storms and newest high water lines around Miami.

But that couldn't be, Bud said. Even when people did disappear in those big storms, eventually they were reported as missing, counted among the dead and so accounted for.

Shara shrugged. Maybe that was true of the kind of people Bud knew. It was a problem for Shara because over the last several years she'd been saving to buy Tiki's and now she wouldn't be able to—not if the owner were gone and not listed anywhere as gone but simply, like others, disappeared. She rose to her feet from the lawn chair and pushed her way through green-painted screen door.

Bud rose too but waited outside where the door had snapped on its hinge. He could feel how much colder it was in the room she had entered, far from the small ring of sunlight laser-beaming the yard.

"Maybe it was for the best," he said, noting the sagging roofline of Shara's back apartment. He'd wondered how this place made money and suspected Shara earned most of her income off the lottery tickets she bought from the gas station and re-sold down here, the football pools and other card games. He thought of a stretch of houses that had gone up along Big Eagle Lake. The builder defaulted and then the bank that held the mortgages was bought by another bank out of state and now no one lived in the brand-new houses. No one local knew the name of the bank to contact about the house's overgrown access roads or the downed limbs in the yards.

It was time to leave this place, a thing Allie would not see.

"You don't want to be tied down here," he said to Shara, following her into the apartment, the wood-paneled walls the same as those of the bar's interior on the other side but here was a rumpled bed and Shara pulling her t-shirt over her head. The line of her bra strap rubber-banded the two rounded halves of her back, bridging the surprisingly small bones of her spine.

"I can leave," he said.

But she shook her head and instead of pulling on the sweatshirt she'd taken from the floor drew the wrinkled bed comforter around her bare shoulders. She patted the bed.

"Jeff says I can come out to Wyoming."

"You should do that," Bud said, sitting. The mattress was horrible, spongy and broken. She saw his discomfort as he shifted on it and laughed.

"It doesn't fit through the door frame." She nodded at the screen door with the low overhang that Bud had ducked through. "That's why I can't get a new one."

Had the mattress been built into Tiki's like a ship in a bottle? "I guess you're stuck then," Bud said, and he flopped backwards. He stared up at the stilled ceiling fan like it might be their cork, the one piece in the way of their narrowed exit.

Her hair swept over his neck and ear as she kissed him, full and pressing. He felt a spasm of pain in his back and had to roll to his side, adjusting, and she moved with him. The small hooks and eyes of her bra strap were chipped, and he bent one on accident and then her skin was warm on his, the whole room warming.

It wasn't any more intimate, just in a different way, than swapping stories and jokes over the bar that long winter, and the previous one, all the little details of their past lives.

On Tiki's dock, looking back at Shara's empty—or not empty?—apartment, postal boxes piled on the step in front, Bud was stubbing out the joint he'd found in the electrical box when his cell phone buzzed and, at the same moment, Tiki's screen door opened.

A shadow of a body moved within the vestibule and then a hand collected the topmost package. The screen door slammed shut.

Bud's phone buzzed again, and, confused by what he'd seen, his hand went for that. It was B.J. Bud sighed.

"Are you in?"

Bud continued to stare at Tiki's front step where two more packages waited for the hand, the shadow of the woman's body. "In with what?"

B.J. wanted to bring some adventure racers to Big Eagle Lake. "They'd use your west ramp," he said. "Come in down that old road."

B.J. must have hiked in their old road, checked all of this out. "I don't know that Allie will go for that," Bud said, whispering at first and then talking at volume, turning to look at the lake and clearing his throat like waking from a dream. Allie hardly tolerated their guests, and what would she say to new people trooping through their property, B.J.'s truck and trailer coming and going?

"These people have money," B.J. said. "You should see the gear."

Just where were B.J.'s kayakers going to kayak *to*? Bud wondered. But water levels this month might be high enough to permit travel up that little channel that led into Michigan, and people got a kick out of that, passing into a whole other state.

Slowly, Bud turned back to the house. The shadow appeared

in the doorway again, and he thought how she'd see him like this, against the lake with his phone to his ear, like he'd been here waiting, like it was any ordinary day but also like he'd watched over the place while she was gone.

Then the arm crept forward from the door and a long dreadlocked lock of hair fell forward. Then the whole head. Christina paused in the act of collecting the packages, eyeing him, and gave a crisp wave. The screened door slammed shut.

He'd have to call him back, Bud said to B.J.

"What—after you talk to your *wife?*"

"Yep," said Bud, refusing to take the bait.

Christina met him after his second knock, not as if she had been avoiding him but more like she was surprised to see anyone. Shara had insisted it wasn't scary out here but had admitted you grew attuned to the sounds of arrival when you lived alone—to car wheels turning onto the gravel from the highway, boat motors slowing, boots crunching over leaves.

Bud couldn't resist craning for a view to where the sunlight through the blinds played stripes across the felt of the pool table, highlighted the worn spots in the varnish of the bar.

"It's just me," Christina said.

Okay, Bud nodded. He got what everything looked like from her point of view—that he'd sent her mother packing. But nothing was that simple when it came to point of view.

"I've got something for you," Christina said, allowing the door to shut and then returning several moments later with an unwashed casserole pan and a food-encrusted Tupperware. "Tell Allie thanks, okay?"

Confused, Bud nodded. Allie had known Shara's daughter was living out here alone?

She'd also rented Red Oaks to that new woman and her children past their usual closing date, and as if that were unremarkable.

In the truck before starting it Bud grabbed his phone and texted B.J. back. You know what? They'd take those kayakers. Send them around.

* * *

Cassie waited for the moment her mother resurfaced before turning the keys in the ignition of the F150. Her mother swam in the lake most summer mornings, and this time of year, though it was early, in a blaze orange swim cap. When she looked out on the world, her mother saw potential for death, destruction, accidental shooting, even in the middle of a lake.

Cassie reversed with an arm looped over the seat bench, and then spun herself in the direction of the parking lot's exit. She supposed it was care of some kind, love, that made her wait for that moment of her mother's head bobbing upward, when air spouted again from her body.

But that was mean, her mother as a whale, and Cassie was trying—she was truly trying—to be a nicer person.

Cassie had taken to calling the battered blue truck Bud had given her *The Fjord*. The game of following random cars had started as a lazy way to kill time and then become a way of escaping her own head. In the Fjord, while her mother swam, Cassie had been led to places she never otherwise would have gone: hunting access roads, lost county trunks. Cars she picked to follow (that picked her? Like speed boats tossing tow lines) brought her suddenly upon golf courses, junk yards, hidden boat landings—even the familiar places new for different angles of approach. Once she'd discovered a university observatory. Another time a llama farm.

Cassie only had to pause for a short time at the top of the resort's driveway before a brown sedan chugged by. It wasn't the kind of car that would have caught her on any other road, where she waited for a specific velocity, choosy as any artist. But leaving Eagle's Nest you had to take the first thing that came by. It could be a while.

Tourists were slowest to understand they were being followed, their eyes and ears taken with new sights and sounds, with the task of finding turn-offs onto unnamed roads. Tailing tourists, Cassie found cabins and boat put-ins, trail heads that she—someone who'd lived here her entire life—hadn't known about but that must have been marked in some travel magazine all the tourists received at home.

She also liked to follow locals, people immersed in their daily lives. Once a green Mustang took her all the way to Tomahawk. A woman in a business suit jumped out at a liquor store, went in for a quick purchase, and then turned right back around the way she'd come. She'd passed about two hundred bars where even Cassie knew you could buy an off sale bottle. Cassie had followed the woman all the way home, telling herself she was worried about this person drinking from a brown paper sack as she drove, though per- haps she was drinking because Cassie was following her, a strange giant truck lumbering in the rearview. The woman went faster and slower, and then Cassie went faster and slower.

Today the brown sedan led her into Wild Fire. For just the slightest moment, Cassie thought it might turn into the Taylor Cycle, Nina's family's other business, and what luck that would be, but then it didn't.

Oh well. She took the turn on her own, grudgingly. Yesterday, at the Dairy Freeze, Julia had picked this place. Nine a.m.

Cassie pulled around back, engine ticking even after she killed it. The heat began to seep immediately. She rolled the window down further.

The Taylor Cycle was stickered over the back door's window, a smaller version of what stretched across the front. It was just like Nina's family to have given their laundromat their name, the Taylors a family who were inordinately, obnoxiously, pleased with themselves. Example: Mr. Taylor took photography classes and Mrs. Taylor hung his photographs on the fridge.

Nina was both like and not like her parents. In the evenings, she and her little sister sat at the dinner table with their backs straight, frowning ever so slightly, worrying already about their homework. Cassie could shock Nina by mentioning she was still wearing yesterday's underwear. Nina, as good as any of the orchestra girls, could roll her eyes at her parents, but at the end of the day she swallowed their world view whole.

The few times Cassie had slept over at Nina's she'd laid her borrowed sleeping bag over the plush pink carpet of Nina's room and wondered how to explain the plain wooden floors of her home, their splinters and cracks and spider nests, the piled books and half-finished art projects, random screws and nails sticking from wallpaper-peeled walls. Not to mention the cold. In winter, alone in the woods for months, Cassie's parents were not the relaxed summertime hosts, not the fellow transplants who could smile knowingly at jokes about the locals. They were just like anyone else, people who had to chop firewood for heat, who lived where they risked isolation by snow.

When they made fun of their local neighbors, they forgot Cassie was one of them.

Cassie leaned back in her seat. Steam billowed from an aluminum chute, which meant the laundromat wasn't closed, not like the Taylor's Dairy Freeze, though there were no other cars in the back lot. She had hoped she might find Nina here, and that was why she'd said yes to Julia about meeting here today. This was the first place Nina and Cassie had met—Cassie sitting in the front passenger seat of her mother's ridiculous car and Nina sauntering over to say hello, not knowing the trunk and back seat were piled with comforters strangers had soiled and which Cassie and her family had to wash.

"Nice wheels," Nina had said.

It was her mother's, Cassie had said, covering a split in the seat's vinyl with her bare leg. Nina explained the laundromat was her parents' place.

"So your fortune's in quarters?" Cassie had blurted.

Christina would have barfed laughing. But Nina bit her lip, confused—certain Cassie hadn't meant to sound so snide.

And that had melted Cassie's heart—really it had. Nina was such a good person.

And she was just about to get sniffly about that, like she had some feelings for Wild Fire and its various dingy and dying businesses, for her friend Nina, whom Cassie hadn't seen or heard from all summer and who was now, apparently, gone for good, moved away, when the back door of the laundromat swung open and out tottered Julia in a pair of lethal heels, her black hair a staticky halo.

Yesterday, Cassie had not wanted to ride with Julia to the Dairy Freeze, though Julia had insisted. She was *so lonely* these days, she'd said, her nails digging into Cassie's arm, the embarrassing confession wafting on the air.

Among the orchestra girls, riding in a car with Julia was recognized as mortal hazard. It was something they lured new girls into just for the looks on their faces when they returned, their knees shaking. Julia talked while she drove—and she looked at you, for too long.

"That's *Eau de New Car* you're smelling," Julia said yesterday of her new Range Rover, laughing at the face Cassie must have been making. Here was a car to show off, the year of its make from the future, except Julia had hung a fuzzy carnival toy from the rearview mirror, and the back seat lay buried beneath fast food wrappers and junk mail. "Awww. It's okay." Julia rubbed Cassie's arm. "Legs like that, you'll get yourself a honey who can buy you a jet plane."

And Cassie had softened. That was so Julia, both the tenderness and the joke. Julia loved to draw the protest of the orchestra girls, to say things like that so one of them would say "Julia! I'm going to buy my own jet plane, thank you." Then Julia would roll her made-up eyes. But wouldn't it be easier, she'd tease, to let someone who loves you *so* much buy it for you?

In the end, it was a joke about herself, Julia's way of acknowledging what she assumed people must be saying about her rich boyfriend. And Julia wasn't a supermodel, giving further rise to speculation among the orchestra girls. So how had she lured Mark? And what did she do to keep him?

They'd been driving through Satuit when Julia got around to phones, when she discovered Cassie didn't have one. She hit the brakes though she was looking at Cassie, mouth gaping, before the car came to a complete stop—there in the middle of the road in downtown Satuit, amidst what amounted here to Friday night traffic.

"You know, no phone. No internet." Cassie wasn't sure how Julia could not remember this. Could it be that she hadn't known of the orchestra girls' punishment? "Can you pull off to the side, Julia?"

Julia stomped on the gas again, shaking her head. Cassie wondered just how so many adults had such terrible driving habits. Maybe only teenagers, so new to driving, were so keenly aware of the varieties of death that could happen in or by or because of cars.

"You didn't see any of my posts all summer?" Julia barreled toward a stop sign.

"No."

"Well girl, I'd thought you were *ghosting* me." She laughed and laughed.

Cassie had tried not to think how weird a word it was for her to have used. Ghosting.

"I brought some shoes for you, and some other things..." They'd come inside the laundromat for the air conditioning, Julia surprising Cassie by having with her an actual laundry basket, with plastic netting, like Julia really did do such ordinary domestic chores as laundry. In fact, clothing spun in a machine behind her—whipping flashes of pink and purple and lime green, no doubt Julia's undergarments, no doubt of the variety any other woman, even Cassie's sexless mother, would have known to wash on delicate.

"Can you believe Mark doesn't have a washing machine yet?" Julia shook her head. Cassie had been about to wonder that.

Cassie twirled her keys, their weight wobbling around her finger. Once before Julia had tried to give her some of Hattie's things and it had been weird. She'd hounded Cassie to come over to Mark's giant cabin and then led her to the bedroom she and Hattie shared during the work week when Mark was away. She pulled thing after thing from the closet floor, none of it fresh, pressing the thin clothing, far too small for tall Cassie, into Cassie's arms. *I don't hold you responsible honey*, she kept saying, adding one more bra or pair of leggings to the pile growing under Cassie's nose, all of Hattie's tiny, skanky items.

But Julia had always seemed to like Cassie. It made some sense that she'd picked her to receive Hattie's old things.

She believed, for example, that there was something unkind in how Cassie's parents treated her—that they worked her too hard, used her in their family business. *Do you get a smoke break?* Julia had joked. Other times, after a few glasses of wine, she'd grip Cassie's shoulders, put her palm to Cassie's forehead. *They didn't even send you to school.*

Julia must have caught Cassie's expression. "Don't worry—I'm not trying to give you clothes again." She'd been extracting sweatshirts and knee socks, piling them to one side.

From the bottom of the basket, she produced a phone.

"It's yours. There's data and everything."

Then Julia put both of her hands on Cassie's cheeks. The insides of her silvery rings glinted cold for the warmth of her hands, more like the sharpness of their gems. Her fingertips held Cassie's skull.

"You call me. Anytime you need, you hear?"

Cassie nodded. Julia taught her the code to unlock the phone, running her own hands over the screen quickly, expertly.

Julia fished for her own phone and pressed a button. The one in Cassie's hand shuddered. "I've got you in here already!" She clinked her phone to Cassie's, a toast. "And you've got me."

It was, of course, Hattie's old phone.

* * *

That morning Allie's plunge, one clean forward dive, came to her as entry into another world; it came with the cancellation of all the sounds of this one. She couldn't smell underwater but imagined what that smell would be: composting vegetation, digesting fish, and her own human odor ballooning from her like a loosening net. This was a muskie lake. And though there weren't as many as there'd used to be, there were still fish here as long as Allie's leg, as thick around as her thigh. They'd swim from her smell and the awkward slosh of her kick and stroke. Allie surfaced, exhaling one hot "ho," and settled into her rhythm, heading east along the shoreline.

Their lake was longer than it was wide. Allie usually swam east along the shore until the end of their property, the furthest cabin and its little private dock. To the west was Tiki's, where Allie wouldn't appear in a bathing suit. She could have swum across the lake, though since her rule for Cassie was not to do that alone, Allie didn't either. Near the shoreline she could touch if needed, find the bottom.

At the property line, Allie flipped for the turn. For a moment on her back, the morning sky was like a deep glassy bowl she could fall into were she not stuck like a scrap of fabric, as if by static, to the surface of this world. Sometimes she could see in the dome of their northern sky the atmosphere's sharpened slope to the pole. The Earth wasn't perfectly spherical but warped like an eyeball accustomed to hard contact lenses. Allie wore hers while she swam, though losing one would mean two trips to Wausau, not to mention that without them she wouldn't be able to see her way back to her own house. Even the bright yellows and reds of the canoes and fishing boats tied off the dock wouldn't come to her through the gloom of green, the shoreline trees reflected in the lake.

The woods were beautiful, if a horrible kind of beautiful. Not a year ago, a couple from Upper Michigan had abandoned their two-year-old in the national forest not far from here. They'd walked him in and then slipped away themselves. It was a story that came to Allie often, shifting in her brain like a bubble in a level, a trapped horror, a thing she could hardly tolerate to think about, but she did. He'd toddled his way out by sheer luck, selecting the one direction that brought him back to the road, the one car happening to pass that afternoon on the mostly abandoned highway. And that car, also miraculously, had been driven by people who'd believed their eyes, who'd allowed the discomfiting information of a lone *baby* on the backwoods highway not only to enter their awareness but to force their stop, to disrupt their momentum.

This time when Allie raised her head again, not toward the shoreline but ahead over the lake, she saw the canoe. It was not one of theirs.

What was it that was odd about the canoe? It rode so levelly on the water, though only one figure sat at the back. Allie adjusted her angle to swim toward it, toward Kate.

She realized that she hoped the silver-haired woman and her grandkids weren't leaving, not yet. The front end must have been loaded with something near equal to its rear occupant's weight. One of the kids tied down in a gunnysack? Allie recognized this bizarre idea as scrap of another horrible story—one a neighbor had once told her about drowning unwanted kittens in a river. Maybe it was related to the abandoned two-year-old. As she was getting older, Allie's daytime brain worked like it did in dream, memories clomping together to make papier-mâché creations, new animals all their own.

"Dear God," said Kate.

Allie had nearly swum into her paddle. The whole lake and there they were on a crash course.

"Quite the marine you'd make. If not for that cap, I'd never see you coming."

"Oohrah," said Allie.

Kate threw back her head and laughed.

Allie hadn't seen their most recent guest, she of the odd arrival, since Allie had left her in Red Oaks, their respective children playing dead on the beach. She'd seen the children; they'd even come out to the bonfire last night, but Kate kept to herself, happy enough to let Cassie entertain her charges—her grandchildren if that's what they were. Now Kate offered over a bottle in a paper sack as if Allie had popped over for tea. Hanging one-armed from the canoe's battered edge, Allie tipped the liquid, the heat plummeting down her throat, warming through her ribs and then dissipating.

Now she'd really die out here—halfway across the lake and alcohol cooling her core.

"Who lives over here?" Kate tipped her chin toward the crumbling boathouse, last remnant of Old Ferdy's old resort. They had drifted closer to the lake's other side.

"No one." Allie traded one arm for the other in its hold on the canoe. "Every year Bud dreams up plans to move that old boat house to our place. Slide it across the ice. You can't build on the water like that anymore."

Kate passed her the bottle of Schnapps. "Can't move or renovate one either."

Allie had allowed Cassie to let Kate's grandkids break her life jacket rule the other day, to go in swimming without them. She'd let them dive off their dock. In the water now, her own legs churning, her arms tiring, Allie felt guilty. There was, too, the matter of the wad of cash with which Kate had paid. Last night after they'd returned from the meeting, Cassie had insisted on retrieving the loose stack of bills from the box in the office to show off to Bud. She'd never seen so much paper money in one place and fanned it like a card player in an old movie.

"What do you think she did? Rob a bank?"

"There are plenty of reasons people get paid in cash," Allie had said, realizing too late the set-up she was providing.

"Oh, she's too old to be a *waitress*, Mom," Cassie had said with a wink. Another thing lost since last spring: Allie's ability to enjoy her daughter's jokes. Now anything edgy made her stiffen.

It had occurred to Allie that another explanation for the cash, for the arrival of Kate and the kids without a reservation, and without a plan for the kids to go to school on Tuesday—when schools started across Wisconsin—was that they'd just had a death in the family. It was an old tradition, in a day and age when condolences were signed online and donations made with credit cards, but Allie could remember elderly relatives' funerals where cards with cash were pressed into survivors' hands, the bills as limp as Kleenexes.

"You want to see Old Ferdy's place?" Allie asked Kate, her legs egg beatering alongside of the canoe.

Kate surprised her by nodding.

The person who'd died had been her daughter, Allie decided. The kids' mother.

Allie knuckled something soft—the silty bottom. As soon as she'd begun to worry that it was a long way to swim, that she'd underestimated it, she was standing in the reeds and dripping.

The story of Fyodor Ferdinand, founder of Eagle's Nest, was

one of Bud's favorites to tell around campfires. Before he'd built the set of cabins guests still occupied today, Old Ferdy had tried to homestead on the lake's south shore—a fact that always signaled to Allie that he hadn't been from here either. Who would choose the shaded side, the lee of hundreds of miles of trees? No members of his family had survived that first winter and now even the small family graveyard was disintegrating. At one spot, a small casket peeked through an eroded bank. Of course local rumor—and so Bud's campfire version—had it that not only had Old Ferdy been a bad planner, a poor gravedigger, an outsider who didn't understand, but a crazed man who'd axed his family. It was the kind of story that made Northwoodsers feel good about themselves in winter. At least they weren't killing each other yet.

Bud offered this tale to tourists alongside the region's other historical hors de' oeuvres, the one about the Chicago gangsters who'd hid out during prohibition, the bullet holes still visible in the walls of one restaurant an annual feature of the Chamber's magazine. But they were all *fishtabs*, Allie would have liked to point out. (She too, despite two decades of residence, was still a *fucking Illinois shithead towing a boat*, and in winter *towing a 'bile*.) Worse, those gangsters had been cop killers. A few years ago after an area officer had been killed in the line of duty, squad cars and armored police vehicles had come out in commemoration from as far as Waushara and Oneida County. Miles and miles of roadways of the Northwoods, when there wasn't much road available, had been blocked for an entire weekend afternoon by their slow parade. Allie didn't have anything in particular against cops, but she knew a show of force when she saw one and suspected her neighbors could recognize one too. Maybe their reverence for Dillinger wasn't so hypocritical—even for the flags draped from so many houses for that parade.

The officer had been one of those they were now calling border agents.

"Man, you've got the buckthorn here too." In her canoe, Kate had drifted near the boathouse's opening. The door had long ago been ripped off and water lapped through to the back. Allie walked onto the weedy beach, wet and barefoot, out of breath.

"We have loose strife on our side, but we let it grow. Something to hold the lawn up."

Kate was familiar with the local invasives. She paddled in toward shore, powering the last two strokes to edge onto the sand. Allie reached for the knotted rope on the bow and tugged her up another foot. They talked roots for a while. Digging versus burning, a chemical kit you could buy for ash borer.

"You don't own property on this side?"

"No." It was interesting that Allie had never thought about why they didn't, as it must have been part of Ferdy's original parcel. The Murphys must have sold it. For Ferdy, building this place, naming it, wouldn't have been about money but more like what it was to Bud and Allie, a way of life.

It gave Allie a sense of kinship with Old Ferdy. *You old axe murderer you!*

"You should bring your grandkids out here," Allie said to Kate. There was a ridge to climb that made for a good picnic, and it would be fun for the kids to cross over in a canoe, their lunches in sacks.

Kate didn't answer, busy tugging her own canoe onto shore. Now, of course, was the point when Allie should warn her about the small plot. Just don't let them head up that way, through those trees. Not especially if these were children whose mother had just died.

It made the game Cassie had played with them yesterday even more macabre. Pretending they'd all drowned, the paddleboat capsized.

"Your girl needed some younger siblings to boss around, didn't she?"

Allie laughed. Had Kate been thinking about the kids' game too?

"It's okay," Kate said. "It's good for girls to be a bit bitchy."

What had she heard about Cassie, Allie wondered. Then, had Kate's daughter—the kids' mother—been a *bit bitchy*? It wasn't a question you could ask, though, about the dead. Even if you wanted to know more about whether it had worked in her favor, worked to protect her, or put her at risk.

Kate scratched at the paint on the boathouse with her fingernails. She brought a chip to her tongue to taste.

"What are you going to do with them now?" Allie said. "The kids. Are you going to put them in school up here?"

But, as if she were rooting for something in particular among the buckthorn, swatting at the butterflies and bees coming out with the warming daylight, Kate stepped out of view around the back of the old boathouse.

Allie stood without moving, tired from her swim. Hadn't they just been mid-conversation? Where had the woman gone?

In her bare feet, she began stepping through the sharper, dryer weeds to the boathouse's corner. Cassie organized a night game similar to this when enough kids were available.

Cassie the ringleader.

But Kate was not behind the boathouse. Nor was she along its far side. Allie began to hack through the underbrush, twigs and tiny thorns scratching her thighs. Surely Kate hadn't come this way or there'd have been a broken path. But then where had she gone? Allie came to the shore-facing side again. Now the canoe was gone. A drag mark led into the thin woods.

"There's no portage here. That's at the narrow end of the lake," Allie called.

"There's another lake that way though, isn't there?" Kate appeared, farther ahead than where Allie had been looking. She wagged an arm southward.

"Not for maybe a mile," Allie said, trudging up the beach. "You're better to drive there if you want to fish it."

The canoe was empty. Perhaps there hadn't been anything in it before.

"There are bears here." Allie normally didn't admit this to guests. "If you want to camp, you should tie up your food. You probably shouldn't even take much food."

"Thanks," Kate said, as if she meant it, but Allie flushed, remembering that Kate was from here. She'd know about bears, only little black bears. The wolves were a bigger problem.

* * *

The sun was blinding today on the lawn. In the shade Cassie lay sweating against the rough canvas of the hammock. The new children, Marius and Miranda, kicked a volleyball from one end of the lawn to the other, each calling for Cassie to join their side, but to her they seemed evenly matched, brother and sister. She waved them off and tried to inch toward the hammock's cooler half. The new phone was a lump in her back pocket threatening her balance, and it pinged again, the small squeak almost enough to throw Cassie to the pine needles beneath. In the last hour, the phone had been blowing up—if "blowing up" could refer to a barrage of posts and texts only from Julia.

Yo girl. The small grinning face of Julia's avatar smirked next to her comment. In it she wore sunglasses, which was sort of funny—as if she were trying to go old-fashioned incognito while online. Julia had posted three more pictures since two minutes ago when Cassie had last checked. In each Julia sprawled across the deck of a different white yacht, in a different bikini, a different drink in hand. This was the backlog of Julia's photos from summer—everything Cassie had missed.

You're gonna have to catch up!

Julia leaned over a silvery boat railing. She smiled from under the brim of a boat captain's hat. Where had she been this summer? Some place with an azure lake, where waves came in all those shades of sapphire.

What are you up to????

What had Julia been up to the summer after her daughter's death? Partying, apparently. *Wait until Hattie found out,* Cassie thought—and then realized what she'd just thought. It had been a few months since she'd last made such a slip, embarrassing even in her own head.

It was funny. When her mother had first taken her phone—silent with hand extended after one of the last PTA meetings (and Cassie didn't even go to public school yet)—Cassie had relinquished it as if she didn't care. Whatever. Within minutes, though, within seconds, the time without it began to pile like heavy stones. Her brain fogged and her palm itched. She couldn't shake the feeling of having forgotten something she was supposed to do, or someplace she was supposed to be. Worse, things came to her that she might say or share—a song lyric earworm; the way a guest's patchy back hair made a pattern like a peace sign—but she had no way to convey those things. She wandered Eagle's Nest through half of June bumping into things, dropping things, like a being that had been squeezed from one dimension to a smaller one, all of what she'd lost inexplicable to everyone who'd always lived here.

Did her parents know what they'd done? Maybe they had wanted her—perhaps she deserved—to feel this badly.

Then, gradually, the feeling faded. She came to see the dumb bumbling humor in guests with their phones texting each other between the parking lot and the beach, sending out images of hot dogs on sticks through their flash accounts. Without her phone, Cassie could slip away for hours in her truck or to the woods where no one could find her. She could claim upon her return not to know the time.

In this dimension she was subterranean. Now, from her pocket, the phone Julia had given her tickled again.

What are you up to?????

What's your swimsuit this summa?

Girl you there?

Cassie stood, flipping from the hammock to her feet in a well-practiced move that had startled many a guest. She wasn't sure where she was going. At the same time, Miranda ran into the middle of the lawn, her body blocking the sun as she raised one leg to kick the soccer ball, the sun haloing around her. Cassie pulled that phone that had been blipping in her pocket and raised it just as the girl swung her leg, her face a determined, laughing mask, and caught it: the moment, the image. With another click, she posted.

The image could have been her, was an echo of a younger Cassie, from any of the thousands of days she'd played on this lawn in her swimsuit.

She breathed out a long sigh of relief, and then frowned. She hadn't realized how it had been nagging her—the problem of what post to make first, with what flash to announce that she was back.

Also quickly—because a person could return to her phone world without all the drama, a phone was just a tool—Cassie added a quick, breezy caption, one that would speak (though again not too directly) to her absence over the summer:

Hostage situation.

Then she turned the thing off. You could do that with a phone. You could also take yourself out of signal range.

"Hey Miranda!" she yelled.

The younger girl faced forward from the prow of the Mercury-powered outboard, her elbows jutting like awkward wings. In back, Cassie twisted the throttle, felt the vibrations from the motor through the boat's metal bottom through her flip-flops.

On the lake she couldn't follow people like she could in the Fjord, though there were waves and breezes, things outside the self that could nudge the self, cancel the problem of decision and choice. Perhaps due to the slap of a wave, Cassie found she'd selected north. Then they had passed the willow at the end of their property, then one of the little lake islands, and finally even the parting of thick green tress that marked Tiki's.

She motored past, aimed now for the opening into Big Eagle.

"What is this place?" Miranda had not worn shoes, and she grumbled as she tried to keep up, leaving the boat pulled to the shore behind them. Cassie tried to remember the way, find the path in the scrub. She and Christina had come up over the dune hundreds of times and trudged through this very field—often at this same time of year when the red and oranges of paintbrush weeds dotted the ridge.

Why didn't it look more familiar? Cassie paused to glance back to the lake. She was sure this had been the right spot, if the lily pads that used to carpet the inlet had drowned.

A hundred yards farther through the tall grasses, there it was—the steeper lip of land that marked the edge of the quarry.

"C'mon," she said, scrambling up. Miranda, good girl, followed.

She was a scrappy little thing, even for her bare feet. Hair whipping on the high ridge, Cassie wondered if she should play the trick on Miranda that she and Christina had once played on Nina, bringing her here. To be fair, the land had played it first on Cassie and Christina, from the cover of tall waving grasses giving away all at once just before them, the little rocks tumbling ahead of their feet down the hundreds of yards to the quarry floor below.

Instead she warned Miranda—Cassie's arm swinging out like a rod. Miranda pushed past anyway, and continued right to the edge undaunted, peering down into the chasm. Cassie swallowed her annoyance.

"Those eagles?"

The giant birds swooped below them.

"Vultures," Cassie said, though vultures and eagles were basically the same kind of bird.

The white clouds above them reflected from the thin pool on the quarry's floor, old rainwater. A moment later, the light darkened, the sun smeared.

"I don't get who'd want to camp here," Miranda said.

"Huh?" said Cassie.

"How do you even get down to the lake?" She shielded her eyes.

"It's not a campground," Cassie said. "It's an old quarry. They used to mine something here." She couldn't remember what, though, and felt an itch for her phone, a signal. Just to have one on her person, apparently, was enough to reignite old feelings, old habits.

"Then what are they doing?" Miranda pointed to a green tent a few hundred yards away on the quarry rim. She was still wearing only her swimsuit, the musty orange U of the old lifejacket over her shoulders like a shawl.

A man emerged from the tent, his body growing taller as he unfolded from it. He perched a tall black cowboy hat on his head with one giant palm.

A sickening feeling rose in Cassie's belly. She took in the tent and the tan extension van parked behind it. There was one way someone might have learned this place was here.

Then he saw them and called, his voice echoing once it hit the quarry wall. "Hey!" *Hey, hey.*

Cassie grabbed Miranda's arm and they ran, tripping through the tall grass.

The voice followed them. "You with Clearwater?" *Clearwater.*

They ran the length of the flower-dotted field, the sharp weeds slicing.

Weirdly, alarmingly, Cassie registered that the beeping she was hearing, the pinging, was from her pocket—she was picking up a signal, even out here.

They slid down the dune, Miranda laughing.

At the boat, Cassie checked her phone. The signal came in even down here, even three feet from shore, even ten, twenty. In fact it grew stronger.

CHAPTER 4

PUSHED FROM SHORE, returned to the quiet of the lake, it seemed silly that they had run from the man at the quarry. The mercury thudding against the water, Cassie aimed the outboard through the narrow opening to Little Eagle Lake, where the world shrank again.

As they puttered within sight of Tiki's, the wind took up two tendrils of Miranda's hair, floating the strands into the curling horns of a grazing animal.

"Your friend lives here?"

"No," Cassie shouted over the motor. "She tends bar here."

"Looks like someone's dumpy house."

She wasn't wrong, Cassie thought. The small clapboard structure of Tiki's was set up off the lake under a crowded assemblage of mismatched maple and evergreen, their branches this time of year a tangle of green that wouldn't clarify until fall—*this* shot of orange part of *that* tree, growing *through* the overhang of jack pine there.

They drifted to the crumbling landing, Miranda's head swiveling to the wooden totem that leaned on the shore. It rose ten feet tall with a midsection of giant breasts, the nipples flat wooden discs like toy train wheels. As a kid Cassie had thought of the statue as a griffin—a real one—trapped, turned to wood, awaiting a spell of release.

"What's her name?"

"I don't think she has a name."

"They could give her a swimsuit top, at least." Miranda climbed onto the dock and yanked her life jacket over her head. Pulling up as if for a jump shot, she tossed it neatly into the boat.

Boxes occupied half of Tiki's front porch, a new delivery not yet marked by rain or dusted with pine needles. Someone was still here. Cassie remembered the back room, where a person could live at Tiki's. It contained a queen bed, a small table and chairs, and an old TV/VCR. She and Christina had spent hours playing in the room, one or the other lying in Shara's bed, rolling with her hands clutched to her stomach in feigned pain. It was always stomach pain, something in the middle of the body. The other girl had to be nurse.

Cassie wondered what kind of modem and router system Christina had set up back there now, if she were living here, as Julia had said her mother knew.

And she wondered if Christina were living here now, had replaced Shara as bar manager, and if she ever brought anyone with her to the back room, made any money on the side. Like her mother, she'd been tending toward trash.

Cassie couldn't believe she'd thought that. Nor just how much she had missed her friend.

She and Miranda hopped onto a pair of swivel seats, squeaky and greasy. Sure enough, Christina appeared through the thin door behind the bar, closing it behind her so that Cassie only caught the barest glimpse of the wall of Stoli boxes stacked there as privacy screen.

"Oh. Hey." Christina seemed surprised to see them, as if it shouldn't be the other way around. All summer, she had known Cassie was a mile away, Cassie's mother delivering her care packages.

Christina fired up two Cokes from the gun, the insistent rush somehow embarrassing in the quiet sunlit room, which was a dingy bar but also beautiful, the jukebox and dart machines old but familiar pieces of dust-collecting furniture that never, at least in Cassie's memory, had worked. She suspected the pink gumball that rested on top of the pile in the vestibule's jammed machine to be the same as the one that had been there since she was ten, even then on its way to fossilization. Christina slid the glasses forward without cherry garnish or thin red stir straw, which, Cassie hoped, meant they were free.

Having come here directly from the quarry, having run from the man in the black cowboy hat who was camping there—and having noted the strength of the cell signal she'd picked up, nowhere near any towers but near enough to Tiki's—now Cassie didn't know what to say. Since last year when she and Christina had driven home from orchestra rehearsals in Christina's Corolla—the *Areola*, they'd called it—Christina's dreadlocked hair had grown into thicker ropes, and a new ring clung next to the other two at her eyebrow. Cassie wondered if she had any new tattoos, remembering Christina's first at sixteen: matching elephants with her mother. The two shared the ability to trumpet call. It was their signal for one another through woods or over water.

"You're the girl in the picture," Christina said to Miranda.

"You took a picture of me?" Miranda swung to Cassie, the stool squeaking.

Cassie shrugged. "It wasn't a picture of you but of the hole you made in the scenery." It was embarrassing because of all people Christina could truly read the picture Cassie had posted of Miranda, a girl playing soccer alone on a lawn, and understand what it meant. The post had spoken of Cassie's childhood, her bare loneliness.

She had flashed it out an hour ago—not realizing that of those she might wish to see it, Christina was at the top of the list. All at once that she'd abandoned Christina for Nina last year showed itself for its dumbness. No matter what Christina's mother had done, Christina was someone who got Cassie. She and Cassie would always be connected.

"You remember how we used to signal each other with flashlights? You'd lean out your grandma's back bedroom window. I'd go out on the end of our dock."

"I think we did that once," Christina said to Miranda.

"What I'm telling you is," Cassie turned to Miranda. "We invented flash. The analog, beta version."

"It really worked too," Christina said. Dry.

Cassie looked to the wall behind Christina. Beyond the objects she recognized so clearly they might have been her own family's Christmas ornaments—jars of pickled eggs and pigs feet, a dancing hula girl, sticky dice cups and cribbage boards, and dusty boxes of pool cue chalk—had been propped a new dry erase board across which a familiar block script spelled out the names of shots only Christina could have invented: *Your Cum-Up-Pants. Wood You'd Rather. Titsle Town.*

"Can I have that?"

Cassie thought Miranda had spotted the boob-shaped coffee mug. It was even more revolting now that Cassie had breasts of her own to imagine some old man asking to have his beer served in it, sipping from the spout of the red-tipped nipple. Christina reached for something else. "The hula hoop?" She hoisted herself onto the counter to retrieve it.

"Why's that there?" Cassie asked, regretting too late that if the hula hoop were a drinking thing, a sex thing, she'd given away her ignorance.

"Shara probably put it there one time I was being a shithead."

Miranda stood on her stool and with a squeaking lurch began to work the hoop. It circled her waist and soon with that momentum the stool beneath her began to turn, the whole thing a sort of solar system.

"Damn," said Cassie. "You're gonna win some bar money someday."

Miranda stepped from the stool to the bar top, still hooping, working it up her body and out to an arm. There was something unthinking in her motion—her eyes drifting without focusing, her body having taken over. Cassie remembered the girl's dives from the dock bench, far more difficult than the leaps she and Marius had dared each other to try.

"What else you got, girl?"

Barefooted, she went up on her toes, walking the bar like a balance beam. Cassie yanked an ashtray out of the way. Miranda hooped with her neck, strutting. When she'd reached the far end, Cassie caught Christina's eye, and then Miranda came flipping between them, a back handspring with the hoop rushing up and down her body. She sprang forward into a one-handed cartwheel, the hoop ending as a spinning bangle on the free wrist.

"Jesus," said Christina.

Miranda shrugged.

"You could be on TV," said Cassie.

"You could go to Vegas," said Christina.

"I *was* training," Miranda said, "for the Olympics."

Cassie coughed, looking to Christina to see if they'd laugh.

"I mean, I'm out of shape now," Miranda said. "Don't think I don't know."

"How were you *training*?" Cassie asked.

"With a coach." Miranda rolled her eyes to Christina. "At a nationally ranked gym in Waukesha. With most of the money my mom should have got from the divorce anyway but which my dad lost in his business."

"Is that where you're from? Waukesha?" Cassie turned to Christina. "You know this kid and her brother showed up by canoe?" Christina was stacking coasters. "You two are like *boat* people."

"Jesus, Cassie." Christina frowned into the glass she'd raised to her lips. Shara had kept a glass of clear liquid behind the bar and told the girls it was water, though maybe she'd been lying. The few times she'd agreed to supply their parties last year she'd given only two conditions: Cassie and Christina wouldn't drive, and they wouldn't try to keep up with the boys. The second was weirder to Cassie than that Shara let them take some bottles from the bar. Allie would never, not in a million years, have admitted there was something a boy could do that Cassie could not.

"Did you take the website down?"

Christina made a noncommittal face.

"Clearwater?"

Then Cassie's phone trilled from her pocket just as Tiki's door swung open and in walked the man in the black cowboy hat who'd asked Cassie about Clearwater. Another man was behind him.

Cassie slipped around the bar and through the door to Christina's back room, taking advantage of the moment she'd looked up to assess her customers. She called for Miranda, who followed with the hoop.

"You open for lunch?" one of the men was saying.

"Hey, didn't we just see those girls?" The other man's eyes tracked them.

"Gotta take this call!" Cassie yelled back.

It was obvious someone was living in the back room. Cassie had cleaned enough guest rooms to size the situation: a damp towel hung from a rack, toothpaste spit flecked the mirror. When she was younger, rather than live at the bar, Christina had lived with her grandmother in a little house on top of the ridge, above Little Eagle Lake to the east. As recently as last winter with the orchestra girls they'd hung out there in the wood-paneled living room, Christina's grandmother in bed in the back. She'd died late in the winter, though, and Christina, Cassie realized, must have moved in here. She'd stayed here alone after her mother went west.

Miranda had followed her into the bathroom. "You going to use this? If not, I'd like to." Miranda began to pull her swimsuit straps from her shoulders. Cassie's eyes fell to the top of the girl's head where her roots were a nutty brown, an entirely different shade than the rest of Miranda's hair. Just how old was she? Did she dye her hair—and if so was that a gymnast's thing?

"Okay, so I would like some privacy," Miranda said, "If that wasn't clear."

Cassie wandered into the bedroom where she finally checked her phone to see whose call she had ignored. Julia's, of course. A tangle of black wires and a router box lay on the ground alongside the unmade bed.

It was more powerful than the system Cassie had built, if this generated the signal she had pulled in from the quarry.

Miranda hollered that she needed a tampon.

"You don't need a tampon. You're like what, ten?"

Christina poked her head around the wall of Stoli boxes. "Who needs a tampon?" She saw Cassie inspecting her router.

"Are you running the website still?"

Christina tossed a tampon through the air. On the package was a small orange price tag, like she sold individual tampons from the bar. Cassie felt a wave of confusion—but then remembered the small display of ancient packets of aspirin and antacids, the little cardboard pharmacy near the pickled eggs. This was another part of bar life—of Christina's new life—that Cassie didn't know.

Christina shut the door, muffling the men's voices on the other side.

Clearwater Dumping, the website, had been Cassie's and Christina's project—and like so many of their projects, their strange mutual amusements, it had started as a joke.

They'd built it to learn, a practice space. Cassie had started with a stock photograph of a serene Northwoods lake, and then Christina had added the title, Clearwater Dumping, cracking Cassie up. Cassie had added the page with the full list of locations—stock photos of other streams, lakes, reservoirs, patches of old growth forests—and the price list for the cost of discrete industrial waste disposal at each.

The site grew. Cassie learned to set up a payment system, to embed maps and satellite views. Christina added a picture of the high school's emptied swimming pool, then the dumpsters behind the Taco Bell in Satuit, and then the whole Taco Bell. The other orchestra girls, whose humor was different than Cassie's and Christina's, not quite as nerdy though sometimes as dark, only came to appreciate the joke of it the day Cassie added the photograph of Hattie's open, food-filled mouth.

But even Hattie herself found that funny, or so she'd pretended, reposting the link, which was exactly the kind of thing Hattie would do, taking any gross thing too far. She'd shared and posted from the phone Cassie held in her hands right now (*I'm a dumpster I'm trash I'm a cum dumpster*), sitting on the edge of Christina's bed.

Cassie was standing by the open back door when Miranda emerged from the bathroom.

"You're not ten, are you?" Cassie measured the girl against her shoulder. She was short but Hattie had been about that short too, and she'd been sixteen.

Miranda screwed up her face. "You thought I was ten?"

"Come on." Cassie led her through the apartment's screen door to the little grassy yard with the lawn chairs. A line of trash cans hid this place from view of the parking lot, and here was Shara's, now Christina's, personal yard space. A purple pinwheel fluttered in the breeze. Someone had attempted a small garden, the several squash plants guarded over by a devilish gnome figurine. Cardboard boxes that had been chucked directly from the bar's back door lay nearest to the burn pile, their *this end up* arrows pointing every which way.

"Let's see who these guys are," Cassie said. The cowboys' voices droned from the opened windows of the bar. The girls crept around the building past a propane tank, a discarded deep freezer, and some old plastic tubing.

The tan van from the quarry loomed in the gravel drive, its top brushing the trees' lowest branches. Cassie took in the Kansas license plates. A torn bumper sticker read, in part, *the A in Aussie.*

"Do you have a phone?"

"Yeah, but it doesn't work."

"Take mine. Get some pictures of this." Cassie crept toward the van. If Christina were operating the website now, and if she'd added the picture of their place—their quarry—as a location, Cassie wanted to know what the men planned to dump in it.

She tried the handle. In answer came a heavy thump against the door. Cassie yelled as she jumped back, summoning the two men from the bar.

"Hey," said the man with the hat. "Didn't we see you earlier? Why'd you run?" He shook his head, still annoyed.

Christina came to the porch, and the man turned to her. "What are you two up to?" he said.

"This is my friend," Christina said.

Cassie, stupidly, warmed at this. It erased anything Christina wanted it to erase.

"These guys are Clearwater Camping clients," Christina said to Cassie. "You know, they're renting a camping site from me."

"Oh," said Cassie. Then, "Yeah. The quarry spot is beautiful."

"You said no one would be around," the man said to Christina.

Cassie tried to follow this. Christina had converted their old website to sell camp sites? And it worked?

If so, it was hilarious and brilliant: Christina renting empty air she didn't own, using her knowledge of the tucked away, worthless places of their home county. *Here's a spot you can camp.*

The man with the hat stepped from Tiki's stoop. "We could use your help with something."

Cassie stepped back. Did he think they owed him something because they'd run earlier? She couldn't place his accent. Canadians came through sometimes.

"We'd like to let those guys out, but the back door is stuck." He looked at Miranda now. "Maybe one of you gals is small enough to crawl in?"

"No," said Cassie, at the same time as Miranda said, "Sure," walking toward the van.

"The poor little doggies!" said Miranda.

Cassie looked to Tiki's stoop, but Christina had gone back inside. Maybe for one of Shara's guns, Cassie hoped, and then hoped Shara had left her one.

The man with the hat opened the cab door and Miranda hopped inside, making her way into the back compartment. It was like something Hattie would have done—stupid and dangerous and too obviously attention-seeking.

And Miranda was certainly not ten, Cassie thought again. She was much closer to Hattie's age. How hadn't she seen it? From within the windowless van she could hear Miranda's soft voice, her murmuring to whatever was in the back. Both men leaned in through their respective cab doors issuing instructions, close enough to jump in and take off with Miranda trapped. There was more discussion. How to turn the lock that the creatures had inadvertently engaged. Then the back doors flew open with a whir of color and motion and an overpowering stink as the animals—four, five, six—shot into the woods.

The men were laughing. "Pretty cooped up hey?" and "Sorry guys."

Miranda hopped down. "No worries."

One of them clapped Cassie on the shoulder. "They'll come back for their dinner."

Because Christina had not reappeared, Cassie had to confirm with Miranda. "Were those kangaroos?"

"Little ones," Miranda said. "Yep."

Cassie slipped down to the landing while Christina was cooking at the fryer—not, apparently, a vegetarian anymore. Did she live on

Tiki's greasy pucks of burgers, the matted fries?

She walked to the water, still pulling in Christina's signal. The system she'd set up at Eagle's Nest—drawing from a satellite phone—barely pushed a signal to the end of Maples' porch. The men had explained that they traveled with the kangaroos to summer fairs in the Midwest. They had a gig in Ashland next weekend, but no other place that would let them camp with their animals, much less a place with wifi.

Cassie stepped into the outboard, alone. Miranda had announced her interest in a giant plate of French fries—she hadn't had any all summer, she'd claimed. Or cheese curds. Cassie hadn't been able to convince her to leave. Now, wondering just how far Christina's signal traveled, Cassie unlooped the bowline from the bracket on the landing and pushed off with an oar.

For some reason, the little engine didn't start. Cassie gave it two pulls before checking the line and seeing the problem. Well then, she could row. She picked up the oars. Ten good pulls from the dock, angling east, Christina's signal held as steadily as ever. Even fifteen. Soon Cassie was pulling up webpages on her browser in the middle of the lake as quickly as if at the Satuit library.

It occurred to her that she could type in Shara's name. What might she learn about Christina's mother? A part of Cassie wondered if her father was still planning to join her, wherever she'd gone; if he'd be happy to trade away Cassie, their whole family, as he had her mother. Her mother, weirdly, had been visiting Christina all summer, so maybe she preferred that daughter to Cassie too. It was just the kind of thing Allie would do: demonstrate more affection and human forgiveness to the daughter of the woman who'd had an affair with her husband than to her own child.

It was too bad the internet couldn't answer the most important questions put to it—not the things you truly needed to know.

Though now that Cassie was playing around, entering names, hit after hit returned for Miranda, an Olympic hopeful in Waukesha (so that was true!), and her brother, and their grandmother, a woman whose name generated a mug shot.

* * *

Allie followed the winding path to Hemlocks cabin, a pack of cleaning supplies on her back. Emerging into the little clearing from the dark, from the whispering rustle of the tall old trees out here, she found the cabin's screen door flung wide open. Often distant Hemlocks went unrented. Who knew how long the door had been banging there on its hinges?

"Hello?"

Allie turned to look back the way she'd come. To look up at the trees' waving, dizzying tops was to remember you were on a planet that was spinning, that had an atmosphere that troubled it further.

But no one answered. No one had stayed here in weeks. It was equally unlikely any guest had wandered this far, the path crisscrossed by downed tree limbs and nets of spider webbing.

Allie was reminded, peering in, of the condition in which they'd first found a few of the cabins: the duplex, Ash and Aspen, littered with nests and scat, evidence of a series of animal inhabitants, and Maples, the cabin that would become their family home, bearing the evidence of human visitors, beer bottles and cigarette packs. Teenagers, Allie had guessed, at the same time as the mess spread across the cabins seemed to ask a question: how did they imagine they'd hold these places back from the wild?

"Hello?" she called again.

Bud had said some kayakers were arriving, people B.J. Spring had recommended. If they were regular backcountry campers, they shouldn't find anything to complain about in remote and dusty Hemlocks.

Allie busied herself in the bedroom, stretching bedding and flipping pillows. She left blankets, though who could possibly need them. Fans, she thought. Did they have extras? She relaxed as she imagined her mother's reaction if she'd lived to know her daughter's life would come to include making up beds for strangers. She'd warned Allie against the one typing course she took, backup to her art degree. Don't set yourself up to be some man's secretary.

At the same time, maybe her mother had known something: to be conscious of the things your hands learned; to be wary of the ways that might steer you.

Hemlock's one sink served both its bathroom (a closet with a toilet) and its kitchenette, a mini-fridge, cabinet, and small range-topped stove lined against the wall. Plumbing had come late to Eagle's Nest, the Murphys taking their time over the course of several decades as if indoor toilets were a fad that might not catch on. Only five years ago, Allie and Bud had filled in and boarded over the last of the outhouses, about which, on occasion, some returning guests still waxed nostalgic.

Now Allie gave the cold tap a twist and the water rushed into the sink basin. Immediately, she twisted it back. What was funny about that? The water coming so quickly? Usually you had to wait for the thumping lurch of the pump's draw, and then the water rushing up, the first smell of iron. You'd expect that turning on the water after even a day or two out of use.

Had there been water droplets already in the sink before she turned the knob? She stared at the ones that splattered it now.

Looking around the room, wondering who had recently been here, she first imagined Cassie. She'd left her mark in the décor of every cabin, but here especially her worst thrift store finds had drifted: a lime green afghan and a velvet painting of a moose. On three nails near the two-burner stove hung a battered flapjack flipper, a wooden spoon, and a flyswatter—an arrangement, a joke in juxtaposition, that signaled Allie's daughter's humor. How many times had she reassured her mother that guests didn't come to Eagle's Nest expecting *new* or *nice*?

Had she meant that to sound so cruel?

Hemlocks was also the cabin where Allie and Bud had stayed on their first visit, and where they'd first tried to live. Before they'd paved the new driveway, rerouting the resort's connection with the county road, Hemlocks had seemed the natural place for greeting guests, the face of the resort. After their first winter, where for months the sun didn't penetrate to the forest's floor, where their infant daughter made her howling introduction to the world, their perspective shifted: the lake was the heart of the resort and so where they should be. Over time Hemlocks became an outpost, one of the "hike-in" cabins.

Now Allie noticed something striking about the stove. Four of the burner coils had been lifted out of the range top. She shook her head, blinked. How hadn't she noticed immediately? The empty holes stared back at Allie like plucked out eyes.

Copper? She wondered what the coils had offered.

As strange as it was to find herself burgled, it was odder yet to think she might not have known—had nearly not even seen.

On the Madison trip with the orchestra girls last spring, Allie hadn't discovered what had happened to Hattie until the next morning, emerging from her motel room to meet the other mothers for the coffee and cold cereal of the continental breakfast. Hattie, she heard, had been the victim of a cruel prank.

The girls had performed unremarkably the afternoon before, but it didn't much matter—the entire competition one in which multiple groups could a get a first or a second, and the biggest high schools, from the cities, had their own separate weekend of judging anyway; the farm leaguers couldn't have truly competed. Afterwards, the mothers parked their fleet of cars and the equipment van as best they could under the lot lights and trudged into their motel, where a teenaged clerk dragged his eyes from his computer screen to acknowledge their presence. He blinked steadily at the bunching mothers and twenty teenaged girls at Ms. Tomas pushed forward from the back. Allie realized his view included the tape measure stuck along the inside doorframe. If needed he could report their approximate heights to the police.

Ms. Tomas distributed room keys, thin plastic that wobbled. Mrs. James assumed charge of a pizza order. At least there was a pool, and soon they were poolside, where Hattie was shouting, "Do *not* get me wet."

She hadn't brought her suit, though Allie recalled multiple pre-trip notes as to this matter. Some of the girls wore baggy sweatpants or t-shirts over theirs, padding about the deck with slices of pizza and bottles of Coke in hand. Hattie alone remained in her concert attire, a crushed velvet dress with long sleeves that must have been stifling in the chlorine-steam of the room. Allie could taste it in her limp slice of pepperoni.

"Do not get me wet," Hattie screeched again.

"Don't stand right next to us then," Cassie called. She'd been one of the first to slip from her towel, to cross the deck to the hot tub and lower herself in, fanning her hair on the concrete behind her neck. Nina had joined her, the two with their long limbs and easy strides resting with eyes half-closed as if they'd come to a city spa. As if they knew what to do at a city spa.

"Enjoy getting athletes' foot on your face," Hattie replied. "And whatever else you'll catch in that hot tub."

The mothers settled into white plastic deck chairs, commandeered the wobbling tables. They looked like their daughters in lounge pants and t-shirts, their hair off their necks in plastic-clawed buns. It was something different at least. September through May they lived in the stale air of their forced-heat houses, or if they had wood stoves, like Allie and Bud, with that dry crackle. All winter Allie's fingers and lips bled, and cracks opened along the joints over her knuckles, sharp as paper cuts.

Someone had brought a cooler and from this Tricia James began extracting ice cube trays of Jell-O shots.

"Where's that one's mother again?" she said, tilting her head to Hattie.

Allie scanned for Julia, who had appeared briefly to sit next to her and Shara during the orchestra's ten minutes on stage. The three of them hardly knew each other but Allie had been struck by their closeness in the dark, listening to their daughters, as if something did connect them. (Something would connect them, soon enough.) But Julia had left soon after—not on duty this weekend, it seemed.

"Headache?" Someone guessed.

"Oh sure," said Tricia, still eyeing Hattie. "I'd get those all the time if I had one like that."

But someone else knew that Julia's boyfriend had an apartment in the city and eyes rolled all around at that—her boyfriend. The new rich one.

Another cooler had been packed with cans of beer. One of the mothers offered one to Shara as she and Christina came onto the pool deck, Shara in a black bikini top and shiny pink shorts and unconcerned by the lip of belly overlapping the waistband. Christina wore a hooded sweatshirt and baggy men's cargo shorts. She sat at a table with her phone.

Shara indicated the thermos she carried instead, whatever was inside. "No one wants to watch the performance on TV? Christina and I saw some of it in our room," she said. This was an attempt to bring her daughter into the conversation, speaking loudly enough for her to hear and join, though Christina didn't, earbuds in.

"Oh, I think we all saw it once today," Mrs. James said, and Ms. Tomas laughed.

"It was the violins who were off," Ms. Tomas said, though not angrily, not as if she cared too much. She opened another tray of Jell-O shots, yellow and green, and offered one to Allie.

"What colors did you hope they'd be?" Tricia James said. "No Bears fans here."

So Allie had to take one, if for nothing else than to join in the spirit of Cassie, who was now directing another girl in the workings of the hot tub jets controlled by a knob on the wall. How did she know about hot tubs? The same way Cassie had known how to slide the plastic key card in the room's door, how to open the top of the room's furnace to fiddle with its setting, even though it was unlike any unit at Eagle's Nest. Cassie took to mechanical things, to systems.

"How's your room?" Ms. Tomas asked.

"Here?" She'd meant to say *me*, though. Are you asking me?

"Unless you're staying somewhere else."

"Oh, it's fine. I mean, it'll be fine. How do you suppose they get the bedspreads so thin? Ours are like single-ply toilet paper." Allie looked for Shara's eye. She'd thought she caught the brand of her humor on their car ride that morning.

But it had been the wrong thing to say to Ms. Tomas, who'd booked the motel.

"Once when we were kids," said Tricia, "we got to go down to the Dells for a vacation. All six of us kids and our parents in one room for a night and we thought we were kings."

"You were," said another mother. "A vacation for us was getting packed off to grandma's for strawberry picking. Don't know how they convinced us that was a vacation."

Allie had memories of crowding into a station wagon with cousins for a trip to Lake Michigan, closed windows and her uncle's cigarettes, an older boy cousin pinching her butt the whole way. At the beach one year, thousands of tiny, dead silver fish had washed ashore, their flashing bodies glimmering in the surf like noodles in soup. There were years and years you couldn't swim in the beaches near Chicago or Milwaukee, even Green Bay. Surely they had the same things up here, but no one wanted to remember. DDT sprayed over all those strawberries.

"Ha!" The girls were squealing.

Cassie had climbed from the hot tub and stood dripping, her damp hair splayed over her shoulders.

"Look," she said quietly, and everyone, girls and mothers, did. Cassie pointed to a camera high in the room's corner, a small black device on a swiveling arm. The next thing Cassie said Allie didn't quite hear, but Tricia James did.

"Now that's a good idea. That little hornball out front doesn't need a free show."

"Give me a towel," Cassie called, and one of the girls (an oboe player?) chucked her one from the rack. Cassie dunked it in the hot tub and then stood, steam rising off the towel and from her body. She wound the towel into a tight ball and fired; it caught on the camera, draping over its front lens. The girls and the mothers cheered.

Cassie took a bow before settling into the tub again, the deep concert bow of the cellist, her long arms to the side like wings.

That was her girl, Allie had realized, inordinately proud. A leader.

In the morning she'd been forced to rethink that.

Hattie sat amidst the mothers on a wobbling chair in the motel's lobby, someone's car blanket wrapped around her shoulders, her eyes red-rimmed and welling. Her hair was wet. One of the mothers stirred sugar from a packet into a steaming Styrofoam cup.

She'd been locked in the pool room all night wearing nothing but her underwear, the towel knocked down again from the camera so the hornball at the front desk had his show.

"She had to get in the hot tub to get warm. She could have drowned. She felt herself falling asleep a few times. Then she'd get out to jump in the pool." Tricia James kept repeating the details.

But why hadn't Hattie used the poolside phone? If she were wearing only her wet underwear, and embarrassed about the boy at the front desk, there were stacks of towels on deck. Allie made the mistake of wondering this out loud.

"You think it's her fault?"

"I just don't understand how it lasted all night," Allie said. She could see the girls locking her in for a minute, but not longer. Plus didn't anyone remember Hattie stalking the locker room in her underwear earlier that afternoon—a thing that suggested Hattie herself might have removed her own clothing. And the towel might have fallen from the camera. Was anyone else remembering this victim was Hattie?

And whose room had she been assigned to? Which mother hadn't noticed that she never came in? When all the mothers had drifted back to their rooms before their daughters, several of them having had quite a bit to drink for being on chaperone duty, Allie, at least, had done so knowing she was leaving Cassie in charge—a girl with a head on her shoulders, and who knew how to keep it around water.

But now the other mothers turned to look at Allie. Hattie had been assigned to her room. What she'd said just implicated Cassie.

"Did you see that towel was *off* the security camera?" Hattie wailed, repeating a thing that had already been said. "That gross boy was *watching* me all night."

"I didn't do it," Cassie said when Allie confronted her, back in their room.

But if she hadn't locked Hattie in, she had gone to sleep—she and Nina—knowing Hattie was still out there.

And they must have known how easily they would be blamed for it—though this was another reason to think Cassie hadn't done it. If her daughter could be mean, she was smart. Even after other stories surfaced of ways the orchestra girls had singled out Hattie, played cruel and petty jokes, said horrible things about her online, Allie couldn't shake the feeling that there was some factor still unknown about the poolside prank.

Now in Hemlocks cabin, staring into the four empty eyes of the cabin's range, wondering who knew the cabin was here and how seldom it was used, a new answer came to Allie—both for what had happened on the orchestra trip and the missing stove coils. Hemlocks was the cabin from which Allie had first spied Christina, a nine-year-old girl careening through the woods, lost. Christina had grown into the kind of girl who'd know the value of copper and who might want it, and who might have enjoyed blame for Hattie falling to Cassie, and even her mother.

It hurt to think that Christina, who'd slept at Allie's house a zillion nights (as the girls used to say), who'd spent long winter afternoons working 5,000-piece puzzles at their kitchen table, could have been so cruel—to Hattie and to them.

But what a relief, if only for a moment, to see Cassie again as blameless. Allie let out a breath with it.

Allie was working in Pines—surveying that familiar rubble, the remodel now perpetually underway—when Marius knocked on the door's thin frame to announce the arrival of the latest guests.

"Mrs. Krane?" he said.

Allie whirled. The boy's face pressed against the rusty screen.

"Some new people here." He reached for his thigh to scratch a mosquito bite, revealing the tan line he'd acquired in the last two days, the white of his thigh like he wore a second, different pair of shorts underneath. Their mother must have slathered both children in sunscreen. Perhaps she'd kept them indoors. A lump rose in Allie's throat to imagine the mother of the two children who'd shown up by canoe, the one she'd figured now to be dead.

"B.J.'s kayakers." She sighed. "Do me a favor, will you? Run a copy of the lake map up to Hemlocks?" They'd learned the hard way to provide plenty of copies of maps, lost boaters coming in hungry and angry after dark, or not coming in at all so Bud or

Cassie had to go out to look for them.

Allie stopped in Maples for an extra flashlight—the new guests would need that too out at spooky Hemlocks. But the new guests in the parking lot, a couple, had a surprise: a baby.

"You're in time for a good chance at northern lights," Allie said, while thinking *a baby?* She stowed the flashlight in her pocket and held out her arms, having found in her experience with traveling parents that you could always offer to take or hold a child. The woman gave Allie a grateful look and introduced herself as Nadia.

"That was a longer ride than we expected," she said. She had red hair, a match for the baby's curling locks.

"What's the baby's name?"

"Ferdinand."

He was a soft weight in her arms, like a sandbag prepared against a flood. Bud would love it, this reincarnation of their patron. For sure he'd tell around the campfire tonight the tale of Old Ferdy's rough first winter—and the local legend that the gravestones on the other side of the lake were related to his murderous delirium, that he'd axed his entire family one long winter night. Allie should warn him about Marius and Miranda, their possibly recently deceased mother. When Cassie was little, Bud had told her the family had gone in a less grisly way, one by one by the flu, and that the shared end number on the three small tombstones was a common burial and not death date because in the Northwoods you had to wait for a thaw.

"I named him for the explorer," the redheaded mother said. "Magellan."

Allie explained that she and her husband had named their daughter, Cassie, for an uninhabited moon in a fictional solar system in an out-of-print sci-fi novel. "My husband was a librarian."

The redhead introduced the man with her as Fred. He was the baby's father, Allie assumed. As he unloaded their two backpacks and the diaper bag, Fred shouldered the wrong strap, spilling Ferdinand's bottles and wipes and backup onesies onto the gravel. Nadia gave Fred a guarded look before bending to help him repack the bag. Nadia and Fred weren't young but were fit enough to be kayakers, both with the physiques of people whose pre-baby lives must have included hours at the gym and more hours reading food labels in grocery stores. Considering their two small backpacks, Allie supposed B.J. supplied the adventure gear.

"Hemlocks is unique," Allie said. "I think you'll like it. I wish I lived there." She believed this as she said it, thought of living out there under the protection of the thickest trees.

But had she just imagined a future for herself alone? Without Cassie, or Bud?

Then from the lawn, Marius shouted: "Cassie's back!" His voice wobbled with alarm.

Allie found him on the other side of the sheet Bud had strung for the outdoor movie that evening. It luffed in the breeze, though Bud was nowhere to be seen. The girls had gone to gas up, Marius explained. They'd been gone for hours. Now, Cassie had returned without his sister.

Allie met her daughter in her incoming boat at the end of the dock. *Gas up* meant Tiki's.

"Where's Miranda?"

"She wanted to hang out." Cassie shrugged. "And this thing's been gnawed through." She held up a length of old gas line. She'd rowed in.

"By what?"

"By something that must have a bellyache now."

Allie hated the laugh that came with this, the spirit of it that seemed to confirm she'd just left a child at Tiki's—dropped her off, Allie could only picture, near the shoreline totem pole that included, over rat-like legs and a hairy bear's belly, a segment with bared women's breasts. The whole thing leaned comically, top heavy, awaiting the final ice shove that would upend it, pull the rug from beneath her feet with all the men at the bar there to laugh.

"I want to tell you something again and this time you have to believe me." Cassie's tone had shifted, quiet and earnest.

Allie dropped to her butt on the dock and reached to meet the bow of her daughter's boat with the toe of her sneaker.

"Kate kidnapped those children." Cassie's voice was low, looking over Allie's shoulder to Marius, who'd drifted to the far end of the dock. Allie's shoe had met her daughter's boat and now she locked her knee to keep Cassie from docking. Cassie looked at her mother's leg, her face quizzical.

"Mom, I *mean* it. These kids have been missing since June. There's an Amber Alert. The police think their grandmother took them. They were last seen being picked up by her after their last day of school. Miranda's hair has been dyed so she doesn't look like the photographs of her online but it's her."

Allie's face must have given away what she thought of all of this. She still could not believe Cassie had left Miranda at Tiki's, that Tiki's was a place her daughter apparently went.

And how often? For how long?

"Kate has a record. Once she hid out on the Bad River reservation for months."

Allie allowed the boat to bend her knee. "Where'd you come

up with all this?"

Cassie's face flashed blank. Then she said "Christina. I borrowed her phone. It's all online."

Allie had known it; she'd known her daughter, somehow, was cheating the phone punishment. She hadn't known she was in touch with Christina. Now all the possibilities she'd imagined before—her daughter's innocence, Christina solely to blame—popped and dissolved, soap bubbles meeting jack pine needles, or simply disappearing as they traveled upward too fast through layered temperatures of air.

"Their mother is dead," Allie said. She tried to say it quietly, Marius still hovering. But her fury was growing. Miranda was a girl dealing with the death of her mother and Cassie had just left her at Tiki's—a place of sadness incarnate, which was Allie's real problem with the bar that was their nearest neighbor. Not just the drunk men and their illegal fireworks from the beach, or their upended snowmobiles in ditches in the morning, but that it was a place where grown adults greeted the morning with the crack of a beer; where Shara, like everyone's mother in a strange hell, was the only one who worked—where her daughter was going to repeat the performance.

And that Bud had spent any time there—as if all he and Allie had done in moving here, in recognizing the horror of the way they were living and trying to escape it, was in the end no different than what everyone else was doing these days, just putting one foot in front of the other, getting by without a conscious thought.

Allie gave the boat a firm push. "Go get Miranda," she said, so tired.

Marius interrupted, his little voice breaking. "My mom's not dead. She's in Canada."

"Huh?" said Allie. Could Kate have told such a lie to her own grandchildren? Something like the family dog had to go to a different family. *Mom just had to go to Canada for a while.*

"My mom's not dead," Marius repeated. "We talked to her on the phone last night. We're going to meet up with her."

"Their parents are divorced," Cassie said, louder because she was drifting, and struggling with the oars in the oarlocks. The chewed gas line, Allie remembered. Everything was falling apart.

"My parents are divorced. Yeah." Marius shrugged.

They watched Cassie row away. "You don't think Miranda took off, do you?" Marius asked.

"What? No." Allie asked if he wanted to call his sister.

"Kate took the SIM cards from our phones."

"Shh," Allie told him again. Then she told him to sit on the dock, watch for the loons. That always calmed her.

The new couple with the baby had left the parking lot—hiked out to Hemlocks, Allie hoped. If they'd caught the scene, she supposed they'd been given a show of what awaited them as parents of a teenager.

Her hand on the doorknob of Maples, Allie heard the crunching of wheels on gravel—and then more wheels, more gravel. One, two, three, four cars and a truck pulling a trailer loaded with kayaks came snapping through their trees to fill the tiny space of their parking lot. They'd never get that trailer turned around, not with all the cars already parked here.

A woman with a red bandana and an expensive pair of sunglasses balanced above her forehead leaned from her window. "B.J. sent us. You're holding some cabins?"

Allie would never be able to explain it to Bud, how she'd thought the couple with the baby were the kayakers. Who would bring a baby on an overnight kayak trip? How could she have made that weird mistake?

Except he'd never said there'd be a dozen of them.

And except Allie herself would have brought a baby into a kayak, if she felt she had to. Long ago she'd run pregnant here to the Northwoods.

CHAPTER 5

MIRANDA'S ABILITY WITH the hula hoop reminded Allie of Cassie's skills with the Ford's tricky innards. It was the mark of a child who'd spent plenty of time alone.

"Kate had one of these at her place," Miranda said. Allie was walking the young girl, now returned from Tiki's, to her grandmother's cabin through a new tent village erected on the lawn. The kayakers with the giant trailer had not managed to get it turned around or unloaded, but in answer to Eagle's Nest's lack of vacancies had produced a store's worth of gear, multicolored tents and intricate cooking utensils, sleeping bags and latrine shovels. Allie had drawn the line there. They could use the bathroom off Maples' kitchen.

"Where's Kate's place? Where does your grandmother normally live?"

Miranda shrugged. She didn't know.

They passed where Bud was working, building a kindling tee pee.

Ceremoniously, for an audience when he could get one, Bud's trick was to start bonfires by rubbing sticks together and catching the small spark with wool batting. It embarrassed Allie—that he'd spent half a winter practicing it, that there were real Native Americans, Bad River and Lac du Flambeau Ojibwe groups, living, hunting, and fishing on territories around the resort.

In Red Oaks cabin, Kate stood at the stove. Marius, shirtless, read in a chair. Allie was surprised to find Kate. So often since they'd arrived the kids roamed the property without her. For a kidnapper, she didn't keep tight tabs on her charges.

Allie also remembered that Kate, near Old Ferdy's, had been asking about the portages, that she had possibly been hiding something in the canoe. Camping gear?

Miranda pushed her way through the door. Allie lingered on the steps, taking in the scene. "If you'll be fishing tomorrow, we do CPR here—catch, photograph, and release." She had meant to apologize for how the girl had been left at Tiki's. Instead, she was repeating the no-fishing fishing policy, here at the fishing resort.

"There some pets I should know about?" Kate asked.

There were, in fact, Old Mickey and Minnie—fish Cassie had long ago named. Old Minnie, wizened muskie warrior, sported a torn lip and gill from the times she'd had to bite the line to twist away.

"I stepped on something," Miranda said, bent over her bare foot. Before either woman could get there, Allie or Kate, Miranda reached for the hook herself and yanked it out. She yelped and jumped to the other foot, blood dribbling over the cabin floor.

"It was hardly in there," she said, shaking it off even as she hobbled. "The hook hadn't totally hooked."

"Tougher than nails," said Kate, turning to her pot on the stove but addressing Allie. "Girls these days."

As evening fell, their guests returned from the water, from their hikes or naps, and began to congregate by the fire. This excepted B.J.'s kayak group, busy assembling their tiny expensive tools and water filtration devices. The others began to gobble the bits of fish Bud was frying, caught by guests in Ash who'd ignored the fishing policy. Watching the guests pluck beers from coolers, some of the bottles Bud had brought from the city with a new wolf's head label, Allie wondered if the blue gill fishers had used live bait, perhaps from one of the roadside stands south of here blithely selling the exotic earthworms everyone else was trying to keep away from the duff layer of their top soil, their sugar maples.

The bed sheet shivered between the trees. At the start of summer they'd sit out on the lawn as if under shopping mall lights as late as nine-thirty, ten, waiting for enough dark to start the movie. Now the sun had shifted its position and set sooner and seemingly more quickly, a fiery meteor in descent, like they had relocated to a different planet.

"Should be a good sunset tonight," Carla said. "I can *smell* the smoke."

Carla and her husband had been here for a week, birdwatchers from downstate, the Sparta area. They were a bit older than Allie and Bud, gray-haired and retired. They'd spent the day in the canoe, the red of his nose and the already empty water bottle at her feet attesting to how hot it had been again—unseasonal, people said every season.

"There's a chance for the aurora," Allie said. Guests with fancy cameras and specific lenses, with alerts and alarms set appropriately sometimes caught truly great photos. Allie preferred when the green wash caught her by surprise, when she didn't know and wasn't quite sure what she was seeing out her bedroom window.

"Not sure what we'll see with the smoke tonight." Carla's husband scrolled on his phone.

"You don't smell it?" Carla said to Allie. "You've grown used it." She'd noticed the smoke from the Canadian fires first thing and had been coughing all day out on the water. The fires had crossed over to this side too, she said, raging through the Boundary Waters again this year.

Lots of people had to cancel those vacations.

"What will the smoke do to the aurora?" Allie asked. She'd seen how it affected sunsets.

This brought Bud into the conversation, prompted his musings. Northern lights did not involve sunrays but cosmic rays, and so what part of the spectrum might be blocked or distorted? Still, it was somewhat rare to see the aurora with the naked eye even at this latitude, even on a cloudless night. Allie took this rambling discourse as her cue to circulate, to leave, though she only got as far as the nearby lawn—one patch where tents had not been staked and where a woman played with her young daughter.

"That's all she'll wear," the girl's mother said. The girl, about five, wore winter pajamas with feet. "I told her she'll get hot." Mayella, Allie remembered, was the little girl's name. They'd arrived earlier in the week but had kept to themselves.

"You must be from down south." Eavesdropping Carla called over the fire.

"Bruce Crossing," the mother replied.

"That near Oshkosh?" Carla said. "That probably seems south to *you*, Allie."

"Oshkosh? Oh, sure, some folks go there for the sun." Allie played the accent for Carla's enjoyment. Most guests didn't remember that Allie and Bud had lived in the city. People who'd stayed didn't like to notice how many had left. "We go to Antigo to ShopKo," Allie said, and Carla laughed. Allie avoided Bud's frown of disapproval. The fire leapt about in the little home he'd built for it, the night darker around it.

A woman with a white ponytail cleared her throat. "Why not the new Target in Satuit?"

These guests were staying in Birches, another couple Allie and Bud's age, though they looked younger for their better shape. Like the kayakers, they were no doubt the kind of people to be counted upon to declare that there was no such thing as bad weather, only bad clothing.

It was what Allie believed too, in general. But there was weather, circumstance, in which you could die in even really good Gore-Tex.

"We live in Satuit." The woman introduced herself as Frieda.

Bud whistled. "You arrived by bicycle." Allie had seen them carry their bikes with them into their cabin. No license plate when they registered, when she filled out all the paperwork the state required now (and which she never had for Kate, come to think of it, since Kate had paid in cash).

"We go everywhere by bike."

Allie looked to Carla, whose cue this was.

"Surely you've been to Sparta then."

Frieda said they'd get down there this winter with their fat tire bikes. This trip they were traveling back to Satuit from their summer place in Canada.

Carla found this hysterical. "You winter in Satuit?"

Allie wondered at that too—and they biked between their Canada place and their Satuit place? Then she asked a question without thinking. "How do you get up there?"

"We had a harder time getting back *in* this year," Frieda's husband, Phil, said. "If you can believe that."

"Oh, there was such a wait on the bridge!" Frieda added.

"We've owned property there a long time," Phil said. He smiled, having come to the end of what was polite to discuss. Allie flushed, thinking of how long it had been since she'd been around people like Frieda and Phil that she'd brought up money so directly. They simply paid the visas, of course, the exit and entrance, both times they crossed the international bridge at Sault Ste. Marie, the Soo as people said.

It was past time for Allie's campfire job: running to the house for extra sweatshirts and blankets. The lights from Maples spilled across the lawn, where Allie came across the mother and her little girl again, this time playing on one of the hammocks.

"Be careful, be careful," the woman chanted, swinging her girl in the net of the hammock, laughing—and then the girl did fall, the hammock dumping her unceremoniously.

The mother looked sheepishly at Allie. "Don't tell me these years pass *so quickly*," she said.

"I would never." Allie remembered the woman's name. Gwen. The merest whiff of laundry detergent recalled to Allie the long winters she and Bud had spent alone with a baby and then a toddler, trapped by snow in their cabin. One late night after a long dark day—baby crying, food stores low, the wood stove clogged and smoking, Allie had come downstairs to discover a chimney fire and had sat a long moment watching it, wondering what might happen if she just went ahead and *opened* the doors and windows.

"Where's Bruce Crossing?" Allie asked. That was where the woman had said she was from, but Allie didn't think that was near Oshkosh.

"North of here. The Upper Peninsula." Gwen named the

highway that ran there. "We're refugees."

"I heard you flooded." Allie had read that in the brief headlines that occasionally flashed across the family laptop.

"They say that's why we were closed," Gwen said. "Yep."

The little girl climbed into the hammock again, tipping precariously and drawing her mother's attention. Before Allie had a small child, it had never occurred to her that her attention might not be a thing that belonged to her, but that it could be taken over and piloted by someone else, a remote IT worker taking over your screen.

The house was lit like a jack-o'-lantern. They'd have to extinguish those lights to see any of the aurora later.

In her kitchen, Allie found Marius and Miranda filling backpacks with food from her pantry: granola bars and cereal, a loaf of bread, can of black beans, a bag of jelly beans. Allie blinked, her eyes adjusting. The children went on with their pillaging.

"Find everything you need?" she asked, bemused. On the countertop sat the weird tool from the other day, the one with the row of spikes. Allie picked it up again. Was it out because Bud had been inspecting it? It would be just like him and his ex-librarian friends, lurkers of chat rooms, to have researched the name of the thing, its use and provenance, all the information that would ruin the tool for Allie—the mystery of it. Intuition had led Allie to most of what she knew or needed to know about the world, and she'd been waiting for the moment to know this tool, its purpose and use.

"Kate said we needed this stuff," said Marius. "She wants us to leave right now."

"Are you going to let them go, Mom?" Cassie sat in the kitchen booth, watching the children stuff the backpacks. They still wore their swimsuits. Only Marius wore shoes—flip-flops.

"Are there wolves out there? I heard wolves last night." Marius filled a water bottle at the sink.

"Kate said those were loons." Miranda rummaged through Allie's junk drawer and extracted matches.

"They're detectives," said Marius. "Those people with the baby. They're looking for us."

"Oh they are? With a baby?" Allie looked to Cassie. Was she the origin of this latest addition to the story—new implausibility on top of the wild idea that Kate had kidnapped her own grandchildren?

"She posted a picture of my sister online," Marius said, his small voice breaking with betrayal. He pointed at Cassie. "That's how they found us."

Allie looked out the small kitchen window. The parking lot was dark now, but she could still see the redheaded woman's small car behind the hulking kayak trailer. Wherever the kids had come from with their canoes couldn't have been too far away, and yet Kate had asked if they could stay here. There *was* something they were running from, or to.

Allie didn't know what to believe. It was the perennial question: was anything more or less dire than it seemed? Everything was in such perpetual process of ruin that the difficulty lay in assessing the weight of each disaster—and then in deciding on the worth of action, or when to act.

She knew her default move, her go-to.

On their porch sat a small bag of Bud's kindling, bundled. "Were you going to take our firewood?"

"I was, but I'm not sure I can carry all this down to the canoe." Marius was trying to zipper the backpack he had filled.

"Your *canoe?*" Allie asked, now for the first time startled.

The trek about which Kate had been inquiring, the one on the other side of the lake, was not one to make in the dark with children.

Allie pulled the big flashlight from the cabinet below the junk drawer. She held it beneath her chin. This game had made a very young Cassie squeal with delight, with a terror mixed with glee. "If you're on the run, there's really only one place to hide out safely."

The kids looked to each other before looking to Allie.

"Jambajune," she whispered, flicking on the light.

Their feet snapped on branches, Allie only half certain she'd found the right path. It may have been years since she'd gone this way, and it occurred to her that Jambajune could have changed. There used to be a perfect clearing into which moonlight shone, a bower of blackberries and a giant balsam fir with a place to crawl inside, like beneath a woman's hooped skirt. She'd first showed the place to Cassie and Christina, helped them christen it, teased them into their first solo overnight camp outs. It's not scary, Allie had said. It's like any other place in the woods. At the same time, she knew what they felt, could hardly believe she could deny to them the feeling that there was something singular and otherworldly about the clearing, in the way the limbs of the ringing pines moved and shook in the wind.

Jambajune lay close to the logging road that led up to the Old Lapham house, now collapsed in the way of a baby's smashed birthday cake. No one came down here anymore.

The clearing, when they found it, hadn't changed. The throne—a tree stump—had only crumbled more, mushy in its middle. Allie turned on the flashlight and used it to rummage in her backpack. She'd show the children how to lay the blankets down over the soft needles and cones under the big fir, to make a perfect nest.

"Are you leaving us here?" asked Miranda.

Allie handed over the funny tool she'd grabbed off the counter. It had a heft to it, and the girl gripped it, nodding.

* * *

Cassie climbed the stairs to her room as quickly as possible. She stashed the phone Julia had given her—Hattie's old phone—deep under her mattress.

Cassie's mother—upon hearing Marius' claim that something Cassie had posted online had brought police detectives to their home—had chosen to take Marius and Miranda into the woods. To hide and protect *them*.

There was no other way to understand it.

She pulled the phone back out from under the mattress, staring at its darkened screen. Were anyone to check it, they'd see not only that Cassie had posted a picture of a missing, wanted child, Miranda, but also that she had known it. *Hostage situation*, she'd written, of all the dumb things. There was the state police department's Amber Alert page in her browsing history. Thumbing furiously, Cassie began erasing, though she knew deleted search histories and even flashes that had faded could be retrieved. Even the most clueless parents had pulled so much from the girls' confiscated phones last spring.

When Cassie set up the satellite system she'd discovered a spot where the signal bounced best—the roof just outside her gabled bedroom window. Now Cassie pushed up the sash and eased out, moving carefully. It was only a one-story drop into grass, but spraining either ankle would make driving the Fjord a challenge—and then where would she be? Truly stuck.

In Hattie's old photo files, Cassie came across copies of pics

Cassie had once snapped. Why had Hattie saved them? The pictures had first been posted on flash without Hattie's knowledge—Hattie drunk and stumbling around a bonfire pit, Hattie with chest and hip thrust flirting with some older guy who was clearly more interested in the keg. The unflattering pictures that Cassie had flashed out that night continued like a horror movie with a lurching, slow-moving villain, one impossible to stop.

Maybe this was what Hattie had felt when she'd seen them— the possible roads ahead of her closing, the inevitability of her fate.

* * *

Alone in the semi-dark of the logging road, the children safely hidden at Jambajune, Allie allowed herself to think about Elmira Lapham and the Lapham house, though it had been a long time. They'd been four months into their ownership of Eagle's Nest when they'd discovered they had a long-term renter, that the falling-down house just east of their access to the county road sat in fact on their property; that though it wasn't one of the rental cabins of the resort, the decrepit two-story with its already-collapsed garage was also their responsibility.

Allie was sure the Murphys had not disclosed this, nor could she imagine how the extra building could have been missed on the paperwork, but what were they going to do? Kick the woman out? In the end, they'd allowed her to continue living there, the rent check helpful those first years, at least when Elmira did hike down the logging road to pay it. Now she and her boys had moved on and grown up, and each year the empty house sank further into itself, erasing the problem the way all problems, eventually, would be erased.

Elmira had even become a friend to Allie in those early years. Allie had just given birth in a remote outpost with winter descending. It was a gift to discover their nearest neighbor was a mother too—if in another era Elmira's four wild boys could have formed their own circus troop, each as capable of walking the roofline of the tall rental house as he was of riding in a handstand on a dirt bike. They ripped pieces from the old house's kitchen cabinets for sleds and catapult platforms and deer stands from which they zip lined on other homemade devices. Baby Cassie and the youngest boy, a few years older and marked by a cleft lip, played on a mouse-chewed rug during Allie's visits and Allie absorbed everything she could about teething and soothing, diaper rashes and crib death, Elmira's easy way of balancing Cassie one-armed against her hip a physical emblem of her deep expertise.

One time, when Cassie had just turned two, they even left her with Elmira for a weekend. Allie remembered this as she left Miranda and Marius, as she followed the old logging road back to Eagle's Nest.

She'd had this same feeling then. She'd felt fine at the house—she always felt an extreme comfort at Elmira's, even with its bb-gun-shot-out and plastic-garbage-bag-covered windows. Elmira brewed tea in a cracked pot and baked tiny sugar cookies from her home country, Albania. Allie's dread only came as she left, like a flu setting in.

The fear had compounded with their distance as she and Bud piloted back to Chicago, without their baby. It would be the only time they would ever go back, a thing they didn't know then. In fact, at the time the trip was to see if they wanted to return, if they could. And so they'd traveled on even as Allie's dread about leaving Cassie grew—until, at some point, it popped. Emerging from the trees, passing city after city, their former life pre-Cassie enfolded them.

Years had passed since Allie had seen so many cars or people, so many lanes of traffic. Even with her forehead pressed to the passenger side glass, Allie couldn't see the tops of the buildings. Intersections were thickened mazes of motion and missed collisions.

On the street, Allie could hardly move for bumping into or being bumped into by people who walked faster than she walked now. Yet staying in place was not possible. The motion of people on the sidewalk, having to flow around those who sat, or who lay with their plastic bags and cardboard signs, worked like a sucking, varying-paced tide. At the same time, from the corner of her eye, she saw women in heels step from cars that no longer looked like cars. They held phones that didn't look like phones. Then, in their hotel lobby, the glass doors canceled all sound of the exterior world. They entered a cathedral of metal and glass. Allie heard thrumming, caught a hint of clean chlorine on the air, and turned for the sight of an indoor waterfall, the smooth pour of it braiding from a third-floor height along a fabricated rock course to settle into a chattering river and finally a placid pool. The crystals of the rock picked up the gold glint from the frames of the lobby's artwork and banister posts. In their bathroom on the twentieth floor they found an ecosystem in their shower: a stall tiled in limestone with sprigs of green—living plants—growing in the cantilevered ledges. Each tiny soap released a different smell of woodland flowers.

They hadn't told Elmira they were considering moving back, that they had an appointment with a realtor. They went to a restaurant they'd once loved, a Ukrainian place with old world candlelight. Allie remembered it affectionately as a dive but now the prices, like with the hotel, were bewildering, as if there'd been a misprint. She mistook the appetizer list for the entrees. She wondered if they'd come to the wrong place—but she knew the building. To get to the bathroom one wound through a shared back hallway where different doors led to other businesses—a brewery, a gym—or upstairs to apartments. All of it was familiar, or should have been, even Allie's peek through the glass door into the gym where streetlight glinted off the chrome of exercise equipment, the curve of a kettlebell.

Except this time when Allie's eyes adjusted to the dark she made out additional shapes amongst the weights and pulleys, the benches and barbells: a family, the children asleep on the mats. The father rested against the wall with a baby on his shoulder, the back of his head and slumped shoulders repeating in the mirror behind him.

It was air conditioned in there, Allie told herself. The father with access keys had likely slipped his family down from an upstairs apartment to escape the heat. Surely these people had housing. She remembered the full, hot stickiness of an overheated child in her own arms—an uncomfortable sunburned child, a crying child.

She preferred that thought, anyway, to dwelling on other reasons people might be sleeping in the gym the same way they were sleeping on the city streets, sleeping everywhere the next day as they drove around with the realtor. As if it weren't that the population had changed, surged from the south and the coasts, or that the city had not kept pace to accommodate them, but as if some sleep sickness had taken over, dropping humans where they waited in the building lobbies or alleyways or beneath underpasses, in the ditches and culverts between suburban shopping malls.

There'd always been homelessness, the realtor said—and in a funny way, as if it were irrelevant to her work.

Allie returned from the woods to find the sky and her house

darkened, though no one had started the movie on the outdoor screen. Guests milled about the property, roaming the front lawn and parking lot, the small strip of beach and the dock. Some had waded into the darkened water. As her eyes adjusted, Allie made out a beaded line of bobbing kayaks, all eight from the adventure group's trailer, each turned backwards toward the house like surfers readying for a wave.

Everyone was looking up at the sky, most with their phones raised.

Gwen, the mother of the young girl, sat in one of the Adirondack chairs, a bundle over her shoulder and a beer in her hand. Her face was one of the few not craned upward. Seeing Allie, she lit into a mischievous grin.

"*No*," said Allie, looking around the yard, dumbfounded. All she could see against the bruised dark of the overcast sky was a thin haze drifted from the wild fires.

Someone standing out in the lake was facing *south* with their camera—oohing and aahing the loudest. Allie had seen guests pretend to make out the Northern Lights before, but never en masse. What a story it made for their social media feeds, though even on a clear night, no clouds or fires, it was tough to get a good picture of the aurora with a cell phone.

"You can't even see the moon tonight," Allie said.

Gwen shook her head, silently laughing.

She was from here, Allie remembered—or close enough, the Upper Peninsula. But she'd had to leave Bruce Crossing because of something in addition to the flooding. Their town had been *closed*, she'd said. And who, forced for some reason to abandon their home, came to a resort for a few days?

Gwen patted the baby on her shoulder—not her daughter, the

five-year-old, but the baby with the tuft of red hair. Gwen held him out to her.

"People are always handing me their children," Gwen said. "What do you suppose that means?"

Baby Ferdy's small mouth found the dried spot of drool he'd loosed earlier onto Allie's shoulder. Allie remembered a time she would have handed baby Cassie to anyone who'd happened by. A time she and Bud had been too many weeks alone with an infant.

"Been a while since I got to hold one that small. His mom didn't even look to see that I'd caught him she threw him to me so fast," Gwen said.

"Where'd she go?" Allie recalled Nadia, the mother, and the man Fred (the father?) she'd sent out to Hemlocks.

Most of their fleet was missing, some guests having joined the kayak group. One boat in particular bobbed quite far out—the one Cassie had showed her earlier with the chewed-up gas line. Rowing, Nadia and Fred had nearly reached the far shore.

"They seem to have somewhere in mind to be," Gwen said.

"My daughter thinks they're detectives," Allie said.

"What?" Gwen had stood from her chair to stretch but stopped stretching now. "Border patrol you think?"

Allie considered her, this woman from Bruce Crossing. Then from above them a voice said, "They are."

Cassie sat on the roof outside her gabled bedroom window, just above her mother's head. As comfortable as you please, as if she perched there every night. She'd been hidden in the shadows, even as every set of eyes on the lawn trained upward over the top of the house. Allie thought of the dozens of nights this summer she'd paused outside Cassie's closed bedroom door, hesitating, listening, not sure if she heard breathing, except Cassie's truck was in the driveway, so surely she was home.

Maybe those nights she'd been out on the roof on her secret phone, online—gone, in this different way.

Blood ran to Allie's shoulders, across her torso; her eyesight sharpened in the dark.

"Mom!" Cassie hissed.

The baby burped on Allie's chest.

"I can *see* them," Cassie said. "Kate left in one of her canoes and those agents are chasing her. She's nearly to Old Ferdy's now, but they're right behind her. She left without the kids."

They were agents now? These parents of the baby in her arms? Allie noticed the glow in her daughter's hand—the phone. Was she attempting to take pictures too? Citizen journalist. Live streamer.

Allie's jaw stiffened, her neck and back. She handed the baby to Gwen.

Where was Bud? Someone would have to turn on the house lights to lead the idiots on the water back to shore.

"Mom!" said Cassie. But Allie walked away.

She crossed quickly, moving faster than was safe in the dark. Surely, she was about to find a croquet wicket, break an ankle, but no, she kept sailing.

A memory of an old sensation came to her. It had used to be you'd step on frogs out in the lawn at night. First the small crunch of bone, then, if you were barefoot, the warm release of their urine. But how long had it been since she'd heard or seen frogs out here? Much less when there'd been so many that stepping on one in the dark had been inevitable. It had used to be that you couldn't sleep at night for their throaty chirping.

But one season the frogs had disappeared, like Hattie, the flutist who'd run a hose from the exhaust of her mother's SUV in through the driver's window, who'd been a Northwoods girl like the rest such that she understood engines and exhaust systems and the usefulness of a new, well-sealed garage. She used a bracelet, one with a complicated clasp, to lock her wrist to the steering wheel, insurance against last-minute doubt.

And she'd left her phone open, unlocked, its long stream of received messages and social media feeds ready and waiting. If only it weren't that way with so many things, with everything: that in retrospect, one could read all the writing on the wall.

PART II

CHAPTER 6

IN THE MORNING, Bud heard the couple with the baby drop their keys in the box.

No, he didn't suppose Hemlocks had been that comfortable for them.

He depressed the button on the coffee bean grinder. He could have told Allie those two weren't the back-country kayakers by the serious, worried way in which they negotiated the simple task of packing the car. The man didn't seem to know how to put the baby in the car seat. The kayaking group, though they might fuss with their techy gear, were big picture thinkers, cool and confident. Talking with them last night, Bud had met oral surgeons and attorneys, CFOs and venture capitalists. They hired people like B.J. and Bud to worry about how to get the kayaks off the trailer, how to turn the thing around and get it back up the driveway, which B.J. and Bud *had* worried about last night, and somehow managed in the dark. That group left this morning at dawn, summoned by the tiny alerts of their fancy watches. They'd left no trace but matted grass, the snail trails of their kayak bottoms in the sand.

After the couple with the baby departed it was so quiet you

could hear the small creatures in the scrub—the squirrels, the chipmunks, the ones that readied year-round for winter.

It wasn't unusual for Bud to rattle around alone in the morning. Cassie was a teenager, her sleep requirements as strange again as a baby's. Allie didn't always go to sleep or stay asleep for long in their bed. She might wake in the night and sit on the beach or, Bud suspected, she let herself into unoccupied cabins when they had vacancies. On a few recent occasions he had found dents in mattresses in the shapes of bodies.

Cassie came slipping down the stairs in socks. Stretching and wincing, she looked like she hadn't slept.

"Horror movie marathon?" Bud had introduced her to *Night of the Living Dead*. All of the *Elm Streets*.

She slid into her spot at the breakfast nook. "You need to know about something," she said. Then she gave him a story like from a Norwegian thriller—what had happened last night. In her version, the couple with the baby were police detectives.

"High speed chase by canoe," Bud said.

"And row boat."

"But they didn't catch them." Bud gave the only part of the story he knew, the end. He'd just now seen the redhead and her husband leave.

"The kids weren't with Kate," Cassie said.

"And you're on the side of the cops?" Bud said. "*If* they're cops."

"Don't tease me."

"I'm just observing something."

Then Allie came in through the screen door with the children.

Marius looked like he'd crawled from a hole in the ground. Pine needles poked from his hair and mud flaked from his flip-flops.

Miranda set a weird antique tool down on the countertop with a thud.

"We thought they'd never leave," said Marius, sighing, reaching for a cup of coffee.

"They didn't get Kate," Cassie said to her mother. "She's still out there, and now they've left."

Bud didn't like to pry into guests' business, but he decided to check out the situation of Kate—a guest last seen going out alone on water.

His own suspicions tended less toward the criminal than the sad and familiar. A woman who took off on her own, who'd come here last minute and expressed little interest in the children in her care (who'd left them last night under Allie's supposed supervision) was most likely a woman who'd come here, as guests occasionally did, to do some private drinking.

He knocked first on the door of Red Oaks. Once Bud had favored this—the biggest and nicest of the cabins—for their family home, but Allie's point about it was true: it was too big to heat. He'd also known after watching his wife go through one pregnancy that they wouldn't have more children. What would she have wanted to do then—move to the bottom of the ocean? To a compound surrounded with barbed wire?

Still, why hadn't they chosen the biggest, nicest cabin for themselves?

When no one answered his knock Bud risked opening the door, poking his head in to call Kate's name.

By the shoreline waited the signs of last night's excitement: boats poorly tethered, garbage and recycling bins spilled over, lawn chairs pulled to spots that didn't make sense in the light of day.

Bud didn't mind when guests stayed up late, had a good time. And unlike Allie, he had thought that if you squinted last night you could see a few faintly streaking columns of the aurora borealis, despite the smoke and haze.

He counted the canoes twice. All present, except for one of Kate's two silver ones.

He motored past Old Ferdy's, buzzing the shoreline just close enough that he'd see the silver canoe parked somewhere in the reeds if it were there. His theory ran that Kate had wandered farther than Little Eagle anyway. There was another bar on Big Eagle, Rosie's.

In the passageway Bud caught sight of Bridget, overhead with a fish in her claws. It had been a good number of years since eagles had been declared phoenixed back from near extinction. Now their Bridget nested in a tree between the lakes reliably enough to send guests for photographs, and across the county eagles were so ubiquitous people joked about hunting them, like the Canadian geese who ruined beaches, lawns, and boat covers and had earned themselves their own unofficial open season. Eagles could dive bomb your small pets and were, fundamentally, lazy. Some, including their Bridget, didn't bother to migrate anymore. Others had been observed to eat their own young rather than protect them from predators—and imagine that, the supposedly regal, majestic bird. Bud gave Bridget a salute anyway as he motored beneath her nest through the passage between the two lakes. She flicked her beak after him like thumbing a nose.

On Big Eagle Bud might catch sight of one of the smaller craft B.J. was hawking these days. Along the north ridge of the bigger lake perched a row of new two-story "cabins," each with its own staircase winding to the shore, its own new aluminum dock and multiple lifts storing jet boats, high-end pontoons with grills, and jet skis—the mosquitos of watercraft. It all represented downstate or out of state money, though. Weekenders with more to do than spend too many weekends at their weekend places.

Bud left the north shore, crossing for Rosie's bar. He hadn't been there himself in a few years, and that was all the time it was taking these days for big changes, for reboots and course reversals.

He didn't catch sight of the kayakers; they had long moved on.

"You have to guess." In the bar, Rosie herself pulled Bud a tap, said she'd scramble him up some eggs. The bar was not crowded but there was news: two guys had come in with something odd they'd caught. Now there was a betting pool—was it animal, vegetable, or mineral? Cash and a Bloody Mary on the line.

You don't need genus and species, Rosie explained, just give us your guess. As she talked Bud read a sign advertising a waffle special. A Sunday brunch on Big Eagle?

"What's the buy?" Those in the bar wore scruffy beards and fish-gut-spattered jeans. Some of their hats wore themselves, stiffened with sweat. Still, they were out for Sunday bloodies, maybe brunch—and so vacationers, no matter how they were trying to dress.

A guess cost two bucks. Bud was surprised by how many people rose to go take his look with him. He hoped it wasn't a lamprey variety—some new invasive horror. Also, he needed to work in a question about Kate without going so far as to label her a missing guest, which sounded more serious than Bud felt it was.

"Hey," he asked Rosie at the top of the stairs leading down to the dock, "You seen a lady with silver hair in here? Kind of a butchy cut?" He didn't know that he thought Kate's short hair was butch, but he was conscious of asking around about a woman. "In her sixties?"

"You're gonna have to be more specific, lover boy," said Rosie. She was already watching his expression, curious to see what he'd think of whatever was in the boat. From this angle, Bud could see the size of it, draped over with a tarp.

"What kind of test line you got on?" Bud called to one of the men behind them.

"Didn't pull it from the lake," he said. "Shoreline. Last night."

Bud thought of the noise he'd heard and told guests was a cherry bomb, common enough Fourth of July remnant. But it *had* been gunfire then—this guy "pulling in" something from the shoreline.

The hunter pushed past them on the dock, stepped down in the boat so he could peel back the cover. Whatever was down there, at that size, had to be a mammal.

"You got a hodag?" Bud joked and got his laugh.

The hind leg was covered in brown fur. There was a curve of haunch. Bud knew the animal immediately but was too surprised to name what he was seeing.

But why not? Big Eagle Lakers who installed hot tubs on their outdoor decks, who used their million-dollar places only three weekends a year, probably kept exotic pets too. Lizards, snakes, baby tigers. Why not kangaroos.

Now the hunter revealed himself to be as astonished as proud, as confused as cocksure. "Honest to Pete," he said, "I thought she was a deer. One's been eating right through our marigolds."

"You gonna mount it?" Bud asked, unable to disguise his disgust.

"What I should do is call the DNR," he said. Here he shrugged. "But then I'd have to tell them I took a shot at a deer."

It was a conundrum, Bud agreed.

Motoring back, Bud decided Kate would wander home in her own time—if she weren't back already, sipping coffee with Allie on the dock.

The two of them had hung out yesterday, gone for some tour of Old Ferdy's old boathouse. It may have been that budding friendship—or at least, mutual regard—that led Bud to feel suspicious about Kate today, to doubt there'd been a mishap just because she was missing.

Allie didn't have the best track record when it came to choosing friends.

There'd almost been Shara. During the early years of their daughters' friendship, Shara and Allie had danced at the edge of their own. A few times Bud had come home to the two of them sharing a beer, once out on the raft, their faces tipped to the sun. But once their daughters grew older and didn't need rides to one another's houses, slept over less often with their different work and activities schedules, their mothers drifted too, which was something to marvel at. Only Allie could manage immunity to friendship with easygoing, fun-loving Shara.

Before Shara, Allie had chosen Elmira Lapham to befriend. Their inherited renter lived with four unruly boys in a falling-down house one uphill hike through their woods. Discovering the state of the house, and their responsibility for five lives subsisting within it, Bud had voted for eviction, kinder than waiting for lawsuit or injury. But Allie had just given birth to Cassie and latched on to Elmira as if she were the only other woman in the world.

Yet through all the winters Allie strapped baby Cassie into a backpack to snowshoe to Elmira's unsound house, or the summers she drank tea in that kitchen where insulation hung from the ceiling and mouse turds dotted the floor, Allie failed to learn the most basic information about Elmira. When Elmira announced her paperwork had come through to move to Manitoba and she vacated the house in a period of hours, Allie said she'd hadn't known Elmira had been waiting all that time for relocation, that her legal status in the U.S. was so tenuous. Nor did Allie know what Elmira had fled in Albania, why joining her extended family north of the border still meant more to her than staying where her adult sons had by then decided to make their lives. (The youngest, only a boy, even chose to stay.) We don't talk politics, Allie had said, shrugging—but that was preposterous, a typical Allie evasion. Bud knew politics were often people's lives.

What his wife wanted to avoid, Bud knew, was discussion of the hard stuff of life, the things that bent and shaped people. This was related to her own story—the culture of the monied family in which she'd grown up and the specific ways that had bent and shaped her.

Bud doubted Allie had told Elmira about her ex-husband, or the boyfriend she'd had just before Bud.

The first husband had been from the same or same enough Chicago suburb as Allie's family. He was someone putting in time at his father's firm while keeping an eye on public office—Bud knew only enough to know he was a douchebag. Allie left him in the end, fleeing her home and both pots of family money, literally leaving all of it behind except the clothes on her back and their old car, her getaway vehicle. She'd hoped that would make for a clean break, and for a few years it seemed she was right, the ex uninterested as long as Allie didn't ask for anything. Bud had only dealt with him once, answering a middle-of-the-night ring for a drunkard's slurred bragging that all of Allie's things had been piled into a bonfire in their drained pool, that if Allie wanted her stuff she could climb in and try her chances at getting it.

And yet, even he wasn't the worst. Between the first husband and Bud, during the summer Allie was living with her aunt and working as a receptionist at a small museum (the aunt, another family outcast, had found her the job), Allie had some kind of relationship with a web designer named Gavin. Ten years younger, with a face and earlobes full of metal, Gavin would later be arrested for setting off a bomb in a downtown parking garage—this during one of those crazy summers—in what, he claimed, was a political act.

Maybe it was no wonder Allie said she didn't talk politics—the two men the two poles from which she'd swung. And a smarter man than Bud might have taken these stories of the kind of people, and kind of trouble, to whom his wife was drawn and wondered about himself. Where did he fit?

In his memory of Allie from that summer they'd met she wore the same flimsy yellow skirt and white blouse every day—as if constantly on her way to a garden party, even when checking out legal resources at Bud's library or price comparing generic cereals at Rite-Aid. He thought she was putting him on. She drove a Mercedes, if it was an old one, beat up and battered. Did she require the discount brand?

But finally he'd understood. She was a woman in revolution, in the throes of changing her life. Bud had fallen in love with her spinning energy. It was the same energy she summoned in moving them here, and the energy Bud believed they needed to find again now.

It was time to leave this place. Time to get out, to *move*.

Bud angled for the boat ramp on the west end of their property. Here a rusted chassis of an old truck stuck from the grassy embankment, just one of the buried treasures the resort's former owners had left them. Bud used it to tie off—and as he did so caught sight of something silver behind the dripping curtain of shoreline willow. Kate's canoe.

Also, the boy.

"Oh good. I've been looking for you." Marius stood from his squat on the dry concrete of the boat ramp, today sporting a hot pink t-shirt with a Wild Fire gas station logo. He was a city kid of a modern era, Bud thought, thinking again of where they'd chosen to raise Cassie.

"Your grandma show up?"

Marius nodded, and Bud's relief was matched by sheepishness. Had a part of him been tempted to believe Cassie's story about Kate? The border patrol chasing the silver-haired woman?

Marius swung a stick—the kind of stick a boy that age will always have. "I want to show you something."

He seemed to have learned their entire property, every road and trail. He led Bud up the old access road to Hemlocks cabin. Berry bushes overhung the shoulder and weeds had grown through the median. Marius stopped halfway, swinging his stick like a water witching dowel.

"What happened?" His stick pointed to the two rows of battered white boxes set off the side of the road.

"Bee boxes."

"I know they're bee boxes," said Marius. "I mean, what happened to the bees?"

Bud could still remember the day the bees arrived. The man had driven down from Ashland with one tiny box containing the queen in the bed of his truck. The rest of the buzzing hive simply followed, a darkened, dotted cloud. It was Allie's idea to keep bees—she of the perpetual belief that her own small efforts were going to help save the world. This was also during the years they were trying to teach Cassie themselves—if Bud now realized the sad limits of that plan, the too-small size of their own understanding, its short shelf life in the fast-changing world.

The hive had failed, of course, despite Bud's hours of internet research, his windows of bookmarked tabs. (Allie had wanted to divine what to do, hang around the bees as if the bees would tell them.) One day they'd come out to find the bees had simply departed. Out for the day? they'd wondered, but then the workers didn't come back. Soon it was apparent that the queen and the larvae had been abandoned, as inexplicable a thing—given the essence of what bees were, how they functioned as an organism—as a dead kangaroo in a Northwoods lake.

But you heard of it everywhere, colony collapse, a kind of suicide.

"Will other bees move in?" Marius asked.

That was an interesting question, Bud said. He didn't know.

Further up the overgrown road, he saw Kate.

Oh yeah, Marius explained. Allie was moving them into Hemlocks.

"Oh?" said Bud.

"It'll be quieter here, and you guys are closing down every place else."

Marius began walking up the road, but Bud said he'd bring the boat back to the main dock.

It was a thing you learned in a small cabin with three people, over months of winter, over years that stacked like ice plates. People needed their space.

At the willow near the base of the ramp, he pulled out his phone. A signal came in well here, which was a new thing he'd discovered the other night, the guests asking after local reports of the northern lights. Bud redialed the last number he'd called, the call soaring through the weeping branches, bouncing however it bounced on its way to Shara.

CHAPTER 7

IT HAD NEVER been the case before, watching guests pack up after Labor Day weekend, load their cars and take their last swims, push their point of departure one hour and then another, that Cassie was leaving too. Never mind reports of lost items, of broken blinds or ripped screens; never mind either the new occupancy of the criminal Kate and her kidnapped grandchildren in a distant western cabin, off record in her mother's books. Monday night Cassie took her time organizing her things, washing her long hair. Early Tuesday she was gone before breakfast. Her mother could take her swim on her own without Cassie's watchful eye. Her parents could stare at each other across the table and wonder if, finally with Cassie gone, they could quit each other too.

Then, coming into Satuit forty minutes later, the first day of her first real school finally about to start, Cassie realized the same little red Honda with the aftermarket spoiler and racing tires had been following her since Eagle River. Though it was behind her, she felt the familiar attachment of their shared vector, the sense of linkage between their vehicles. For all the times she'd dogged other cars—tailed tourists for fun—it was now an outrage to be so dogged herself.

She made the turn into the Taco Bell lot quickly and without her signal, but the red Honda wedged itself behind her anyway. Now she was stuck in the drive thru line in inexorable progress toward a breakfast burrito with only ten minutes before the first bell.

Hattie had worked at this same Taco Bell for all three weeks of her food service career. If that was now the only job she'd had in her lifetime, was that *who Hattie had become*? What little kid imagining their future would name that fate? During those weeks Hattie commanded the fugly window, the drive thru, taking orders while recording on the long-graffitied interior wall a tally mark for each passing customer: Fuckable? Or too ugly to fuck? *Fugly?*

Now Cassie's tail climbed out of his red Honda, where, Cassie saw, a parking pass just like her own swung from the rearview. A fellow student, since Cassie was no longer a pretender but, as of this morning, starting in ten minutes, the real deal.

"Haven't seen you around all summer." Sam Sandy leaned in her window.

Sam had been Hattie's shadow, and he hung in Cassie's window now the way he'd hung on Hattie, brown bangs in his eyes, shirt and pants too long. *Smell something?* Hattie would say whenever he came around. *Someone get this piece of toilet paper off my shoe.* It began to seem like he'd only leave if she stopped, so Hattie wouldn't stop. Here in the Taco Bell drive thru, Sam gripped a McDonald's cup. He was using it to spit.

"That's gross."

Sam inspected his cup, shrugged. He was easy to wound, yet he'd always chosen to hang around Hattie, so some part of him must have found wounding familiar. A car length space opened in front of Cassie, and she put her truck in gear, but Sam wouldn't step back until she started rolling forward. A moment later, he was leaning in her window again. "You going to school? Yeah, I heard that you were."

Cassie sighed. "I'd like to get out of this line, actually." There was curbing to her right, which the Fjord could handle but she'd take out landscaping.

"They fixed up your windshield good, huh?" He leaned in to inspect, peering around the dangling lanyard of her parking pass, as if it were still possible to see the cracks. Hattie must have told him about it. Cassie's own parents hadn't noticed the new windshield on the old truck, didn't know that last spring Cassie had rolled the Fjord in a ditch and Hattie, her only passenger, had cracked the glass with her forehead. Two weeks later the story of the accident, and Cassie's bad driving, was subsumed by Hattie's death. Cassie was glad for that at least, though maybe it would have been better if people had remembered that some of the time, to some extent— and most especially in those last two weeks of her life—Hattie had been her friend.

"Would you mind backing out?" Cassie said. "I don't want to be late."

Sam nodded, spit, and tripped over his too-long jeans lapped over the back of his shoes.

"You know Julia's been looking for you," he called before he got back in his car.

Oh, she knew. Julia had been texting and messaging her on the hour. She sent comments on shows she was binge-watching, as if Cassie were right then watching the same show. She sent screen shots of things she wanted to buy online, and then of her regrets after she'd hit *purchase*.

Cassie missed her own phone at the bottom of Little Eagle

Lake and even imagined what Hattie's phone might look like joining it there, with only the fish to take notice, their big tails swishing
silt over the screen, their glassy eyes utterly indifferent to Julia's
urgencies.

She followed Sam to the high school—home of the hodag, myth-
ical beast town residents had invented and stage-photographed
about a hundred years ago, fooling folks "back East" (or so went the
legend) to the extent that someone was sent out from the Smithso-
nian to investigate the horned and clawed, forest-dwelling, pig-like
Wild Thing. To anyone with a modern eye, trained to read a posed
shot, the famous photo of the pitchfork-wielding men cornering
the sewn-together beast was clearly a prank—fake news of the time.

Now what traffic clogged the Northwoods on a weekday
morning in September gathered outside the SHS lot. Five minutes to first period made for a veritable Who's Who of the county,
kids with the same last names of the original hodag hunters, of
parents, aunts and uncles, and grandparents who'd queued at this
same entrance on similar mornings in previous decades, some in
the same vehicles.

Hopeless she'd make her first class on time, Cassie caught
a double flash of Sam's brake lights and his nudge backwards.
Taking the cue, she threw the Fjord into reverse too, knowing this
dance of theirs from the drive thru. Sam pulled out and began to
race around the block; he was showing her a way into the parking
lot from the other side. She'd wondered why no one used the far lot
entrance, but instead, lemming-like, lined here.

Sam rounded the big block of practice and playing fields and
hooked the final left with Cassie following. She was so intent on
catching him that she didn't notice how he slowed at the entrance

for the string of speed bumps, which Cassie took at full power, in full sight of her lined classmates waiting their turns at the far end. With the first bump, her hand flew from her wheel to high five her own interior roof. With the second and third she jounced against her tightening seatbelt, her foot flying from the gas pedal. She came to rest in the first space she could slide into, near a blue Range Rover, her parking pass swinging.

Even with the first bell rung, this whole back half of the lot was empty. Waiting out here was the only woman in town who owned a vehicle like that.

"That's my kind of entrance." Julia leaned from the window in dark glasses.

"New girl," Cassie said.

Julia laughed. She'd been the one who'd taught them to say that last year when she'd started as Ms. Tomas' assistant.

Julia said she needed a favor. Cassie wondered if Julia could possibly have set up Sam to lead her here. Cassie hadn't been answering her texts.

"Last name." It wasn't eight thirty and the school secretary sounded tired. Cassie leaned over the counter on her elbows, hoping she wouldn't notice Julia lurking outside the glass of the front office, still gesturing at Cassie as if she'd forgotten what she was supposed to do. Mrs. McAdams's three gold bracelets clanked against her keyboard. She pulled a hand away and thrust it in the air so the bracelets dropped up her arm. She'd been in orchestra a few years back, Cassie knew.

Mrs. McAdams pressed a few quick keys. "You a senior?"

"A new one," Cassie said. "I'm so embarrassed I forgot my combination already. Locker 223." Cassie gave her Hattie's old locker number, trying not to feel Julia's breath—from out in the hall—on her neck.

The rumor went that during her senior year Mrs. McAdams had an abortion. She was pretty enough to have that kind of problem. But then why was she married now? You'd think the abortion would have meant she didn't have to. Cassie could ask Julia later—Julia never failed to answer a love or sex question.

"Do you still play the cello?" Cassie said.

Mrs. McAdams looked up, startled. It was always the younger girls who knew the older ones, who were watching to see what was going to happen to them.

In the empty hallway, Julia's body took on the green glow from the locker rows, even her teeth glinting, and for that appearing extra crooked. For the other "work" she had done or did herself (shaping, injecting, tweezing, painting) Julia was opposed to cosmetic dentistry. *Girls,* she said, *never mess with your teeth. It's how they identify your body.*

She'd said that before anyone had to identify Hattie's body—if anyone had to do that.

Cassie produced the piece of paper with Hattie's combination, not too surprised that she did in fact remember it from the one time she'd been to Hattie's locker before. Cassie had come with some of the orchestra girls to a basketball game—they let you in even if you were homeschooled—and they'd given the slip, playfully, to Two Barrel, the school's rent-a-cop, and his real-cop friend and roommate Trent Lapham, two doofuses not long enough out of high school that they still hosted parties themselves, ones Cassie and Hattie had plenty of the other girls had attended.

Did knowing Hattie's locker combination mean she and Hattie

had been close—had been best friends? It was also true that Cassie had an odd ability to remember numbers, like Julia's new Range Rover plates. She'd noticed the other day they weren't the same as her old SUV's.

"Didn't they let you in here last spring?" Cassie asked, twisting and turning the dial.

"They did," Julia said. "But only twelve times."

Cassie smiled, though probably it wasn't funny.

Pulling upward on the latch, Cassie could already feel the emptiness on the other side. How was that a thing you knew about a locker before opening it? For a moment she felt a pang of protectiveness for Hattie, what she'd feel if her own mother went through her stuff. The night of the basketball game Hattie had a bottle of vodka in her locker, siphoned from her mother's supply into an emptied Sprite. Not that Julia would give a shit about some smirched Smirnoff, not now.

Julia stood on her toes to feel with one hand along the locker's top shelf. Tall enough, Cassie could see there was nothing there.

"I keep thinking maybe I missed something. I wake up in the middle of the night and I just want to check." Julia's arm fell limply by her side. She sunk an inch into her wedges. "Also, there's something I want to tell you."

"Okay," said Cassie, the annoyance Hattie had often sparked in her leaping, then falling back to the earth as guilt.

"Come to my house after school so we can talk about it?" Julia pleaded.

There was orchestra after school, which Julia should have known. Not that Cassie had decided to go—she was having second thoughts about orchestra. Cassie hadn't lifted her cello all summer, couldn't imagine listening to any of the music they'd played—Hattie always coming in late or loud, so terribly that it was noticeable even for a flute.

"Can you tell me now?"

"You're late to class."

That was true, and Cassie didn't know yet what happened to tardy students. Perhaps they were locked out in the hallways.

Julia was still grieving, Cassie reminded herself, and agreed she'd meet her, accepted her hug. There was Julia's smell again, orange blossom and coconut, which was somewhat surprising. Her girl gone, her mind still consumed, apparently, with trying to find out why, and Julia took the time to shower and condition, to apply all her lotions and make-up and scent. She must have woken at the same time Cassie had this morning just to be here in this hallway, breaking into this locker, but looking and smelling like her same old self, as if nothing had changed.

It was like how the new SUV, the Range Rover, was an even better car than the one Hattie had killed herself in.

Halfway through the day, and then with rolling, ramping speed, Cassie found she was already over high school. Too many things were so much less in reality. For starters, the school was empty. It would have been possible to cartwheel in the hallways during class changes. In gym, an awkward group of seven batted one shuttle-cock with three torn rackets. The lunchroom attested to the story: the trays on the lowest level a different shade than the fifty or so on top that were used, washed, and replaced every day.

Julia and Mark's driveway led through aspens. The house was new, but such care and expense had been taken in its construction that the wooded lot remained intact, even the soaring pines that ringed the house closely. The height of the trees added to the trick of the house, which looked like a one-story from the outside. Cassie had been here twice before and knew that once you stepped through the front door the ceiling vaulted and the floor dropped. A back wall made entirely of glass revealed the house had been built on a long sloping hill.

She'd come to the conclusion that Julia wanted to ask her about the kids—Marius and Miranda; that she'd discovered they were at Eagle's Nest. *Hostage situation.* Cassie had made the flash post and eerily coincidental caption before she'd googled anything about Kate, learned that the children were missing. Now she knew that her post of Miranda may have brought the people who'd been looking for them. She wasn't sure if that was good or not. It hadn't resulted in the kids being found. But neither had it led to anything bad happening to Cassie.

Could her parents be arrested, now, for harboring kidnapped children? Just what kind of people were her parents? What if Cassie herself were an abducted child, snatched from some crib long ago and hidden here? It was a ridiculous thought; Cassie had her mother's hands, her father's mouth and jaw, but it didn't mean some part of that idea didn't ring true. Cassie shivered.

Julia answered the door and Cassie stepped into the front room—the *foyer*, Hattie had called it. Bright natural light from the wall of windows at the back of the house flooded the room. Cassie avoided looking up to the glass catwalk that crossed between the second-story bedrooms. The first time she'd come over, Hattie had waited for her up there. *Dare me to jump?*

Julia wore leather pants and a tank top and jewelry like she was going to a club. She gave Cassie a look of confusion. She peered beyond Cassie, out the opened door, shaking her head as if Cassie had done something wrong—maybe in using the front door?

Julia had asked her to come over, though that had been hours ago, and Julia *hadn't* been texting her constantly since. Maybe for her that was a disinvite. Cassie followed Julia to the kitchen where a bottle of wine and a glass sat on a granite island.

"Guess you don't have the pull you used to," Julia said.

"Huh?"

"People used to listen to you, didn't they?"

"I don't know that anyone ever listened to me," Cassie said.

"Well no one's here, are they?" Julia threw out her arm, causing Cassie to notice again the wall of windows, which extended even here into the kitchen. They were spotted with something greasy, the remnants of birds, their bits of feathers and blood. All day long birds must thud against that glass.

"Julia, did I miss a text?" Some half of a conversation was missing. Julia was upset about something that Cassie couldn't grasp.

Julia held out her hand and Cassie handed over her phone—Hattie's phone.

"Oh, silly," Julia said, her face breaking into a grin. *Silly* was an odd word for her to use. "You haven't been checking Hattie's *photo*bomb."

Cassie had logged into her own photobomb and flash accounts but wasn't accessing Hattie's. Julia held out the phone to show her. Apparently, she'd sent about twenty photobombs since she'd last seen Cassie at the high school directing her to bring all the orchestra girls with her this afternoon, declaring they'd have a party. She'd included pictures of herself cleaning the house, getting dressed, buying grocery carts of frozen pizzas and low-calorie hard seltzers.

Cassie stared at Julia in her leather pants and jewelry. She'd wanted Cassie to use Hattie's accounts, to check and answer from them.

Julia sighed. "Well, now we know." She turned to open the oven door where a pizza rested, uncooked. "God damn it," she said, and then turned the oven on. It clicked through its pre-heat cycle. "This is the worst stove in the world. The *worst*. Fucking cheap."

The second and last time Cassie had been over to this house—summoned by Julia to receive Hattie's clothes—she'd learned Julia talked to herself when alone. It was a surprisingly doddering thing for Julia to do, but then she had been blinded by grief, handing over tank tops from the laundry bin still stiff in the armpits.

Julia's phone rang. She pivoted to where she'd left it. "Fucking Mark."

"He's out of town?"

Julia snorted. "He's at the Super 8 in Satuit."

"Oh," Cassie said.

"You always stay on the property, girl," Julia said, wagging a long finger. "You stay. That means something later when they count everything up." She twirled the finger, tabulating. She poured the rest of the wine from the bottle into her glass.

Cassie understood why she was supposed to have brought people over with her—the orchestra girls—for a very particular kind of party in which Julia would be upset and the orchestra girls would comfort her, listen to what Mark had done now. It seemed like and not like something Julia would do: admit to such a failure as fighting with and possibly losing her rich boyfriend, owner of this house.

Julia didn't know about the kids staying at Eagle's Nest, and if she had she wouldn't have particularly cared. Nor did she care that Cassie had come here instead of going to orchestra rehearsal—she hadn't even remembered there was rehearsal this afternoon. Cassie pictured Ms. Tomas's raised arms and her own empty seat in the cello row, but so many seats had been vacant at that first meeting, like parking spaces at the high school this morning. It was funny that Cassie had been raised to think of Satuit as big—a real city—with its Target and Fleet Farm, its high school. She'd outgrown it in one day.

Julia drained her glass and stared out the glass wall. Cassie wondered if they were looking at the same wad of feathers.

"What happened with Mark?"

"I kicked him out."

Cassie doubted this.

"You don't believe me." Julia advanced toward Cassie and stabbed her in the sternum with one long pointed nail. She was so ugly at this angle, this drunk. At the same time, Cassie liked her more than ever. She loved her. This was how a person should look if their daughter were dead, had died the way Hattie had died. Julia had the right feelings, at least. Cassie was the monster.

Julia hiccupped, or sneeze-hiccupped, a glob of snot shooting from her nose. She wiped it imperfectly, streaking her hair.

"I should go," Cassie said.

"No, no. Come over anytime." Julia waved her hand, dismissing Cassie, catching herself from stumbling by reaching for the island. Then, oppositely and desperately, "Will you sleep over? I hate sleeping alone." Hattie had slept with her mother most nights in that big king bed at the end of the catwalk in the upstairs bedroom. Mark was never here during the week.

She couldn't, Cassie said. She just couldn't. She waited until the pizza was done cooking before she left. She made sure the oven was turned off.

CHAPTER 8

THE WEATHER DIDN'T know fall had arrived—that school had started, and the tourist season ended.

Allie lolled on the raft with the children. Beneath them water tinked against the hollow barrels that floated the platform, the wooden planks as dry and hot as a sauna's. It was nearly too hot to lie in the sun—a slice of summer preserved for them. It was hard not to marvel that Cassie had given this up for high school. For three days, Allie's daughter had risen early, got herself dressed and out the door. She returned at dusk after orchestra.

All that morning Allie had attempted to involve Miranda and Marius in the resort's end-of-season chores. They'd started with laundry, going cabin to cabin to gather sheets and the light blankets they could do in their own machines. Neither child knew how to operate a washing machine, where to pour the soap or that final complex step of pushing a button.

"What will you do on your own?" Allie asked.

"Have a maid." Miranda shrugged.

It was difficult to pinpoint the kids' social class, even where they'd lived. Marius' stories involved desert creatures. Miranda claimed to have been surfing "for years." Allie had thought they were city kids, pale when they'd arrived, but Marius and Miranda were comfortable out of doors, poking things with sticks, flinging dead fish.

Above all, she trusted they were safe at Eagle's Nest. If any part of Cassie's story were true—that they'd been abducted by their grandmother, that private detectives or police had been sent to search for them—Allie bet Kate had her reasons. Determining the details of the kids' background seemed one way to discover these reasons, to confirm Allie had been right in allowing them to stay on here.

Marius had declined breakfast, saying it wasn't like he'd "gone to bed with his belly on E." Was he often hungry in the morning? Allie asked. Then Miranda had recognized the designer of Allie's wedding ring—well-known in Chicago but not here, and not by kids. Confounding it all, the kids swapped their swimsuits (finally!) for clothes, returning from Hemlocks in jeans with bells on the bottom and t-shirts featuring *Star Wars* characters. Allie had fingered the hem of the material. It was hard to know if the clothes were thrift or recently bought; those movies come back around, and that thin, threadbare style was popular in new clothing.

Not that wealth or class mattered for knowing if the kids had been treated badly. Was there something in their lack of basic skills, though, that signaled a life without much attention from adults around them? Did all kids exhibit such strange assortments of knowledge?

Rocking the raft, Marius sat up in the middle of a story involving shark baiting and diving cages.

Allie braced herself against the swaying platform. "Are you talking about something from TV?"

"No. The Gulf," Marius said with some patience, like he'd told her this already.

"That's when Mom and Remmy took you." Miranda wore an old pair of Cassie's sunglasses, looking as bored as Cassie ever had. "*I* was living with Dad."

This was a new piece of data: the kids split between separated parents. Perhaps Kate had removed them from the sidelines of an ugly divorce. Maybe she'd felt what Allie had that night of the canoe chase: an overwhelming desire to protect these children, to secure them someplace safe.

Deer did what Allie had done—hid their fawns in soft patches of forest moss, under trees.

Miranda sat up, rolling in one smooth motion.

"Wanna see something?" Marius said, grinning.

Miranda walked to a corner of the raft, turning to square herself, arms at her sides. Before Allie could think of what the girl was about to do, get out a *no*, Miranda was in motion, turning a cartwheel that ended with her planting both feet on the last inch of the raft's far corner and then springing into a high backwards somersault into the lake.

Marius clapped as she surfaced. Allie was still holding on, the raft bounding and rebounding beneath her, jerking at the end of its anchor chain.

"I'm out of shape," Miranda said, shaking her hair, bitter.

While they'd been on the raft, a high buzzing had been growing in Allie's ear. It could have been a mosquito—those had lingered this season. The buzzing became louder, and Allie turned to see a jet ski skimming the water.

Occasionally they caught a stray from Big Eagle, and today it could have been someone up to take their dock in, out to run the excess gas from the jet ski they'd hardly used.

"Gary!" Marius stood to wave his arms.

Behind the driver—Gary, apparently—rode Kate. Allie hadn't seen her yet this morning. It was like this mystery woman to arrive by water.

Gray-haired Gary wore a drooping moustache, and in some immediately discernable way he struck Allie as competent. While sun-browned on his neck and hands, he wore a hat and long sleeves—not the usual garb of men around here on a hot day. Kate stepped from the jet ski onto the raft and Gary invited the kids for a ride, soon looping them around Little Eagle, teasing them with runs toward shore. *Don't break up the milfoil*, Allie wanted to call to him. *That spreads it.*

"He's a geologist," Kate said. "He's been working on some maps for me."

"Okay," said Allie. Now Kate was mining something?

Kate smiled. "And he's helping them at Tiki's with their solar panel project. He's good at that kind of stuff. He could probably help you with your wifi problem."

Allie didn't know she had a wifi problem. Kate waved her hand as if at a fly. Shouldn't they lock the wifi access with all the people wandering around these days? She said Bud was concerned. Allie wondered if Bud had shown her the letter they'd received from the sheriff's office. Hotel and resort owners were being asked to report trespassers or "suspicious strangers"—such as those who tried to book a room but couldn't produce identification. The online system required ID.

"What are they doing with solar panels at Tiki's?" Allie asked. It sounded like a project with which Bud would involve himself.

"I know," Kate said. "Why not invent a form of energy that runs on the hot air of old men?"

Then she said that she wanted to show Allie something. She wanted to take her to her place. She nodded across the lake.

A half hour later, Gary, Kate, Allie, and the kids loaded into one of Eagle's Nest's outboards. Allie had contemplated what to tell Bud. While she'd been putting off her seasonal chores, he'd thrown himself into his. Awake before Allie, he'd stripped half their tomatoes for freezing. He was partway through a re-carpeting of Aspens and talking about going ahead with Ash though it wasn't due for floors until next spring.

Allie finally wrote that she was going on a hike. Kate had advised her to wear tall socks and good shoes, to bring water. The boat trip took them in one neat line southeast across the lake. They pulled onto shore not far from where Nadia and Fred had seemed to chase Kate that other night.

Allie hadn't explored this shallower, boggier end of Little Eagle, where northwest winds shunted most of the lake's debris: downed logs, otter carcasses, trash. Neither did she know of any streams leading in or out. Like most of the county's lakes, Little Eagle drew its water from below, a result of the water table. Gary looped the bowline of the boat to a thin, leaning oak tipping into its own morning reflection. Not too far in, the bank climbed steeply, though it was not yet visible for the poplar and birch, the scraggle of underbrush—Japanese barberry.

The kids set off behind Gary as if they knew exactly where they were going. Allie recalled that when they'd first arrived they'd done so in advance of Kate, knowing their way. Had they been leading her? Or fleeing her? But it wasn't as if now they were trying to get away.

Kate bent to tie a bootlace, grimacing. Far more grandmother than kidnapper.

It would be a three-mile hike, though Allie couldn't imagine proceeding one mile in this direction. They'd run into the highway soon and would appear to passing drivers as if emerging from swampland. Before they'd set off from the boat, Gary had produced the walking stick, something from his belt that expanded. He looked at the top from time to time, so that Allie suspected he was reading a small GPS device. A vest with zippered pockets promised more gadgetry. To some degree, both he and Kate were the kind of people with whom it felt safe to trek off into the woods, the kind of person Allie had fantasized she might become, first moving here. But it had been years now since she'd hiked farther into the woods than she could get out again within in an hour—maybe a sign of becoming a local. People from here knew the woods and the lakes for their winter selves, for their danger.

"The kids have traveled a lot, huh?" Allie asked. She and Kate caught up with the first half of their party outside a drainage tunnel that cut underneath the highway. Gary was poking his foot in something someone had dumped from the side of the road, ashes.

"A cooking fire."

Kate whistled. "Pretty damn close to the road."

"Maybe they cooked under the lip of the tunnel," Marius said. "Kept their light low."

Gary ruffed Marius' hair. They recognized something in each other. Were two of a kind.

Gary gestured to the tunnel, which was big enough for a person to walk through. It was dry but with leaf and soil debris that suggested times of year when water, snowmelt, rushed through. A trace of matted dirt meandered through the trees behind them showing the route water could take down to the lake, if it wouldn't register on any map as a creek. No cars passed above on the high-way. Daylight telescoped from the tunnel's far end.

"I had no idea this was here," Allie said. She didn't often travel that highway, but she was sure she'd never realized she was crossing a culvert, never thought she might see people crossing below. What took your vision on that highway were the trees that towered above. Next to her, a thin pine tree shot a good hundred feet into blue sky.

Kate gestured that Allie could go first. With this trip she was showing her something, Allie understood, giving her something. The tunnel smelled a little like the basement parking garage of the museum where she'd used to work. Wet concrete.

Bud had spent summers up here in the Northwoods as a child. Not enough time that he'd say he was from here, but he knew the roads and towns, had been able to teach Allie the trees. That first trip they'd hadn't stayed in Vilas County but in a cabin that belonged to Bud's second cousins in Cable, a town near a big annual ski race that now, with changing snow patterns, had become more popular for its bike course. That had been a very old cabin, with a pump and ceramic basin instead of running water, with an outhouse in which someone had installed a tiny, perfect stained-glass window.

You just needed to get away, Bud had said. You would have liked it anywhere. He was joking because he didn't like her friends—the group of kids who worked with her at the museum and whom she was calling her friends though they were a good decade younger and hadn't lost any time to divorce, to bad first marriages.

Allie wasn't sure why Bud found them so distasteful, maybe because they thought he—her new librarian boyfriend—was old. Allie accepted that they were amused by her, or half amused, half horrified. She drove a giant, honking car. At the time, she still ironed her skirts and her hair. She hadn't known about—had never even previously heard the term—global warming.

Wait—are you serious?

Was it like the hole in the ozone layer?

You're kidding, right? said Gavin, who was one of them. Maybe their leader. For a time, he had selected her, taken an interest in Allie despite all the younger girls.

Just where, he asked, pulling lightly on one loose end of her straightened hair (she had to do it with her aunt's faulty, shorting iron), *had she been living?*

She'd gone on hikes with the museum kids too—urban explorations, Gavin had called them, leading them to some distant El stop first and then thoroughly turning them around as they followed him through neighborhood pockets trapped by expressways. The others got a kick out of Allie here too, her distaste for sharing water (she just hadn't been prepared for someone to reach for the bottle she'd brought), her unwillingness to eat a sandwich they'd gleaned from the dumpster, her lack of interest in the new device Gavin wanted to try out, a phone app that showed their location as they moved, updating as they went. Soon everyone would have access to this kind of technology, Gavin claimed. Better than a street map, which only showed streets. *Sure, in case you get a cabbie who's fresh off the boat,* Allie had said, though this had left the museum kids to walk off, shaking their heads, with only Gavin to explain to her that she'd been insensitive.

As if his expensive gadget were going to be an equalizer, she'd thought at the time, bristling and embarrassed.

Now everyone did have GPS in their phones and even their cars, though Gary's wasn't losing its signal, even beneath all these trees. As they emerged from the tunnel into daylight, he held his walking stick to eye level for a reading. Allie thought of telling him about her city hikes, years ago, but accurately relating the whatever-it-had-been into which she'd fallen with ten-years-younger-Gavin would have been as difficult as it had been that summer to explain her married suburban life to the museum kids, the hours she'd spent in committee meetings to determine the color theme of the country club's Christmas décor.

"Wait," said Allie. "That's just a regular compass?" She had caught sight of round glass eye at the top of Gary's stick, and he held it out for her inspection.

She would have guessed they were heading southeast and was pleased to see the confirmation. Though if satellite signals could be spotty in the Northwoods, so too were compass readings, where certain rocks and minerals could pull a needle, where the gap between true and magnetic north widened. Allie looked for evidence that anyone else had passed this way, another campfire remnant, but could see none. Then Kate pointed to a blue reflector, the kind that would have marked a driveway. This one stood in the middle of a field and had been bent at a perfectly right angle.

They came into trees, dense and old, and found Kate's place in the thick of it. The trailer had been parked so long in the woods that trees had grown around and over it. Instead of grass, the spongy ground that ringed it was a compost of moss and needle, downed branches and leaves. Dark shadows shifted as the distant treetops swayed. For a moment, Allie thought she had floaters at the edge of her vision. A palm to her cheek came away sticky where one of the glittering droplets had landed. *Pitch*, from where trees high above had been damaged by wind. Her hair would be netted with it like she'd been out in rain.

It made sense that the children had been so pale just a few days ago, at the same time as they were comfortable out-of-doors. Allie wondered if they *had* been getting enough to eat. She saw no access road.

The kids were the first inside, the metal door slamming behind each in turn. "Top bunk!" Miranda yelled.

Following—Kate held open the trailer's metal door—Allie blinked in the dark interior. The front room was more spacious inside than she'd assumed. She took in the shagged rug, the giant television set, the sagging, gold-flower-printed couch, all of a decade closer to her own childhood than the current one. Now she'd guess the children's clothing had been original *Star Wars*, first release, if it had come from the closets and drawers here.

"Looks like you did a pretty good job," Kate said to Gary.

Allie raised her eyes to the roof patch in the kitchen—a newer spot of glinting metal above the stove.

"How's the smell?" Kate said, wry. Then, "Don't worry. It wasn't meth."

Kate explained the trailer had been her father's. He'd lived here alone for decades. She'd grown up here. Allie took a seat on the gold couch and accepted a beer Gary had retrieved from the fridge, another with the wolf head label on it.

"We're not staying here," Kate called in the direction of the back bedroom, to where the kids had run. Allie's eyes returned to the patched-over hole in the roof. She couldn't imagine spending a night here during storm, under the swaying and creaking of the high tree limbs above.

"A small explosion," said Kate. "My dad had that stove since the sixties."

"You were here when it happened?"

"A good thing it was daytime," Kate said. "We were awake. I was able to put out the fire, and the kids made their way to you."

Allie absorbed this. The day the children had arrived in that canoe they'd been fleeing an explosion in this tucked away hideout. They'd come ahead of Kate. Miranda, Allie remembered, had submerged when her grandmother appeared in the second canoe. Had they been trying to get away from her? Using the situation of the fire to escape? "You found us," Marius had said.

But the kids had never said anything to Allie—in all the time she'd spent alone with them—nothing like *help us*.

"You lived here long?" Allie asked.

"I made their father a lot of mac and cheese on that stove," Kate said.

Now Allie recalculated. All this time she'd been assuming Kate's daughter was the children's parent. It was easier to accept a woman absconding with, kidnapping, her daughter's children. To take them from your son was to take some other woman's children from her.

"Yep, I'm responsible for their father," Kate said, leaning back into the cat-scratched recliner she'd chosen. She'd brought Allie here as much to show her the trailer as to tell her this. She seemed to assume Allie had heard stories about the children's father.

In the corner of the room stood a wood stove. Allie followed its pipe to another hole that had been cut through the trailer's roof. No power lines led in here. Allie guessed a generator since she saw a TV, old VCR, and row of VHS tapes. She stood to scan the hand-printed titles—game show episodes taped from TV, most from the eighties—and several of Marius' conversation topics from the last week came back to her. Highest mountain ranges, deepest sea trenches, animals of the African plain.

"Where's their mother?" Allie asked.

"She left them," Kate said, as if she'd been waiting for Allie to ask this, knew exactly what she was thinking. "*She* thinks she's going to be a social media star."

Allie nodded, while hearing the advice Bud would have given her in her head: to believe about half of what Kate said, a person who'd so far kept all this from her.

"She went to Toronto. She films and posts from there."

Allie remembered Marius saying his mom was in Canada.

"Wouldn't your son know to look for you here?"

Gary had gone outside and returned now (from where? A truck or shed Allie hadn't seen?) with a large cardboard box. He lugged it down the narrow hallway to the bedroom in front.

"You're assuming he wants them back," Kate said.

Allie heard the kids in the back bedroom, their bossing, a thump.

"Don't get me wrong, he has to act like he wants them. Wring his hands for the TV, send people to look for me… It doesn't hurt *his* career either."

Allie decided not to care what his career was.

"What was your plan though? Or what is your plan?"

"The Nicolet starts just two miles that way." Kate tipped her chin.

The Nicolet referred to a few thousand acres of national forest. It ran to the border with Upper Michigan, and on the other side continued as the Ottawa, a more expansive tract of state-owned land. Every few years a person or a group—sometimes a family— made a headline after emerging from the woods, having managed to live there for a few months.

She remembered that Kate had been scouting the area around Old Ferdy's, looking for a passage, a portage point for their canoes.

All along they must have stored those silver canoes down by the distant, boggy shore of Little Eagle lake, readying them to leave, not knowing they'd use them first to flee a fire.

Kate seemed to take pity on Allie's horror. "We weren't going to live in the woods," she said. "I was going to get them closer to the Soo, see if we could cross into Canada someplace around there. Marius wants to get to his mother." Here she shrugged, like she couldn't imagine why. "And I have a sister in Ontario—so if we can get across, we don't have to worry about trying to get back."

Then she took a gulp of her beer and smiled, her pity for Allie run out. "Maybe we'll get lucky. If we wait it out, the border might cross over us. They're inching the southern line further every day, moving the checkpoints south."

That was what Gwen had been talking about—the residents of Bruce Crossing asked to move. Listening to Kate, Allie suddenly understood the border as a line that could widen, with a no-man's land created in between. The places at which people could cross would be fewer. But how would people—and mining and lumber companies—access Lake Superior? There would have to be permits, ways for the people who could pay to pay.

Allie followed the kids' voices to their bedroom. Here were the bunkbeds, though they were piled with cardboard boxes. Allie saw toilet paper and soap, canned goods and powdered milk.

Marius played on the floor with California Raisins figurines—another toy not of this decade.

"How did you sleep with these boxes on your beds?" Allie asked.

Marius shrugged. "I don't know. They're new."

"Who knows?" Kate said in the doorway. "Maybe we could get as far as Toronto. Their mama's pretty busy, though. A busy, busy woman."

Allie saw Marius' back stiffen. "She wants to see me," he said.

Kate pursed her lips here, not saying anything. "You might have heard of her?" She said to Allie, her voice dripping with sarcasm. "Monica Morello?"

Allie didn't know the name though, didn't follow celebrities. Kate laughed, but just briefly.

"What about your dad?" Allie asked Marius. "Do you miss him?" Allie remembered too late Miranda's comment that Marius had been with his mother "and Remmy," while she had been "with dad."

"I miss him," Marius said, "but it's not like we could live in that house right now."

"Dad's *fixing* it," said Miranda.

Was he a politician? Allie asked.

"Real estate." Kate laughed. "It's amazing what a coat of paint will do to a subdivision condemned for mold."

Out the window, the sky seemed darker through the trees, but she guessed it was still afternoon and hot above the tree line; that the sun shone brightly on her beach.

Then Allie told Kate she'd smuggled someone out of a city through a checkpoint before. Gavin, though Allie didn't say his name.

"Did you do it for a trade?" Kate asked, suddenly more interested in Allie than she'd been all week.

But Allie didn't know what she meant. "It was almost twenty years ago," she admitted. She brushed past Kate into the hallway, led her back to the living room where Gary crouched over a box in the kitchen, unloading supplies into already full cupboards. (Who was going to live here? Did Gary live here?)

It hadn't been easy, she told Kate. His hand was bandaged and bleeding and police dogs had sniffed around her trunk where he was hiding. Though she wouldn't hear the news until later of the number of bombs set off in the city that day, she knew enough at the time to know he'd done something. For months she'd listened to the museum kids talk.

She'd driven Gavin through the police check point without much thought or fear. She was a white woman in a luxury automobile, and close enough to her old life that she couldn't imagine she'd have trouble. Her life was different now. She remembered a local officer coming to the house to question Cassie after Hattie's death, and how her hands had shook when she hadn't let him in, had refused to call her daughter downstairs.

She'd punish her own daughter, take away her phone, give her a form of the silent treatment for a summer, but damn if she'd hand her over, let anyone else blame her.

Before she'd dropped Gavin off, at a gas station in a distant suburb outside the city, he'd tried to kiss her goodbye. He'd got part of her cheek. He knew she was going to do big things herself someday, he said. He knew she was on the right side.

Only some of this she filled in for Kate, who sucked in her breath.

"I knew I liked you," Kate said.

Allie didn't know if she liked herself. She'd never told the story of Gavin to Bud.

The next time she and Bud had driven north—leaving the city to buy Eagle's Nest—they'd had to pass the suburb where Allie had recently deposited Gavin. She had to pretend it was all so strange to her too, the city's new exit checkpoint, the high fencing around the water reservoir, the dearth of songbirds so remarkable for the time of year.

On the hike back, Kate explained more about what she'd meant by *trade*. People who wanted to cross the border unofficially, without paying visas and showing documents, could do so by arranging a trade with someone who wanted to cross the other way. The friends or family or sponsors of the travelers would agree to mutual aid—a ride, a safe house, further transportation out of the extended border zones. This was done via websites very much like those where people swapped vacation rentals and arranged ride shares, if these particular websites didn't come up easily in Google searches. This was why Kate and Gary were fixing up the trailer and scouting routes from here through the national forest. Gary would help whoever came in trade for Kate and the kids.

Who wanted to come south? Allie asked. Why here?

What do you mean *why*? Kate stopped. They'd come almost all the way back to the highway tunnel. The kids ran ahead—something in the tunnel's dark passage inspired running—and Kate's eyes flashed as she turned to Allie.

People had all kinds of reasons to go where they wanted to go, she said. Some crossed for work. Some to be near family or away from family, or near or away from a lover. Some wanted to travel, wanted adventure, wanted different freedom or different health care, or wanted different weather. Some felt safer in one place rather than another. And some, who knows? But who was Allie to ask why?

Allie absorbed this. She thought on it.

Think of your daughter, Kate said. You don't think she has a right to movement on this planet? To make her future wherever she needs to?

But that her daughter might leave home was Allie's worst fear. Thinking of it, her heart pressed against her lungs, like her body had been designed without room for it.

The women came out into heat and daylight on the other side of the tunnel. Unlike Allie's, Kate's mood brightened with their emergence, with the glint of the lake not far ahead of them.

"You know who introduced me to Gary?" Kate said. "That girl at Tiki's. You have to know someone who can get you on to the websites."

Allie found Bud by the fish house.

Not only was it drier in the sun than it had been in the woods, but a static seemed to snap through the air, like in winter when socks sparked against carpet, or when flannel pajamas clung to flannel sheets.

Bud had been smoking, the smell almost enough to cover over the remnant odor of entrails. For decades the fish house must have served as a focal point of the resort—where everyone had to meet at the end of the day to scale and clean their catch, its screened interior a necessary relief from the flies and mosquitos drawn to that work. Now the fish house was used for storage. Here they stowed their paddles, oars, bocce balls, and volleyball nets, their horseshoes and life jackets. Yet the other night when those guests brought in that string of blue gill Bud had cleared the old sink and scaler and put on a revival fish cleaning show. Now the drain was plugged for his efforts. Allie found Bud with a small rolled joint pressed between his lips and his arm plunged to the elbow, fish guts and scales reflected in his blond forearm hair like sequins.

"I forget, sometimes," said Allie, "how you got your name."

It had been his one cred with the museum kids—Allie's librarian friend who always had a little pot to sell. Now that it was legal, Bud's habit made him seem more like an old man than a young one.

They were both getting old, of course.

"Someone took the stove top coils out of Hemlocks," Allie reported

Bud paused, though with half his arm still stuck down the drain. "Too bad they didn't take the whole stove. That one never works right."

"I replaced the coils. But I wonder if someone's been going out there."

"I'm going to tell B.J. he can bring more kayakers through," Bud said. "If we don't say yes, he'll just bring them in through Tiki's."

"Who's over at Tiki's now?"

"Just Christina. You knew that."

Allie nodded. She told Bud she'd offered one of their cabins to a visiting scientist, a geologist doing some work in the area. She had extended the offer to Gary on their hike back and he'd taken it.

"Wildlife count?"

"Geology, I believe, is about rocks," Allie said.

She watched Bud's face carefully. He didn't let on if he'd already met Gary or not, if he'd seen him at Tiki's, where Kate had said Gary was helping with a solar panel project, where she'd implied she'd had conversations with Bud about their wifi.

Allie reached for Bud's arm and brushed away fish scales. Shimmering in the slanting sunlight, they floated to the ground. The fish house had the best screens of any of their buildings—a kind they must not have made anymore, with tiny, crosshatched fibers like rebar. Years and years ago, on one off-season day like this—maybe it had been spring, the mosquitos especially terrible—they'd met for a lunch break in the fish house, eaten their sandwiches and drunk from the lemonade thermos and then made love on one of the half-inflated rafts stored here with the moldy lifejackets, with the remnant anchors and discarded tackle. After, they'd read out loud to each other from the many markered recordings on the interior pine walls—guests' names and fish type and weight caught over the decades.

"Kent and Kendra closed up," Bud said. "They sold." He was working at a clump of fish bone stuck in the grinder.

"People should go where they want to go, I guess," Allie said.

Later that night, she ran into Cassie in the kitchen. Allie couldn't sleep. First she'd walked down to the dock, one of her usual routes. She'd been spooked, though, by something moving in the far trees. Could it be people? Kate's story of trying to trek through the Nicolet-Ottawa to avoid the new border zone and get closer to the big lake for possible crossing, possibly in trade with someone else, was a big, bizarre idea that had stuck in her mind.

"What are you doing?"

Cassie was working at the kitchen table. She snorted and indicated the homework in front of her, one very worn textbook with a peeled cover and a cracked spine.

"What's school been like?"

"They combined junior and senior English," Cassie said. "Only the Mexican kids have their own class."

Allie started. Moving here, she and Bud had talked about the problem of raising their child without much exposure to diversity—to people, cultures, skin tones. We'll just have to read good books, Bud had said. Now Allie had sent her daughter to public school for less than a week and already she'd become a racist. So much for handwringing over social media as the culprit.

"There's no football team either," Cassie added, though Allie didn't know her daughter to care about football.

For everything Allie had thought she'd done to remove Cassie from the world, that world had followed them here. You may as well try to get away from dandelions, their seed heads borne on the wind.

CHAPTER 9

CASSIE WAS STANDING in her window in her jeans and
bra when she realized a man was on their dock, turned around and
looking up at her house. She dove for her closet. Then from the
floor she laughed at herself. As if anyone looking in this general
direction was looking at her; as if anyone, these days, could *see* her.

She crawled forward on her elbows and reached for her phone.

Peeper on my lawn.

Free show! Julia texted back.

Cassie could see the sky from this angle, lying in her closet.
This time of year geese arrowed by in their formations. Owls and
bats followed in the night, afterimage. But the sky today was clear—
an unbroken wash of blue.

She hadn't slept well, and something in the wide sky produced
a memory of a book her mother had read to her as a child, one in
which a small mouse who wants to reach the "far away land" keeps
getting distracted from his journey by other animals in need. He
gives away his eyesight, then his sense of smell. It seems he's never
going to get to the far away land because of his own stupid generos-
ity until a magic frog appears and turns him into an eagle, returning
his senses and permitting him flight. What's funny is all along on

his journey he'd been afraid of the shadows passing far above him. Eagles. Were they just other mice who'd ascended? Why then did they prey on their own kind? Why were those who remained so tormented by those who'd left?

It was just like something Hattie would do, were she still eavesdropping on this world. She'd fuck with the living.

Perhaps the man on the dock was another of the new strays her mother seemed to be picking up. In addition to Kate and the kids, a man named Gary had moved into one of their cabins. Then her father had rented Red Oaks to a couple with a fancy tandem kayak and expensive fall camping gear. The resort was far from closed, from quiet.

What was it like, Julia had asked her once, to live at a place where strangers were always coming and going?

"Every week you say goodbye, don't you?" Julia had said.

Her father stood on a chair, a precarious position from which to handle jars of home-canned tomatoes, yet he needed to stock the high shelf. He'd resorted to canning after filling the deep freezer, the garden a wonder this year with cherry tomatoes as thick on the plants as blueberries. It had been funny to see him canning— boiling jars in his apron. It was both like and not like him, her father one who looked to the future, who always bought the newest gadget. Her mother refused to think past lunch. She had her own way of ignoring things, and then when she did notice something, her own way of communicating about it.

Cassie set the heavy tool she'd found in her closet down on the table with a thud. It looked like an ancient weapon, with a row of spikes on the end.

"Look what mom left me."

Specifically, Cassie had found the tool on top of her cello case, which she'd wedged into the crawl space at the back of her closet when she'd decided to drop orchestra. Leaving the tool there had been her mother's way of saying she knew Cassie had tried to hide the cello back there, that she'd stopped going to orchestra. Maybe her mother had seen the case from her end. The crawl space ran between their two bedroom closets, along the eave.

"Is she going to murder me with it?"

"Probably not until winter," said her father, now poking his head into a cabinet below the sink, looking for more room for his jars with their fleshy, red-orange contents. "Don't forget your lunch."

"I buy lunch, Dad."

Her mother would have noticed that Cassie was running late for school. She might have seen the outline of the cell phone in her back jeans pocket and would have known it couldn't be hers.

She wasn't looking forward to school. She hadn't even brushed her teeth—a thing some girls did, bizarrely, in the school bathroom after lunch. Satuit High School was a place of sad mysteries, the library stocked with out-of-date encyclopedias and pull-down maps in classrooms with the wrong names for countries. *Just ignore those political boundaries,* the history teacher had said, a strange response that Cassie couldn't get out of her head. In general Cassie found school too distracting for thinking, with different smells overwhelming her in each room—chalk dust, formaldehyde, carpet cleaner. And constant sounds. All day long boys' giant basketball shoes squeaked against the flooring in the hallways, and electronic bells like fire alarms sounded at random, unnerving times. 11:07. 3:06.

She was about to throw the Fjord in reverse, to head dutifully to school, when two things happened: Marius' little face appeared in the bushes in front of where she'd parked, and, next to her on her seat, her phone wiggled.

Cassie broke into a sweat. If the Fjord had lurched forward as it did sometimes upon starting, she might have just hit Marius. The image of his face coalesced inches from her front bumper. Strangely, the ringing phone had stopped her, put her foot to the brake. Win one for distracted driving.

"Shit, Marius." She leaned out her window, the engine tinking cool again.

"You didn't get me yesterday. I ate your dust."

"So like a little genius you're hiding there again? Get *out* of there."

Somehow this led to his climbing into the passenger seat.

"Someone's old cup is down here."

"I know." Cassie reached to check her phone. It wasn't Julia this time but a general alert from the high school. School was canceled.

Cassie put her head against the seat. She'd read books in which kids woke to snow days or Saturdays they'd forgotten, and so knew to expect relief—if not this tidal wave. She didn't know how her stomach had been clenched, her toes flexed, until she released them.

Marius stretched the weathered seatbelt over his small shoulder.

"What do you think you're doing?"

"Can I go with you today?" He smiled a jokey smile. Of course he didn't expect her to tilt her head like she was considering it, or to throw the Fjord back into reverse.

Follow up information arrived moments later from Julia. School had been called due to a bomb threat.

Never mind, read her next text. A power outage.

Cassie wondered if she would have gone to school anyway. Something had been telling her she was done with that.

She let Marius choose the turns. This he did with an indication of his head, jerks to the right or left, for the effect that he was her horse, choosing their direction with a strain of neck muscle, a snort. Cassie was the rider, her hands on the wheel spinning to keep up.

He didn't have any idea where he was going. The game wasn't unlike Cassie's own of selecting a car at random and daring herself to follow it until it stopped. The time she'd brought Hattie along, Hattie had called it stalking. She'd liked thinking they were creeping someone out. But they weren't scaring anyone, Cassie had said, two teenaged girls.

It hadn't happened to Cassie yet that a car led her too far. She'd dipped into Michigan, just over that tree-blurred border, and looped as far south as Tomahawk. What if one day she picked a car headed someplace warm and south? The Carolinas? California? Would she go? Last winter when Christina had been accepted to Stanford, she'd said she wasn't even going to pack a coat. Cassie remembered, with embarrassment, her shock at that idea of living somewhere without a coat.

She and Marius had nearly made it to Conover when Cassie first defied Marius' heading. She pulled into a gas station.

"Hey!" Marius said.

"The reality here, kid, is that we need some gas."

"I thought your Dad made all your fuel?"

Cassie scrutinized the boy before climbing down from the cab. *That* he must have heard from her mother—that Bud was making biofuel from lake algae. Cassie's father knew that Cassie was using regular diesel because of the distances she travelled, the odd places she stopped. *You go through it, don't you*, was all her father had said.

On the marquee of this particular Esso station the letters for *beer* and *bait* clung loosely to the yellowing board—they hung there through summer and winter, both seasons in which people needed beer and bait.

She couldn't see Marius when she returned with a loaf of bread and a jar of peanut butter. Cassie hurried to the truck.

He'd slid down in the seat, head tucked and eyes closed, hands folded over his chest. Cassie tapped with the peanut butter on the glass. The boy opened his eyes, then shook his head, still angry. He'd thought he'd locked the doors but didn't know the locks in the Fjord didn't work. Cassie's driver's door popped as soon as she pulled the handle.

"I didn't say to *stop*." He was still mad.

"I got us some lunch, okay?"

"I don't need lunch." Marius said. "I can go for *days* without eating."

"Sure. I'll remember that in three hours."

"Where we going anyway?"

Cassie pulled from the gas station. She'd picked north because one small black car had been heading that way, had zoomed past them with just enough momentum that it seemed it could carry them too. Marius cranked down his window and put his elbow on the edge where the glass had retreated. That window didn't work well, either. She'd have to get the pliers to pull the glass back up from the foam. Today the breeze was good, though. With the peanut butter, the risen sun, and maybe their new direction, the day had brightened.

She'd felt sad this morning, Cassie realized. Restless too. She reached for the radio dial. Maybe she'd find the radio station she'd used to listen to with Christina, the one with the girl DJ from Houghton. Then her phone chirped again. As she slowed, reaching for it, the cup that had been Hattie's rolled from under the seat beneath Marius' raised feet.

"Hello?"

This time it wasn't Julia, or high school robocall, but Sam. He was stuck. Could she pick him up?

It turned out that Sam was not far down the highway, in Eagle River. He waited outside his car, uncleanly parked on a residential street with its hood popped. Mostly he looked surprised to see Marius—this more than that they'd arrived so quickly, or that Cassie had answered Hattie's phone.

He'd *called* Hattie's phone, Cassie realized—filing this away to consider later. Had Julia told him Cassie had it?

"What happened to your car?" Marius asked Sam.

"Overheated, I'm pretty sure."

Marius gave Cassie a look of doubt. There was some reason this answer was not acceptable—*he* knew, Marius, small knower of things.

"You can get in," Cassie said, sighing. Marius surprised her by climbing through to the back seat, making room for the new guest. Cassie put the Fjord back into gear, turned around on the side street.

"So who do you think called it in?" Sam asked. "The bomb threat to the school?"

Cassie looked over to Marius. She hadn't explained either of Julia's texts to him, that her classes had been cancelled today. He wasn't enrolled in school himself, Cassie realized.

"It was just a power outage," Cassie said. In saying it, though, she wondered what it would mean, if a power outage were serious too.

"Which way you headed today?" Sam asked.

From the back seat, Marius indicated the direction: north. Sam nodded. Sure.

This time Cassie slipped off highway 45, choosing a side road that twisted along the edge of Land O'Lakes. In spring, none of these roads were passable, washed out and too potted even for four-wheel-drive trucks. Even today there were places where Cassie had to slow, overgrown tree branches scraping. But at some point, they'd cross into Michigan and not even know it—a neat trick that appealed to Cassie.

They'd been driving in silence a few minutes when Sam turned to Marius.

"You're one of those kids, aren't you?"

"I don't know what you're talking about." Marius looked out his window.

"You were kidnapped by your grandmother. Your dad was on the news."

"Well," Marius said, stiffly. "I'm not a *kid*."

Cassie caught herself grinning. Determined and cocksure, Marius was such the little man. At the same time, she was startled by the new thoughts: that Marius wanted to be with his grandmother, that he didn't want to return home. Could this possibly be what Allie knew or was thinking in harboring the children? Yet that seemed too empathetic for her mother, selfless. She wanted the kids to stay because it fit the story of how right she'd been to move here all those years ago, to live in what she still thought of as a tucked-away corner of the world.

Yet to the people who lived here, this was the whole world. To Cassie, it was all she knew, or had been allowed to know.

Also, had the kids' story appeared on the local news?

"We don't have a TV," Cassie said to Sam.

"But you have internet." Sam turned in his seat and addressed Marius, filling him in. "Your dad's afraid you're dead."

"Nah," said Marius. "He didn't even try to look for us until this week."

Cassie tried to imagine a similar circumstance with her parents but couldn't. She'd never had any space from them.

The wind blew in through the open windows. Rounding curves, topping small hills, they came across one stunning secret lake after the next, an opening of trees parting like a curtain and then closing again after the next rise. Occasionally a dock and pontoon jutted from a shoreline, the only indication of some hidden cabin. Just as often the lakes appeared untouched, unclaimed, disappearing again behind shaggy, leafed out trees in Cassie's rearview. Only when they reached highway 2 did Cassie know for sure they'd crossed into Upper Michigan. She turned west.

The ghostly Paulding light floated not far from here. Sam claimed to have seen it. Surprisingly, Marius knew about the light too. Scientists had deemed it inexplicable, he said. Cassie recognized the word and realized Marius had seen the same taped documentary she once had, and for some reason this was deflating—all of Marius' odd bits of knowledge about the world due to hours of television watching.

Not true, Sam argued. Students from the college in Houghton had proved it was just a trick of atmosphere and high beams from cars on 45. Why else, Sam argued, had the legend only sprung up since the sixties?

There was that college in Houghton, again. What was it like? Cassie asked. She'd seen the Keweenaw Peninsula on maps. The college girl DJ broadcast from there, from halfway out into Lake Superior.

There wasn't a college there anymore, Sam said. His mother, who was in the service, said the navy used the buildings.

They came into another little town, following a detour off the highway, and Cassie realized she'd been here before.

It wasn't the damaged road that she remembered. Here too, though this was the detour route, the main road that wound through the small town was missing chunks of its concrete, and one edge hung, crumbling and precipitous, over a creek bed of sharp rocks and fallen, twisted guardrail. But she remembered the corner with the little red brick bar that they idled next to at the town's one stop sign. She had come here with her father once, years ago, to meet a friend of his, a fellow librarian whose small library was to be closed too, as her father's had been long ago and before Cassie's memory of it as anything other than a low yellow building with empty windows.

Her father's friend was a man with a red goatee and shock of red hair on top of his head that stood up in starched sweat the moment he removed his stocking cap. He didn't take off his ski jacket, and neither did Cassie's dad. It was a thing you didn't do in a bar, Cassie remembered thinking to herself, filing away for the future. The bar's door was thrown open for what was considered to be—here anyway—a warm breeze. The goateed man was angry about the library, which had been closed despite his efforts, awake over a forty-eight-hour period, to rescue books from low shelves to save them from flooding. He was already working without a paycheck, he said, so it wasn't the overtime that did the library in.

Cassie might have been nine or ten. Old enough that she

judged the bartender, a woman like Shara, for having delivered her fries without ketchup. The bartender wasn't paying attention either to the swearing red-haired man or the plight of her own town's library but leaned steadily against the back rail as if she planned to disappear into it. She was unmoved by the sound of Cassie tapping her fingernail on the tab of her coke can, a sound she knew to register keenly in her mother's hearing. Finally, Cassie did what Christina might have. She stood on the rungs of her stool to reach over the bar to root for a bottle of ketchup herself. It was from that angle that she caught sight of something amazing: a baby in a rectangular bouncer on a low shelf underneath the bar, just in front of where Cassie had been sitting.

The baby wasn't sleeping but lying still with open eyes. It wasn't even watching its mother, and she wasn't watching it. A few minutes later, a man called from the kitchen and the bartender left, swinging through the doors. Cassie's father and his friend moved on to discussion of other libraries that had closed, the problem not the disasters themselves but the lack of concern and action about their closures, the lack of shared, communal belief that libraries could or should be preserved.

When her father put down money on the counter, and when he and Cassie and the librarian stood from their stools, Cassie hadn't said anything about the baby under the bar. They went out the opened front door, past the gumball machine that took quarters, back into the street.

And from that moment Cassie had forgotten about the baby.

She'd never seen such a skinny little thing. Somewhere now it was a child. Did it still live in the detour town?

Marius had to go to the bathroom.

"Why didn't you say anything at the gas station?" Cassie asked.

"I can use this cup."

"No! That's gross." Cassie said she would pull over.

She and Sam dropped from the truck while Marius made the short hike into the trees. It was weird for it to be such a nice day and not to see any cars on the road, Sam said. And just think, at school it would have been third period already. He'd have been in... Statistics.

"You're in Stats?"

"I'm good at math," Sam said defensively. He'd inserted a plug of tobacco, unwrapping the package from his back pocket, removing a pinch with his fingers. Watching him, Cassie had the idea that he wasn't actually very good at chewing it. Like he could read her thoughts he said, "You know who got me hooked? Hattie."

Cassie laughed. She'd never seen Hattie chew—but it was just the kind of thing Hattie would do, as a girl, and for the attention. Cassie remembered watching Hattie pull up her pant leg in the front flute row and start shaving her leg with a dry, disposable razor. What? She'd said to Ms. Tomas. I've got a hot date tonight. Everyone, including Ms. Tomas, had groaned but Hattie hadn't been kidding.

Sam was chewing with only limited success, his face showing the appearance of straining, of having to think about what he was doing.

"You know what's the truth about Hattie? I mean, the thing no one says?"

A brown squirt dribbled from Sam's lip as he turned to Cassie. Just the right amount of fear flickered in his eyes. He didn't know what she was about to say.

"She didn't know what she was doing. Not more than anyone

else. She acted like she knew, like she had everything figured out and had everything the way she wanted it, but she didn't."

Sam leaned, pressing his coat to his chest before spitting. A brown stream made its way to the hard gravel near their feet, the highway shoulder.

"Course she didn't. You think she knew what she was doing when she gassed herself?"

Cassie hadn't expected this reaction. While she thought most of the time that most everything Hattie did was instinctual, was poorly planned and then only repeated or continued if she received attention for it (any kind of attention), she hadn't until now applied that to Hattie's death. But Sam had—Sam who'd followed her, who'd truly been Hattie's closest friend.

But it was too cruel to think a person could die because of some dumb, everyday mistake; that suicide could be anything less than the grand gesture it appeared and instead an everyday slip-up, like if Hattie had nicked her leg that day while shaving in orchestra and had somehow bled to death right in front of them.

A car flew by, a trio of leaves rising in a small whirl from the back tire. Where had these dried leaves come from? They were the first that heralded the next season.

Cassie was reminded of spring days when out on the roads you could tell who had come from where, the truck beds and cab tops of those from further north heaped with snow. These days, her father said, it also meant they might have come from west, where weather patterns were growing wetter. In their pocket, it was getting drier every year, which worked, ironically, toward the spring flooding.

"Where's Marius?"

In the wake of the passed car, a moved cloud, Cassie felt the sun return to her face and realized she and Sam had been leaning there long enough that the engine she'd turned off had stopped ticking.

"Marius!" Cassie began to call for him.

"That kid. Come on," she said to Sam, who leaned to spit.

From the truck she grabbed the gas station sack with the food and then her sunglasses too. As she and Sam worked their way back into the woods, she looked for a wide bush, something with coverage. Meanwhile Sam found every possible branch to step on.

They came to a clearing. Under her shoes, she felt strewn chunks of gravel, flung this far from the highway by passing cars. A cool breeze from a different direction lapped her neck. Was the smell of the lake on it? Several miles still lay between them and the little beach she'd begun think about, not the big beach as far as Ashland where her parents sometimes led caravans of guests for daytrips, but the little one her father had shown her, tucked off highway 2 not far from where it meandered back into Wisconsin.

"Have you ever been to the ocean?" she asked Sam.

"Yeah. My grandparents live in Maine."

"Yeah?"

Cassie felt something drawing them ahead. Maybe they were closer to some inlet from the big lake, which had a way, her father told guests, of luring people; several Great Lakes shipwreck tales featured in his campfire stories collection. The land ahead of them dipped and then dropped off entirely. Cassie blinked, seeing that below her swayed the tops of trees.

They heard water too—maybe a small falls. She knew Marius had scrambled down if only because of how inviting it felt to do so herself, the slope dotted with shingles of rock, built in handholds and steps.

They found Marius not far from the stream near a small cave

opening, rubble around his feet. He'd been stacking the reddish stones into a hiker's cairn.

He smiled. "She says she has a sixth sense for it, but I guess I do too."

"For what?" Cassie asked. She understood the "she" to be Kate, his grandmother—a woman who had undergone earlier transformation in Cassie's mind: in addition to kidnapping her own grandchildren she was capable of allowing someone—her own son—to believe his children were dead.

And Cassie's own mother, in allowing Kate and the kids to stay in Hemlocks, was an accessory to that.

Marius held up one of the flakes of ore from his pile. "We're rich!" Even he knew to say that was a joke. "I think I can *smell* it," he said, confidingly. "Isn't that weird."

Cassie thought the banded stones had a gravity more than a smell. She surveyed the small scraps—the slag, the crap that was probably poisoning the stream.

She wanted to get back to the car, but Marius noticed the grocery sack. "Can we have our picnic here?"

Sure, said Cassie, shrugging. She had brought the lunch stuff, if now she itched for the lake. If anything happened to them here, something creepy in the woods, she supposed her own truck would work like a flag. Her parents, and Sam's mom, would discover their bodies here. Marius' father would find out he wasn't dead by finding out he was dead.

They made peanut butter sandwiches with sticks for knives. They each ate two. On the air wafted the hint of metal, of cool stream, and yet the sun warmed the tops of their heads, the part in Cassie's hair.

And what if somewhere (she knew it could not be true but

now she found it comforting to imagine) someone was sitting with Hattie in just such a weird location, eating something as ordinary as peanut butter on gas station bread without any jelly, musing at the thought that somewhere someone thought she was dead? And wasn't that funny? What a thing to think.

She remembered the rise of the land near the mostly hidden turn off to the secret beach. They bounced over the dirt path to a cleared area that made a kind of parking lot. Beyond that, on the other side of dotting grasses, the horizon razored the sky and lake.

Only one other car occupied the lot. They parked on the opposite side and trooped down the footpath to where the grass gave way to sand, where they pulled off their shoes.

It wasn't a particularly wavy day, but their ears filled with the gurgling slaps of the shore waves. Unlike the beach in the Ashland harbor, this one fronted open lake. From here, Cassie and her father had watched tankers pass, ships of the Great Lakes fleet headed from Duluth or Ashland through the Houghton channel or around the far top of the Keweenaw all the way to the Soo.

"I didn't bring my swimming suit," Marius said.

"That lake is *cold*," Sam said.

Cassie thought of her father again. Superior was the most indifferent of all the lakes, he said, more ocean than lake. At the same time, most of his ghost stories ascribed the big lake personality—memory and vengeance, and occasionally an indecipherable mercy.

Cassie had never been to any of the other Great Lakes, she said. And she'd never seen the ocean. Maybe because the boys had been jawing at her all day, telling things, she volunteered this.

"Are you serious?"

Nothing apparently could have amazed Sam or Marius more.

"You've never even been to Lake Michigan, even?" They began to pepper her with questions.

She'd been to Minneapolis a few times. It wasn't like she'd never been anywhere.

Sam sat in the sand, rolling his pants cuffs. "You shouldn't feel bad about it," he said. "Most kids from here haven't been any of those places. Haven't left the county. I just have because of my mom."

Cassie still had no idea who Sam's mom was or exactly what work she did and was becoming less interested in his family the more he bragged about it.

Marius listed the times he'd flown, the oceans in which he'd swum. Cassie began to peel off her pants. She was wearing dark underwear anyway. Then she took off her shirt, because why not. Marius was just a kid. Sam was just Sam.

But both boys were embarrassed, turning away. Jeez Cassie. Oh my God.

She walked to the edge of Superior. The way to go in, when you were going to go, was just to do it. You walked into cold water the way you walked into your first day of class—your first day ever as a student among other students, like some straggling member of a species discovering it wasn't the last of its kind. Everyone watching or no one watching, it didn't matter, you had to show resolve. You walked into cold water the way you walked into the funeral of a girl whose dirty cup still rolled on your floorboard, not a week after she'd insisted on borrowing your smaller bra so her boobs would look bigger; your friend (had she been your friend? She'd never told you what she was going to do), who'd been so dumb as to do something so stupid that people would later think it was profound because to imagine it wasn't was unimaginable.

The water wrapped around her ankles like ski boots. Thigh-deep, she dove.

The truth was that Hattie would have loved a day like today—out of class, the randomness of Marius and Sam along, the peanut butter sandwiches eaten off the side of the highway at the edge of an abandoned quarry.

She came up for air before she wanted to, the water more tolerable than she'd thought, than it had seemed with her first steps. Superior was so funny this way, some of its pockets swimmable and others unbearably cold, and even that depended on the day. It wasn't related to depth or angle of the sun but seemed more connected to some mood of the lake. She swam a few strokes.

Soon she'd swum farther than she'd thought—the boys on the beach shading their eyes though Superior carried their voices.

"She's crazy," Marius said.

"She's from *here*," Sam corrected. "Girls from here are crazy as F."

A wind came up on their walk back to the car. They'd stayed to watch a freighter likely heading toward the locks where Upper Michigan and Canada, and Lakes Superior and Huron, all came together. The ship looked like a toy on the horizon except when a bird passed or wave crested in the near distance, altering the perspective.

Nearing the parking lot, conscious again of the phone in the pocket of her damp jeans, Cassie turned to Sam. "How'd you know to call me at this number?"

"I didn't." He flushed, looked away.

"You *thought* you were calling Hattie's phone?" Cassie's body beneath her clothing was cold from the water, and though she could tell the sun was beating down around them, see its hard refraction off chrome in the parking lot, she couldn't feel it, like the sun was deflecting from her wet and chilled skin.

She wrestled the phone from her pocket. "Have you been leaving Hattie *messages?*" She began tapping as if to call them up. She didn't know the password to listen to the voicemails, but Sam didn't know this.

Sam protested. "Come on! That's private." He made a grab for the phone, but Cassie was taller.

Then Marius interrupted them. "Whoa. Look at that car," he said.

They'd forgotten about the other car in the lot, a red Neon, when they were down on the beach alone. Now they noticed the front tires were half buried by drifted sand.

Sam tried a door and it swung open, for a smell that made Cassie step back. The stale air had been heated and cooled and heated and cooled, trapped a long time in the confines of the car. A pack of cigarettes rested on the seat; a candy wrapper littered the floor. A half-drunk and now completely thin and flat plastic bottle of orange Crush protruded from the cup holder. CDs out of their cases spilled over the passenger seat.

Cassie thought of the age of the driver that they'd still listened to CDs. It was easier than thinking of how and why a person came to abandon their car by a lonely beach.

Sam went for the cigarettes.

"Not in front of Marius," Cassie said.

"*I* don't care," said Marius. "I'm not a *kid*."

"We need to go," Cassie said. "Let's just go."

Neither boy questioned where they had to go or why—other

than that Marius announced he was hungry and began making another peanut butter sandwich in the back seat.

After a while, Cassie cut down from highway 2 onto 51, heading south into Wisconsin on a main road, which would be faster than the winding way they had come earlier—or so she thought. Soon enough they came upon a stopped line of cars, though a single truck sailed past in the opposite lane.

Construction, Cassie thought, which was fine. At least the road ahead was passable if they'd have to wait their turn.

"A deer," said Marius. "I bet."

Cassie shook her head. No one would stop for a deer.

"It's a check point," Sam said.

"Checking for what?" Cassie said.

"My mom told me about these. She's probably going to be stationed at one."

Cassie knew there were checkpoints along the border with Canada in Minnesota, north of Grand Marais, and even new ones in some of the passes through the boundary waters. At the Soo locks you'd get caught in a long line and processing too. But she'd been driving—even canoeing—back and forth over the Wisconsin and UP border her entire life and never heard of a state line checkpoint.

"We don't have any fish," Cassie said.

"I think they're looking for people," Sam said.

"What?" Marius' mouth was covered in peanut butter.

"They'll just want to see your driver's license," Sam said. Cassie reached under her seat.

"Will they want to know why we're not in school?" Marius asked.

Cassie had never been pulled over. The only two police officers she knew were the bumbling school rent-a-cop, Two Barrel, and his roommate (a real officer, at least) Trent Lapham. Once recently she'd puked beer in their backyard. Before that, she knew Trent from childhood; his family had rented from Cassie's parents. Now more annoyed than nervous, she spun the radio dial. Sam's mention again of his mother, and the navy using some of the college buildings in Houghton, made her think of the station, and the college girl DJ. Cassie's father had said the school was pretty much all male, but the DJ had somehow commandeered a microphone. Cassie found the station right away today—the girl's voice coming through as clearly as if she sat in the truck with them. *If you're back on campus*, she was saying, *then you know what I'm talking about.*

"The college *is* open," Cassie said to Sam.

"That's not what she said," Sam said.

Cassie listened further and heard the DJ describe the campus this semester as a ghost town. She'd be playing Halloween music early, she said, beginning with "Thriller" and the opening beats of the song followed.

If young people were disappearing from the world—at least its rural places, its Midwestern places—there must have been other places they were arriving, where their numbers were increasing. Cassie thought of how her father explained the changing water level of their lake to guests. All that water went somewhere, sloshing in the tub of the Great Lakes basin or traveling as mist or snow.

Were rising sea levels affecting the Great Lakes? Every once in a while a guest would ask this. Superior's six hundred feet above sea level her dad would say, shaking his head. And then proudly (as if it were their lake, as if it weren't still an hour's drive away), that Superior was the largest source of fresh water in the world. More valuable than all the copper of the copper range in its day.

"Um, Cass?"

She'd pulled out Hattie's phone, texting as they crept forward, her foot on and off the brake.

"I don't think you want cops to see you texting and driving."

They were approaching a small brown shed. (This was the checkpoint? Cassie could have driven through it with the Fjord. She'd hit smaller deer.)

"I'm texting a cop," she said.

Trent didn't text back right away—but then he was standing by her door.

Cassie grinned, rolling down her window. He didn't look up until they were right in front of him, the next vehicle. Cassie stopped where the sign said stop. Though another sign warned a canine was in use, she didn't see a dog anywhere.

"Cass?"

Trent's squad car, the one with a big deer guard, was parked next to the shed. Another officer sat on a folding lawn chair—not Two Barrel, thank God. Cassie couldn't imagine the two of them working together in any serious grown-up capacity.

He was the same Trent Lapham, then of the cleft lip, with whom Cassie had played as a little girl, his mother a renter on a far corner of the resort's property. Trent mostly ignored the younger kids at their house parties, but he'd greet Cassie with a shout. *My old tree-climbing buddy!* That had not been bad for Cassie's developing regard among the orchestra girls. Hattie would have been pleased to know Trent and Two-Barrel had come to her funeral. So many boys their own age hadn't.

The scar still crossed Trent's upper lip, though now for the effect of making him appear tough. He looked in at Cassie and Sam in the front seat, squinted through to Marius in the back. "Where you coming from." The question was routine.

"Lake," Cassie said. "There wasn't any school."

Trent nodded. "That's where they've got our dog today. I was there all night." He rubbed his face.

"So it was a bomb threat?" Cassie asked.

"No." Trent sighed. "But enough people on social media were saying that. It was a computer outage. None of the IT is working, none of the security cameras. Everything's a mess."

Cassie didn't know why classes couldn't be held if the cameras were down. "What's all this about anyway?" She indicated the stopped line of cars on the perfectly fine road. "And look—I just texted you."

Trent pursed his lips and pulled out his phone. His shoulders flinched.

"That's kind of a shitty thing to do," he said. "Text from her phone." He wiped his face again with his hand.

Cassie felt heat rush to her face. "Julia gave it to me."

Trent grunted. He knew who Julia was.

"You better get on," he said. He slapped the hood of the Fjord.

Cassie wondered that he hadn't noticed Marius, that he hadn't said anything about the boy in her backseat for whom there was an active Amber Alert. Trent wasn't a terrible policeman, or she didn't think he was. It was seeing her, though, recognizing her face and putting her into a category in his mind, *people he knew*, that had rendered Marius invisible to Trent.

"I have to tell you something," Cassie said. She felt Marius shift behind her. Even Sam.

She'd felt sympathy for Marius briefly when he'd declared he wasn't a kid and that he'd wanted to go with his grandmother. But it was wrong that, somewhere, his father was worried he was dead, like Cassie's mother was wrong for keeping the kids, for hiding them, complicit in Kate's crime.

"Yeah?"

And then Marius made a small sound, a whimper, and behind Trent wind ruffled a tree. Instead, Cassie told about the abandoned red Neon they'd seen at the beach, the sand over its tires, the stale cigarettes and CDs—as if the medium of the playlist also attested to whatever might have happened to the inhabitant. The more of the scene she described the more its urgency appeared to her. What had the driver done? Who didn't yet know?

"Okay," Trent said, nodding. Was there anything else?

He looked at Cassie vacantly. He appeared to have forgotten completely the night he and Two Barrel helped Cassie and Hattie after Cassie had rolled the Fjord.

That had been the closest Cassie had come to seeing Trent and Two Barrel in actual police action. Hattie had texted them, and they'd come out in Trent's cruiser but without the lights. Cassie and Hattie had just left one of their parties; they were sort of responsible. The Fjord had rolled so far over that it had rolled right back up on its tires again, the only changes their location (now in a ditch), the new dent in the passenger door, and the elongated crack in the windshield from where Hattie's forehead had hit it. That had been two weeks before she died.

They'd cleaned Hattie up, pulled the truck out of the ditch. Cassie had waited for a ticket, a breathalyzer, until finally she'd burst and asked. Were they in trouble? Two Barrel shook his head, stepping away and lighting a cigarette. It was poor form of her to have asked. Two Barrel drove Hattie home and Trent followed Cassie in her truck all the way back to Eagle's Nest. After she parked, he got out of his car and followed her to the door like they'd been on a date on a TV show. The lights shone from inside Maples, her parents awake.

You don't seem all right, he'd said finally. I'm not, she'd said. You want me to write you a ticket? he'd asked, and that had made her laugh. Before leaving, he'd looked at the house once wistfully, like he wouldn't mind seeing her parents again. When he was a teen-ager, living with an older brother after his mother left, Trent had done some odd jobs around Eagle's Nest, helped Bud with shin-gling. Cassie remembered the small butter cookies his mother had made—that before she'd lived here, she'd come from somewhere else too.

Borders made a place a home, held it into a shape, gave it some-thing like a trademark cookie; if they also served to sever people from those they loved.

A line of cars had begun to grow behind them, and Trent glanced over at his partner in the lawn chair.

"Your folks know where you are?"

"Of course." Cassie lied.

"They know you're hanging out with Julia?"

"Julia just likes to see Hattie's name come up on the screen when I text."

"Don't," Trent said, grimacing. "You don't need any part of that mess."

He hit the hood of her truck again. She had to go.

Cassie drove but her shoulders and neck ached.

Maybe Trent was the one everyone should have blamed after Hattie. That night they'd rolled the truck, he and Two Barrel had asked her to move her arms and legs, had used a small flashlight to watch the track of her eyes. Neither were health professionals, but they'd put a few band-aids on her forehead, pronounced her fine, drove her home. For two weeks after the accident she'd walked around, talked and laughed in most of the ways she always did; she'd gone to school and rehearsal. For the neat roll of the Fjord and their rescue by Trent and Two Barrel she and Cassie became minor celebrities, briefly. Then Hattie had made the worst, most unthinking, ill-considered, confused and depressed decision of her life.

Cassie's own lungs thickened to think of it.

It was dark by the time Cassie and Marius crunched over the gravel of Eagle's Nest's parking lot. The lowering sun had dipped behind the tree line. They were cold, still in t-shirts. Cassie had been in the lake.

Marius hopped down from the truck and waved good-bye. He headed through the trees to Hemlocks like a kid skipping his way home from a school bus stop. Cassie saw the strangest thing when she turned to face her own house: Maples was dark.

Her mother left the house so rarely that, in her entire life, Cassie had only found herself alone there a handful of times. With someone always home, it was rare to find the door locked. Cassie had to think about where to find a key, and then she remembered the one on the pegboard in the garage. More mystery: both of her parents' vehicles were parked in their usual spots. So they were somewhere on foot or out on the water in a boat. Or in *boats*—if they'd each gone somewhere separately, which seemed more likely.

Cassie roamed the house, turning on lights in each room. It occurred to her that she hadn't called home to say Marius was with her, that school had been canceled—which her parents might have heard about on their own. At the same time, how would they have expected her to call? Supposedly, she didn't have a phone. Let them think about that if she got in trouble for this.

She didn't find her parents in the kitchen, the living room, or any of the bedrooms. In passing she flipped on the radio on the big old-fashioned stereo in the living room. A burst of staticky-crackle transformed into polka. In the kitchen she opened the refrigerator, wondering if she was hungry.

She almost didn't hear her phone for the accordion notes booming through the house, music that gave way to a girl's voice, the Houghton DJ. She had played a polka? Equally strange, her parents' old-fashioned radio—more decorative item of furniture than useful object—had been tuned to that station?

The phone in her hand fueled the confusion—as if the college girl on the radio had called Cassie. *Here's my favorite one*, the DJ was saying: *Titsle town. Now give me a shot of that! That's a Wisco original!*

But it was Julia who'd called Cassie's phone. "It's an emergency," she said.

Cassie had to turn off the radio to hear Julia. At the same time, *Titsle town* hung in the air. That had been the name of one of the shots Christina was advertising at Tiki's, one Cassie had assumed Christina had invented. It fit her sense of humor so perfectly.

Julia was sobbing—sobbing and driving. She cursed someone turning too slowly in front of her and Cassie could hear her swerving to swing around them.

"You've got to meet me," she begged.

Cassie couldn't imagine climbing into her truck again, and felt the ache return to her shoulders at the thought of the Fjord's lumbering bounce along the potholes of their driveway. The very last thing she wanted right now was to drive anywhere, to leave Eagle's Nest again tonight. Plus she was low on gas.

Never mind, Julia said. She was driving toward Cassie. She'd pick her up.

It's really an emergency, Julia said again.

Cassie sighed. If it was to Julia, then wasn't it? What else was there other than perspective—how a thing looked to the person living it?

Cassie walked down their dark driveway to meet Julia. She didn't need her to pull in just as her parents were returning from wherever they'd gone off to—maybe to work or sleep in separate cabins. She stepped along the pits she knew better now from the vantage of the Fjord's driver seat but remembered too from the days she'd ridden her bike through their puddles. Year after year, snow retreated to reveal the same holes in the same places; they reappeared even in the years they re-graveled. There was something underneath, deep underneath, that made the holes.

The moon glowed at the halfway point where the driveway turned sharply and trees had been cleared. Here her mother seeded milkweed every fall. Cassie could never quite keep it all straight: milkweed made food for caterpillars and so supported endangered Monarch butterflies, yet the milkweed itself was endangered, and wasn't helped by being eaten by caterpillars. Then there were the bees, and the humans, tied up in it all as dependents but also as bunglers, since pollination was a kind of bungling, involving thieving, littering, like it was all only accident at the base of the food chain.

As if the plan all along, for all of it, was collapse.

CHAPTER 10

ALLIE WOULDN'T HAVE agreed to go to Tiki's for Friday night fish fry—a thing they hadn't done in years—if she'd known Shara had returned.

The one consolation, if there could be any, was that Allie didn't think Bud had known they'd find the former bartender working side-by-side again with her daughter, Christina. Now Allie and Bud were trapped within three feet of the whirling duo, hemmed in from behind by other patrons.

Gary had invited them. Allie and Bud had been putting off dinner, waiting for Cassie to come home, when their newest post-season guest knocked on Maples' back door to ask if they'd eaten. Gary, in his geologist's vest and hiking pants, had been completing odd jobs in exchange for his board at Eagle's Next, replacing broken lights on the strand between the cabin paths and digging phragmites from the beach. Allie had seen him at work on a trail between Eagle's Nest and Tiki's, and tonight he was to man the deep fryer at the bar.

Even the girls had never tried to establish a permanent path between the two places, through the swamp. Allie wondered that a geologist hadn't been able to tell the way the area flooded, to read the slope of the land.

"Well hello, neighbors. You still here?" Shara was at work on the floor behind the bar taking apart a box. In a kind of ballet, Christina stepped over her mother and Shara rose with the pieces of the box in the air and shouted over Allie's head *who wants some cardboard?* Several voices responded, and Shara handed the scraps over, her armpit in Allie's face. Christina and her mother switched places again, moving as if there were eight arms between them. Christina slid two mugs of beer to Allie and Bud, darker and redder than the usual Lite Allie drank, when she drank beer at all.

We're still here, Allie thought.

"Careful," Bud said, a hand on Allie's arm. "Stuff is strong."

"Cassie here?" Christina asked.

Three of Christina's long dreadlocks had been bleached a yellow-y white. She seemed to have a new tattoo creeping from her shoulders toward her neck. Yet Allie saw in her eyes and mouth the girl she'd known as a nine-year-old, the one who'd walked out of the woods lost and terrified. She saw the girl who'd lived out here by herself for the summer, who'd look through the window curtain before unlocking the apartment's back door for Allie, reaching for the soup pot or hot dish she'd brought over.

What had Shara said to her daughter when she returned? How had she and her daughter negotiated her absence?

Though Allie had to admit she didn't know where her own daughter had been today—or Marius either. At least they'd known the boy was with Cassie since Miranda had seen them leave together—confusingly, as if Cassie could bring him to school. Later, when Allie heard on the radio that the school had closed for an IT issue, *a systems hack*, she'd had to wonder just how her daughter had known school would be canceled, and that she could take Marius with her for the day.

"School then orchestra," Allie replied to Christina, though she knew her daughter wasn't going to orchestra anymore either.

With an upended bottle in one hand, a soda gun in the other, Shara cocked her head. A small TV sat behind the bar—old, but with a digital converter box. "I got bad news for you honey. There wasn't any school today."

Allie nodded. She'd have to admit she knew it. "I remember how, in college, it was the fire alarm they pulled." Then she regretted having said that in front of Christina—*college*.

"You don't have any Miller anymore?" Allie asked.

Christina jerked her head to three single cans in the glass-faced cooler. She told Allie the price.

"Are you kidding?"

"That's why we enjoy the homebrew." Christina glanced toward a man at the far end of the bar, and he tipped his well-worn Blue Jays hat.

They split to find a table. At the same time, Allie tried to understand the crowd. Deer season was a few months out. Bud threaded the crowd toward the wall spot she finally found just as Allie remembered Kate saying that knowing a girl like Christina was helpful for people wanting to cross the border, implying that she could arrange "trades."

"Maybe you should be home-brewing something other than diesel," Allie said, lifting her beer. "What are they selling this for?"

A narrow ledge rimmed the room, just enough for a cube of blue cue chalk, the glass bottom of an emptied glass.

"I didn't know she would be here," Bud said. He said that he had talked to Shara on the phone the other day, that he'd called her, but she hadn't said anything about coming back. Allie felt this like heat lightning, a dry parch in her throat both alarming and far away.

"Do you want to leave?"

But she wasn't going to be seen running away. Allie shook her head. "Let's eat. I'm hungry, you're hungry. We gave our order."

She hadn't looked closely enough at anyone's face to determine just who in the sea of people they might know, but the usual crowd at Tiki's was the one that had fostered the rumor, long ago and long a joke in her family, that she and Bud were nudists, that Eagle's Nest was some kind of commune.

And where and how had that idea first sprung? Had Bud gone about some chore in the yard one day without his shirt on? Had he and Allie been seen making love, sunning afterwards on the raft on one of the still-warm days at the end of the season—those hot September days that were both gift-like and foreboding?

"She's been stocking this place from Wyoming, sending food and supplies," Bud said. He seemed to want Allie to know Shara had been looking out for Christina, that she hadn't just abandoned her daughter.

"She doesn't own Tiki's. They lost their distributors, their beer license." Bud shook his head at this calamity. He looked out over the room and drummed his nails. "But there are a lot of campers in the area who have learned to come here for stuff."

Allie turned to stand shoulder-to-shoulder with her husband, to look out over the same room. In t-shirts and jeans, in flannels, beards, and bandanas, small groups of men and women crowded the tall tables and long bar. Several held drinks to their chests, and some red-checked baskets of food—French fries, sandwiches. These could have been their neighbors, Tiki's usual crowd, but in fact it wasn't. The air was clogged with familiar sunscreen and Deet, but Allie didn't recognize a single person, and now something in the visitors, these campers, struck her. They weren't just casually dressed but dirty. They were also thin, a few with the wild eyes of the sunbaked. At the nearest table, two women in purple t-shirts lined in the sweat marks of their backpack straps shared a single granola bar. A man flapped by with a garbage bag split open over his shoulders, and two more wrapped over his boots.

When the crowd parted Allie saw Gwen, the woman who'd stayed with them last weekend with her daughter, Mayella. They'd been moved from their home in Bruce Crossing, told they couldn't live there anymore because of flooding—though the flooding had been last spring and most recently the problem had been drought.

"You think they're all camping for fun?" Allie asked, realizing her own amazement as it came through her voice, as she turned to look at her husband's familiar face and saw on it instead an assemblage of features she knew individually but not all as one: a hard line of a nose, sky-blue eyes, loose lips.

"I don't know what they are," Bud said. "I know this, though, Shara and Christina have found a way to make it work. They're going to make enough money to get out of here."

"Make it off of people who are homeless, displaced."

Bud changed the subject. "How did you know Cassie's school was closed today?"

"I heard it on the radio."

"But you lied about not knowing it."

Allie didn't answer.

"You think she could be responsible for the outage, whatever it was—that she might have hacked her own school?"

Bud had not been on the orchestra trip. He'd not seen their daughter coolly ball the wet towel to fire it at the security camera above the pool. He hadn't seen the girls at the funeral in their long black dresses, their thumbs twitching on their rhinestoned cases. Didn't know they all admired her, looked to her, Cassie of the long hair and deep cellist's bow.

"You think I've been unfair to Cassie?"

"Why did you put that thing on her cello case? Why doesn't she have her phone back? You know, all day long we had *no way* to get a hold of her. *No way*."

"Just because a person has a phone doesn't mean you can get a hold of them."

"I know! She doesn't always answer. She's a teenager."

"I'm saying, even if she answered."

Bud still thought it was possible to get a hold of people—to keep a hold on anyone. He thought she didn't want their daughter to grow up or leave home. Allie knew Cassie would do both. She didn't want her daughter to grow up or leave home at this *time*. When the world was like *this*.

And then Bud set down his glass and left.

He left their spot at the wall. He left their side of the room. Then he left the bar entirely. And the room closed in around Allie, keeping her there.

The man with the Blue Jays hat who'd brewed the beer—at whom Christina had nodded earlier—watched Allie order another at the bar. She raised her glass to him.

"How do you like it?" He called, his moustache tipped in the yellow foam.

"I'm glad I walked," Allie said. At the same time, she worked on placing his accent. French?

It wasn't like Bud had left her entirely alone. She knew Gary. The bartenders. Plus she *had* walked. Her own home, and her own bed, were only a mile away.

Then Kate and the kids walked in. Miranda slipped through to claim a stool right up at the bar. Kate doled a few quarters to Marius, and Allie saw him make his way to the jukebox. It didn't work, Allie could have told him, but then heard the music swell.

Allie also knew Gwen and Mayella. She maneuvered to their high table at the center of the room where Gwen looked thinner than she had just a week ago, her leg with a bandaged ankle propped on the stool rung beside her and a pair of crutches leaning in reach.

Allie had known they'd been forced to leave their home but hadn't asked where they were headed. She had simply assumed family or friends in another city awaited their arrival.

"I tripped," Gwen said. "Marten hole I think."

"Is it broken?"

"Broken but healing. Some people came along." She nodded over her shoulder to two men at the next table. Allie tried not to think what would have happened if no one had come by—if Gwen and Mayella had been left out in the woods. Or what might have happened, Gwen found defenseless by the wrong passersby.

Allie squatted to talk to Mayella.

"Well hello."

The current was different down here near everyone's knees. Light and shadow played. The adults' talk drifted. Allie observed the footwear. Boots, but also softer, less sturdy tennis shoes. Patches made of duct tape.

"I'm going to get some French fries," the girl whispered, but she didn't say it like it was such a treat.

"What would you really like?" Allie asked.

"Orange juice," the girl whispered, and Allie thought, well, that was something she could help with.

She'd seen juice in the fridge beneath the overpriced Miller Lite cans. Allie worked her way back to the bar, but it was even harder to get a spot now. She watched for Christina's eye. Gary was dropping baskets into the fryer, pulling them out and shaking contents into wax paper lined baskets, pulling paper tickets on a clothesline above his head. Allie ducked under the trap on the side.

The fridge was right here. First she had to locate one of the small plastic kids cups and lids she remembered so vividly from those years long ago when they had had come to places like this with young Cassie.

So many different supplies populated the shelves beneath the bar now. Alongside the fishing lures Allie took in propane canisters, shovels, tent stakes, nylon patch kits, matches, small compasses, medical kits, flares. There were battery packs and two battery powered stoves. One type, Allie saw, utilized copper coils like the kind they'd lost in Hemlocks. She noted the row of disposable phones and phone cards, the stack of blank postcards and the set of postage stamps. When she reached for the juice in the small refrigerator, she saw the bottles of insulin. The amoxicillin. Doxycycline.

"You can put that juice on your tab," Shara said. She was standing right there when Allie turned, pointing to a ledger taped to the bar's back mirror.

Allie gave a grimace before ducking back under the trap with the juice.

At their table, the brewer with the Jays hat had come to talk to Gwen. He was telling a story.

"I heard that sound and knew I was someplace safe." He pointed out into the bar, waving generally.

What sound did he mean? Not the Eagles emanating from the jukebox.

He held up a finger, grinning, and there came the sound: a very particular thud and roll, the rumble of pool balls falling through the internal tunnels of the wooden table behind them. In the tray at the end the celluloid balls knocked into one another, coming to their rest.

"It was the middle of the night for me," he said. "I mean, trees and trees and trees. How do you know where you are? And I was still a bit seasick. Then they brought us into a dark room. That was when I got scared. I'll admit it. Why couldn't they turn on the lights? But then on the other side of the wall I heard that sound. That rumble, rumble, the thwack and crack. The sound of people playing pool! I mean, you hear that, and you know you've landed somewhere ordinary. Somewhere safe." He held up his glass. There was a punchline coming: "You know you're most in danger of getting a beer."

"Someone took you over the border?" Allie asked.

"I left one bar and ended up in another." He shrugged. "It was like any other weekend!"

"Why were you trying to come south?" Allie asked. She understood why people were leaving here. Bud seemed to think everyone should.

"Don't like to stay anywhere for too long," he said. "It's best to keep passing through."

Later, Allie drifted with others outside. Freed from the grill, Gary was explaining plans for a system of solar panels he was hoping to install on Tiki's roof.

Allie wandered to the driveway. Here, to confirm what she'd begun to understand, she noted the half empty parking lot, and that no cars or trucks lined the gravel drive that led through the trees to the highway, as they would have on a night like this in the past. A few jon boats and kayaks bobbed off Tiki's dock, though not in the usual vibrant yellows and reds but greens and browns. Most people in the crowded bar had arrived here on foot.

"Have you seen the kangaroos?" Mayella asked, having followed her outside.

"What?" said Allie.

Mayella grabbed her hand, her small paw warm in Allie's. She led her around to the side of Tiki's, near where a big RV was now parked. It loomed larger than Tiki's, and Allie wondered how she'd missed it back here. But they'd come around the other side of the building, the lake side, when they arrived. Shara must have returned in this vehicle. It was probably where she was living.

Here against the north side of the bar, protected from the wind, someone had built a makeshift pen. Inside Allie saw a water bowl, a bed of straw, and two small creatures blinking back through the dark with the glassy, reflective eyes of deer.

She jumped back.

Mayella stood on her tiptoes, attempting to peer through an opening in the slats.

"They're part of a zoo." Marius and Miranda had come up behind them. "And they're wallabies," said Marius.

"Kangaroos," said Mayella.

It happened at every level, Allie thought—one person's reality not at all the same as someone else's. Not even their names for things.

"They came with some guys on their way to a show in Ashland," Miranda said.

"What are they going to do with them during winter?" Allie asked.

"That's why people are trying to find the rest of them," Miranda said. "There were more. Bud said one's been shot."

Allie felt this like she'd been shot—Bud had seen a kangaroo hopping around their woods and he hadn't told her? There'd been times in their marriage they'd shared hourly updates on the progress of a robin's nest.

"Well they can't live here," Allie said, and she leaned forward to lift the latch on the gate.

All creatures deserved a fighting chance.

She returned to Maples late, for sight of light streaming through the first-floor windows, the front door flung wide open. Inside, Bud lay on the living room couch beneath a Birchfield watercolor print that had been among the very few possessions Allie had moved with them from their house in Chicago.

Her heart fell. She'd looked around for him before she'd left, wondering if she'd been mistaken, if the whole night he'd only been somewhere on the other side of the bar, trapped in some other conversation. But he had simply left her there, walked home through the dark on his own.

"Do you really think Kate kidnapped those kids?" Bud said, stirring as Allie came into the room—ready, it seemed, to accuse her of something. "She wouldn't have brought them to a public place then would she? Where anyone could see them."

Allie stared at him. So he had stuck around long enough to see Kate and the kids arrive. Just what was his story to himself about them?

"Call Kate and ask." Allie held out her phone.

He was going to bed, Bud said, lying back on the couch.

In the morning, they slept in—though the sun hadn't yet floated above the tree line when Kate and Marius knocked on their door. Allie came downstairs to answer it. Bud sat up from the couch.

"Hey," said Kate, "Is Miranda here?"

"She could be upstairs with Cassie," Bud said. "I'll check."

Bud clomped up the stairs. Allie had seen Cassie's truck in their parking lot on her walk back but hadn't had the heart last night to wake and confront her about her whereabouts. She remembered noticing in the moonlight, though, a new dent in the passenger side door of Cassie's truck. Or had it always been there? A few months ago she'd thought it was just her eyesight when one day there appeared to be a crack in the windshield, but the next day it was gone.

Bud came downstairs and announced Cassie wasn't home either—not in her bed or her room.

Allie flew to the window, looked out across the lot where her truck was still parked.

"Did you leave the bar without Miranda?" Allie asked Kate.

"I assumed she was with you." Kate shrugged.

Allie had found many of Kate's actions mysterious. But this response was one of the first for which she couldn't conjure sympathy, invent an explanation. Now she thought newly of all the times Kate had simply left the kids for the day—assuming they'd be minded by Cassie or Allie, or maybe not assuming anything at all. She'd picked them up from their school and driven them north without telling their parents, perhaps without telling the kids where they were going. She'd let the children spend the summer confined to the living room of a trailer parked in the middle of a dense forest, where they'd watched recorded TV shows from another decade. And what was their life going to be like in Canada—how was Kate planning to take care of them there?

It was the first time Allie had considered that she could have been wrong in taking Kate's side all this time.

Marius pulled a piece of paper from the top of Allie's laptop. Cassie had gone to an orchestra gig, a last-minute thing, the note read. Ms. Tomas had needed another cellist, and they'd be gone overnight.

"Why didn't she just text you?" Marius said, turning the hand-written note around in his hands.

Allie knew her daughter had quit the orchestra—or at least that she hadn't been going to rehearsals. Would Ms. Tomas have called her for the gig even then? She looked at Bud, who picked up his phone, started thumbing a text. But *he* knew Cassie didn't have her phone, Allie recollected. After a few moments, Bud's phone buzzed back.

"Shara says they're not at Tiki's." He didn't apologize for having messaged her.

"Why don't you text Cassie?" Marius asked again, insistent. "She has a phone. Why don't you just ask her?"

Allie winced, thinking what she'd done to Cassie's phone, now somewhere at the bottom of Little Eagle Lake, discovery to be made by some future archeologists, or, if not, material to be ground up whenever the next glacier, someday, swept through. Bud's phone buzzed again. This message took longer to read.

"Some people at Tiki's saw a girl Miranda's age hitch a ride with someone."

"Oh my God," said Kate, and she took a seat.

"Miranda didn't want to go to Canada," Marius said, turning to comfort his grandmother. "She's been trying to figure out how to get back to Dad. She doesn't want to give up her career, you know. She missed too much training this summer."

CHAPTER 11

CASSIE HAD BEEN under the impression that Julia's boyfriend would be their host at the cabin in western Wisconsin. Hattie had sometimes told people Mark was her stepfather—if he'd just put a ring on it. Cassie and Julia had driven through the night, slept briefly in a parking lot so as not to arrive before dawn. Stepping from Julia's Range Rover in the early morning light, Cassie understood there was much she might have asked about in advance. Mark was nowhere in sight.

Neither was the cabin any kind of cabin. The structure had been built in nod to cabin as concept, the cross-cut ends of the logs meeting in corner rungs, two chimneys belching a wood smoke smell that fit the scene: the acres of privately owned woods through which they'd driven, the long gravel road that had crossed and re-crossed a stream. The cabin stretched three stories with two wrap-around decks, with rows of shined windows, sets of double doors. In contrast with the old growth density of the surrounding acres—private hunting land, Cassie understood—the cabin loomed in a clearing the size of a Walmart. Both American and Wisconsin flags drooped from a pole in the yard for the incongruous effect that they'd arrived at some other sovereign nation.

"Thanks for coming with me," Julia said, from behind dark glasses she didn't need in the early morning light. "I didn't know if I could face him alone."

Among other assumptions Cassie could have asked about then: if Mark were expecting them, if they were invited.

Julia tugged at her tank top on her way up the steps. Cassie reached to touch the wood post on the end of the porch railing. It had been carved into the snout and snarling teeth of a bear.

They walked into a room of strangers in pajamas lingering after breakfast.

On an L-shaped couch, three men spooned grapefruit from bowls, their heads craned upward at a giant TV mounted above the fireplace. Past the couch and long dining table at the back of the room, a row of windows revealed a deck and a backdrop of a long grassy field. A staircase ran up one wall, revealing an open hallway with multiple doors. People could ascend or descend in their pajamas in search of bagels and herbed cream cheeses like royalty.

A woman in a pink t-shirt crisscrossed with crosshairs and camouflage leaves came to greet them. Julia went in for a hug, though she didn't say the woman's name for Cassie.

Julia, of course, looked like no other woman, no other person, in the room. Her black tank top and cleavage were the wrong thing. So too her dark mascara, heeled sandals, the tiny pink purse with rhinestones.

"They all went out," the woman said. Her voice reminded Cassie of Shara's, deep and scratched. "Took the four-wheelers out to the muddy spot to horse around."

Cassie introduced herself, offering a hand, grudgingly glad for this one thing her mother had taught her to do.

"Melody," said the woman, as if flustered by her own name.

"Is Mark out there getting muddy too?" Cassie didn't have to look at Julia to know she wanted Cassie to ask this, to take charge.

"Mark? Oh yes. Thought he'd be hung up in Washington all weekend, but he made it."

Julia put a hand on her hip, finding her pose. "He's hung up down there so often he should just get an apartment. I'm always telling him that."

But instead of going to look for Mark, Julia allied herself with Melody, who'd been fussing with something in the kitchen—making hamburger patties?—as if this were the kind of thing with which Julia had any skill whatsoever. Cassie pictured the cold meat stuck under Julia's false fingernails, the gouges her press-ons would leave in the soft sides of the buns and deviled eggs.

Fighting the tug of sleep, the long stretch of the day ahead, Cassie took herself outside for a tour. From the deck she saw two more buildings—one a bunkhouse for even more guests, the other a machine shed.

Cassie learned to drive on the series of ATVs they'd kept at Eagle's Nest and had taken at least two others apart down to the bolts, working with her dad or just fiddling around on her own, making go-boats with the engine parts. In this machine shed she found a gymnasium-sized room crowded with what men in the Northwoods and marketers in newspaper fliers called *toys:* ATVs, snowmobiles, jet skis, and the attendant gas cans and spare tires, tow ropes and trailer tie downs. The room was high-ceilinged and clean, and lit like a storeroom. Along one wall ranged a rack of carefully organized helmets and snowmobile suits, blaze orange vests and even spare boots from which guests, presumably, could help themselves. The abundance was dizzying. Cassie thought of Sam Shandy's stretched-out hand-me-downs. Kids at Satuit who ate chips from the vending machine for lunch. On another wall hung the locked cabinets behind which, Cassie would guess, were the bows, crossbows, guns, and ammo. Rich people knew what to lock up.

Even the garbage bins smelled new. The two large refrigerators next to them were stocked with beer, the brand that went with the politics that Cassie had already made a guess about. Bud had taught her to size guests in that way. She spied an unlocked cabinet and was just opening it when she heard the high buzz of ATVs and laughter from the driveway. Inside the cabinet hung the keys for the vehicles on correspondingly labeled hooks.

The ATV riders had circled around the garage and now passed the open window as if single-filing by on a TV screen. The riders, mostly men but a few women too, ranging in age from twenty to fifty or sixty, began to dismount and remove their helmets. At the edge of the field Cassie saw archery targets.

She startled to hear a sound behind her—applause. Someone had come into the garage and used a remote to turn on a large television high in the corner. The applause had come from the TV, on which bicycles were zipping by.

"You watch the Tour?" the man said, addressing Cassie as if he knew her.

Another man entered, medium-sized and fit, though in his late fifties probably. He went to a cabinet, returning a key and helmet. It was Mark. Cassie had seen him once or twice, with Julia at orchestra concerts and last at the funeral. He'd been the only man there in a suit but hadn't seemed aware of that.

"The Tour de France?" the first guy repeated, grinning at her. He had dark hair and tanned skin and wore a gray t-shirt over khaki cargo shorts, similar to what anyone might wear around Wild Fire except for the material, which seemed shinier, stretchier.

God, she was like her mother, looking at people's clothes. He also had a beaming smile, a dimple.

"Antonio," he said. His touch was a quick grasp that wasn't exactly like a handshake. He nodded his head again at the TV. "I wonder if they'll move the race even further into fall next year. Two already dropped out from the heat."

"Huh?"

"You here to shoot?" He tried a new topic. "Half the people here are into shooting. The rest of us just drink." He patted his trim belly. Cassie doubted he drank. If he did he'd have a belly like Two Barrel.

"Guess I'm here to drink," said Cassie.

And he laughed—like what she'd said was funny. Maybe he had no idea how old she was.

"Oh, God. *Cassie*, Cassie." Mark had recognized her.

"Hello," Cassie said. She should have used his last name, called him Mr., but she couldn't remember it. If she tried, she might let slip one of Julia's dozen pet names for him—all inappropriate. Despite that, though, Cassie understood Julia really did love Mark. That was what her mother, all the other mothers, missed when they looked at Julia, couldn't see for everything else about her that was so distracting.

Mark ignored Cassie's hand and pulled her in for a hug, leaving the shoulder of her t-shirt wet with his tears and snot.

In all the thinking she'd done about Hattie, she'd not considered once Mark's grief for her.

"This was Hattie's friend," he told Antonio—which likely revealed her age. Oh well, flirting had been fun.

"I've heard so much about Hattie," Antonio said. "I'm so sorry."

Mark wiped his nose on the long sleeve of his shimmery shirt. He asked if she just got here, if she'd had a tour, if she wanted one. It wasn't his place, but a friend's, a business associate. Everyone met here this weekend in September, every year. They walked out to the field with the archery targets.

"Is Julia with you?" He stopped walking.

Cassie nodded. She was the one who had brought his crazy, grief-stricken hot mess of a girlfriend here for some kind of confrontation in front of all his friends and business associates.

Mark wiped the corners of his eyes with the back of his sleeve. "Good," he said. "I've been so worried about her."

They watched the target practice before Antonio joined them again, holding out a bow. Did Cassie want to try?

"You should," said Mark. "Hattie loved it."

Maybe later, Cassie said, feeling weirdly shy, though she liked watching the high sail of the arrows from the others' practice, the dull thud as they hit the far targets. Hearing that Hattie had been here once made the place different, made Hattie different, revealing some part of her Cassie hadn't known. It was hard to believe she'd been here and no one had ever heard about it. She'd talked about the time she'd visited her dad in San Francisco until even Sam rolled his eyes, and Sasha, the youngest flute player, her mouth a small pink bow, had told her to shut up. Hattie's real father was a bike messenger. One of his roommates did heroin. The life he lived in San Francisco was exotic.

Antonio offered the bow, and Cassie decided she'd better take him up on something. Maybe she'd feel what Hattie had felt. Cassie had played darts before and had shot a gun with Christina and Shara at the range but felt nervous that Antonio was watching. He was younger than the other men, but different than Trent Lapham. In some kind of different league than Trent Lapham.

There weren't as many women out here as men, but Cassie paused to watch one—another tall girl about her age—take aim. Even before she released, Cassie could tell by the confidence with which she raised the bow, not dissimilar from the way in which Ms. Tomas raised a baton, that she knew what she was doing. There was whistling from the others before the arrow hit the bullseye. They could tell from just the arrow's flight, maybe her release, that she was on course. Antonio cheered too, and Cassie excused herself without shooting. Her job was to help Julia.

Inside, one of the men on the couch scooted forward, now eating from a bowl of peanuts. The people inside, Cassie understood, ate all weekend. Now they were watching the Tour, too. A group of men hunched forward on their bicycles pedaled so closely to one another they could have reached to hold each other's handlebars; one could have stopped pedaling and just rested his feet on the seat of the next, the motion of the group enough to carry them all along. Except, Cassie could see, if even one of the group made a mistake all of them would crash.

She didn't realize her heart was pounding, or that she'd put her hand over it until she saw the grease stain from the peanuts on her t-shirt.

"Do they crash?"

"Some years," the man replied. He was older than her father, or just looked as if he were.

The other man on the couch had his foot in a black boot. Crutches leaned against the end table.

"I was in a crash."

"You bike?" This was the man with the cast.

"No. Flipped my truck. It was winter. Pretty slippy."

"Mess up your truck?"

"Not that anyone can see but me," Cassie said.

"A Ford then!" This was the answer her father would have given. Small talk was easy for men because all they needed to know were the names of teams and maybe a few players, who was winning what. Girls had to come up with details, secrets about themselves or other people, and offer these up in trades, their value whatever it cost the person to say.

The funny thing about the roll of the Fjord was that Cassie and Hattie had been in it together; it might have been what made them true friends. For at least those two weeks before she died. In truth Cassie hadn't even known Hattie a year ago. That showed what a year was, what could change.

"You got any more of those peanuts, Mel?" The man on the couch called in the direction of the kitchen. "We're going to have to make a grocery run if I keep eating like this all weekend."

More women milled in the kitchen, the one thing they had in common that they seemed to be, distinctly, either older or younger than Julia. The older ones dressed more mutedly, except for their jewelry. The younger ones wore shorts and ponytails, like Cassie. Daughters or girlfriends, Cassie thought.

Julia was arranging cheese slices on a plate, attempting to stripe the whites and yellows, to alternate the varieties with olives or rosemary, but using her bare fingers.

"Let me, let me," Cassie said, moving to block view of Julia and her unsanitary hands from the room.

"I have to have something to do," Julia said, hissing. "I've been to the bathroom four times since we got here just to avoid standing around like a dumbass."

"Should we go?" Cassie said.

"Is Mark here?" Julia sounded desperate. At the same time, she glanced to the microwave to check out her own reflection. Cassie called to mind everything she knew about Julia: pushing past the images of the woman in the white bikini on the boat deck, the woman from orchestra practice who'd stand behind Ms. Tomas miming gross things with a violin bow. Hattie had said her mom was from here—somewhere in all these woods that counted enough as here.

Cassie took the sunglasses perched on her own head and fit them over Julia's face, which was quickly crumpling, the sobs beginning in her shoulders.

"Say you're allergic to cilantro," Cassie whispered. This was something the only truly rich woman who'd ever come to Eagle's Nest had said. She'd been dragged along by a husband who wanted a quaint get-away, something rustic, both all the while seemingly believing Eagle's Nest's battered kayaks and spitting outboards, thin towels and sheets were part of some calculated project; that the plastic bag of marshmallows from the gas station that Cassie held opened on her bare knees at campfires was some kind of theatrical prop. "Cilantro always gives me headaches," the woman had said every night when she wanted to go to bed early, though there was no cilantro anywhere at Eagle's Nest.

This ruse was enough to get Julia from the kitchen and up to one of the bedrooms. In the hallway, Julia emerged from her mini breakdown long enough to peek into several of the vacant rooms and to make sure she picked the biggest one. Once she had Julia installed in what had to have been a master bedroom, though it didn't seem occupied, Cassie promised she'd send Mark to check on her—and this would give her time to decide if she'd do that. She wanted to protect Julia, even if now she wasn't sure if she should. Mark appeared to be grieving for Hattie—but then what had he and Julia been fighting about? Though they'd spent the summer together (or so photographic evidence hinted; Mark wasn't *in* the pictures), when they'd returned Julia stayed in the house and he'd decamped, which was simple enough math, Cassie figured, to indicate he'd been in the wrong.

There was a meal going on downstairs—lunch? The time of day for a meal seemed off to Cassie, in one direction or another. She was invited to sit down to eat just as Mark and Antonio entered. In relation to the rest of the group, she wondered who she appeared to be—one of the girlfriends/wives or one of the daughters?

She sat down next to the tall girl who'd shot the arrows.

"So you're from here, huh?" she said.

A girlfriend. Cassie placed her after some deliberation. It was the thin gold chain on her neck, pretty in a quiet way.

"I'm from here too, Minneapolis. Well, a suburb of Minneapolis."

Cassie laughed. "Minneapolis is *here*?"

The girl gave her name as Jessica, which she said through a mouthful of food. She pointed around the table with her fork. That girl was from Texas, that one Poland. Where was Cassie from?

At school she said Wild Fire. "Vilas County," she finally went with. "Near the U.P. border."

"Oh, I've been there," Jessica said. "You know, my family travels all over, snowmobiling and dirt bike racing. We stayed at a resort in Vilas County once, this old fishing place with all these cabins named after trees."

Cassie stared at her. Though it was breakfast—*brunch*, maybe that was the word—Jess cracked a beer, the fingernails on one hand surprisingly ugly and stubby like Cassie's when she was practicing cello regularly. Now Cassie wanted a drink too, though she hadn't had one since the night she'd rolled the truck—not that she'd been drunk then. She hadn't thought so. Before she and Hattie had climbed in, to test herself, she'd tossed her keys high in the air, caught them perfectly in one hand.

Cassie explained her family ran a resort in Vilas, with cabins named after trees. Jessica became convinced that was the place her family had stayed.

"But you must have been gone. You'd remember my family," Jessica said. "We were the ones that sank our boat."

"How'd you manage to sink a boat?" In her experience, boats could be flooded, or submerged, tipped or upended. It took a lot more than you might think to fully submerge things that had been designed with modern parts to float. Also, she doubted Jessica had been to her Eagle's Nest. How to explain how similar so many of the small resorts were? With the same moose antler décor though there weren't really moose in the county.

"Oh, the usual dumbshit way. My dad forgot to put the plug in. We loaded it ass-first off the trailer at that little ramp way off to the side at your place. Then he got pissed and didn't try to take it out right away but just sat there in it, swearing. He even drank a beer." Here she paused for hers. "By the time he was ready to do anything about it, or let anybody help him do anything about it, your dad had to call a tow company, and they came and hauled it out, scraping the shit outta the hull, so he could complain about that the next two years."

Cassie shifted in her seat, her shorts too short for the chair so the tops of her legs rubbed against the hard edge. What if Jessica had been to Eagle's Nest? She might have been at Tiki's, or out on that water that day. It was strange to think of life going on there without her—that it had ever, and that it would.

"Your dad was super nice about the whole thing. What a funny guy! Said he's done that before, that anyone who's spent any time on a lake has."

Her father had never put a boat in without a plug that Cassie could remember, but this kind of lie to make someone else feel at ease was him quintessentially.

"Anyway, my dad being who he is, he just bought a bigger, better boat. Like, he went the very next day. Then we had to buy our own cabin to keep the thing at, and since it was such a big boat we had to be on a big lake. Now my parents have this place up on Superior. Ojibwe Bay? You ever heard of it? It's near the Soo, and a major hassle now that it's on the other side of a checkpoint. We got searched last year and it took hours. But that's where we keep our boat, tied up at a dock." She laughed.

After brunch, some of the women began to pick up plates. Julia had not come down, and Cassie didn't figure good odds for her wanting to leave yet. As far as she knew, Julia hadn't seen Mark. Cassie found Antonio and asked him to teach her to shoot.

"It's addictive," he said.

"I have a high immunity to addictive substances," Cassie said.

"Ah. You lack commitment." He pretended he was taking notes

on her, like in a job interview, and it made Cassie laugh—at the same time as she was startled. She'd never been on a job interview, never imagined herself on one.

She was retrieving one of her arrows from a distant target—finally, instead of whiffing into the trees—when her phone chirped.

From the far end of the field, Antonio gestured that Cassie should hurry. It wasn't safe to stand too long near the targets. The chirp had made for a surprising sound—different than the buzz when Hattie's phone received a text. Reluctantly, she put the phone away and worked on the arrow, which was wedged in pretty good. She thought of every fish she'd ever yanked, the guts that came with. It would have been easier if she could have pushed the arrow through.

She trotted back along the edge of the clearing, giving what she hoped was a wide enough berth to the other shooters. She realized the chirp from the phone was a flash post—someone had posted something to Hattie's flash page. She couldn't resist pulling out her phone to check.

It was her mother.

Cassie stopped, tucking the arrow under her arm to scroll. *Cassie, call home! Emergency!* Read the post.

How could her mother have thought to post to Hattie's flash page, that Cassie would see it there?

Her mother hadn't in any other way this summer brought up Hattie, indicated she understood that the girls might have been friends, or whatever they'd been that Cassie missed her now. Cassie hadn't articulated this to herself before but felt the knowledge with a tightening in her throat. She was grieving for Hattie—but like she was some kind of robot monster, only understanding her own human emotions long after they had come and gone, waves hitting the beach after a boat rounded a point. She was feeling things the way her mother did.

"That your boyfriend texting?" Antonio asked.

Cassie hid behind the sheet of her hair for an extra second. "Hardly." She was eager to take another shot. The string felt like one of her cello strings against her fingertips—shooting like something she'd always wanted to do with that instrument, bend one of its long wires to its breaking point.

As she readied to release, another chirp from Hattie's phone made her jump. And then another.

"Just a sec," she said. "I'll turn it off."

She hadn't thought her mother would believe the story that she'd gone somewhere to fill in for an orchestra ensemble. Her mother had left that funny tool on her cello case and knew her cello was in her closet and not being carted back and forth to rehearsal. The note had been for her dad, and a formality. They'd know she wasn't dead if she was bothering to lie.

After shooting, she and Antonio ended up on bikes. From the rack in the garage, he offered her a plastic helmet. She wasn't sure why he was paying attention to her, other than that, perhaps, he had no one else to hang out with either. He worked in some capacity for Mark but hadn't known Hattie—so he hadn't been working for Mark for long.

He was from the Northwoods, too, he said finally, when he picked up on her suspicion.

"Where in the Northwoods?" Cassie asked. His insistence on a dorky helmet didn't square with that.

"Wausau." He adjusted his helmet strap, his brown fingers moving at his chin.

She laughed.

"You think there aren't people like me in Wausau?"

No, Cassie said. That hadn't been what she meant. She'd meant Wausau was a city, not the Northwoods. It was a place with a movie theatre and traffic lights, with restaurants with outdoor seating and orthodontists.

"And you're Miss Authentic Northwoods?" Antonio said, taking off first on his bike. "Tough competition for all three of you who live there. Seriously, they should make first prize a trip somewhere exotic—Dubai, Green Bay."

Somehow it was easier to trust him after this teasing, what he was saying like what Julia was always saying to her, and opposite of what her mother had given her to believe—that everything she needed was right here at home, that there was nothing else out there. They biked in silence in the orange windbreakers they'd borrowed. It wasn't deer season yet, but Cassie understood the orange as even more sensible than the helmets. Not everyone acknowledged the DNR's calendar or planned by it when it came to filling their family's freezer.

In a year from now, wherever she'd find herself, she'd be as far from this moment again as she was now to when she'd first met Hattie, when she'd been just one of the girls in the flute row, no more remarkable than anyone else, no more lodged in Cassie's memory forever.

When they returned, Mark and Julia had found one another.

Face to face in the driveway, they resembled warring birds, one fluttering a step forward, the other hopping back. Cassie pulled off her helmet.

"Well look who it is," Julia said. "Just in time, as usual."

She and Antonio had raced and so arrived out of breath. Cassie's legs were on fire. What would her legs look like if she could ride like that every day? If she lived somewhere people biked—where their jobs and houses and schools were close enough?

"Let me ask you something, Cassie," Mark said. The t-shirt and shorts he wore looked on him like another kind of business suit, wrinkle-free and fitted. Mark was thin, with thick hair like Cassie's father's, but his nose was small and pointed, his shoulders and chest a triangle.

Antonio reached for her bike. Quietly, he began wheeling both of their bikes back to the garage and Cassie felt a stab of hate for him. Had he been entertaining her all along as some duty to Mark? She also missed the bike for something to lean on. She'd perceived from a distance that Mark and Julia were arguing, but now felt the force of Mark's anger, like Julia's, turned on her—a blind and blinding search light.

"Let me ask you, what if your parents found out you'd been stealing from Eagle's Nest?"

Cassie felt her lungs tighten. Her parents—well, her dad—had insisted years ago that Cassie be cut into the family business. Each year a fund was credited, and for more than she'd have made if she worked minimum wage like everyone else.

"Her parents?" Julia sneered. Her hair stuck out and her mascara had streaked. With her arms folded around her body, she resembled a thin mink ready to scramble for a hole. Cassie wondered if she was *on* something—one of her headache pills? She didn't elaborate her point about Cassie's parents, and Cassie was left bewildered.

Her parents wouldn't have turned her into the police, Cassie knew. This, it turned out, had been Mark's reaction upon discovering Hattie had been stealing from him, to the tune of $5,000.

"What if you'd stolen from your parents like that?" Mark asked. "What would they have done?"

Now Julia was crying, and Cassie understood this was the thing they'd been fighting about all summer—that Mark had called the police on Hattie in the day or days before she had killed herself.

But Mark also missed Hattie. Cassie remembered his tears when he'd greeted her earlier. *That* had been real, she'd been sure.

Of course the feelings could co-exist: guilt and grief. Even anger could join the party. Cassie felt the tightness in her chest fly out to her fingers, an electricity humming from their ends.

What would Mark have done if he'd found out she and Christina had listed his private lake as a dump site on their webpage? He'd be as angry as this, and for the same reason. He'd see it as stealing. *He* could have made the money from allowing people to dump in his lake.

"But five thousand dollars is nothing to you," Cassie said, flat and cool. "You're like a millionaire."

Mark flinched, offended. He was something more than a millionaire.

She could understand it for just a minute—like one of those pictures where you had to relax, blur your eyes. But his point of view was a hard one to see.

CHAPTER 12

IT WAS A few hours more at the big cabin in the woods before Cassie thought to check her phone—Hattie's phone. Since she'd turned it off, she hadn't seen the posts that had accumulated on her own flash page. Now all the orchestra girls were flashing her. *Will you call yr mother?* Even Nina wrote on Cassie's page, typing from wherever she lived now, from where she hadn't bothered to contact Cassie about anything else.

Cassie's mother was flashing everyone. Leaving posts over everyone's pages.

Cassie scrolled until she found her mother's original message: *M. missing.* Then she turned off her phone again.

Marius couldn't be missing. She'd last seen him wave from the path to Hemlocks, headed back to where he and his sister and Kate were staying. The thought that something could have happened to him along the short trail in the woods made Cassie's stomach twist (and beneath it, the realization that her mother wasn't flashing everyone because she was concerned about *Cassie*). Then Cassie realized M. might also mean Miranda.

She texted Christina.

Christina filled her in. Miranda had hitched a ride from Tiki's. Someone else reported she'd first asked them for a ride to the bus station in Stevens Point. Cassie could try to get there, but she couldn't leave now because Julia was wasted.

From outside the bathroom door, on the other side of which Julia was vomiting, Cassie said she could drive.

"All you have to do is ride," Cassie begged.

At first Cassie hadn't thought the emergency had much to do with her. What did her mother want her to do about it? Christina was annoyed though—and thought she should have already been helping to look for Miranda. *Whose phone are you calling from?* Christina had texted. Christina hadn't had Hattie's number, yet Hattie's phone held Christina's saved as a contact. Something in this was as sad as the time when, at one of Christina's parties at her grandmother's house, when a few of them had been drawing on their arms, designing their future tattoos, Hattie had written *trash* across her own forehead. She'd thought it was funny.

Later some of the moms had thought the girls did that to Hattie.

When Julia refused to leave the bathroom, Cassie turned off Hattie's phone. There wasn't anything she could do about Miranda from here, not if Julia wouldn't leave.

Cassie spent the next few hours, after another big meal, wandering between conversations and lawn games.

Who was their host anyway? People opened refrigerators, helped themselves.

It was a different kind of rich entirely that you didn't have to be home to have guests.

Though there wasn't much daylight left, Cassie helped herself to an ATV and a headlamp, grateful for the breeze of her own motion. She took a lap down the driveway for a feel of the machine. She was just coming back when she heard it—when they all heard it, and even those who'd been inside came out—a gunshot to the south and east.

"It's them again," said someone.

"Maybe they're after geese," said someone else, doubtfully.

Now people were unstringing their bows, unloading their rifles. This was to prepare to mount ATVs, to ride out to see.

"Don't forget lights," someone said. Helmets were sorted. Keys tossed.

It's them again, Cassie heard. This time the voice was excited, and among everyone in motion, Jessica was walking straight toward Cassie.

"Let's go," Jess said and then she was up on Cassie's ATV behind her. "Hey," someone was shouting after them. And Cassie understood Jess had not unstrung her bow but only slung it over her back—a violation that had to do with form, with politeness, as much as safety. You didn't count a crib out of turn, and you stowed weapons safely on the back of your motor vehicle, the law observed by people who shot animals for sport, if for no other reason than to show they knew the rules around here.

At Jessica's direction Cassie took the ATV trail in the direction of the shots.

Jessica moved her hands from the grill to Cassie's waist, steadying herself. It was already getting too dark to be traveling at this speed, and on a trail she didn't know, but it seemed they had succeeded in their head start. Cassie didn't want to lose it. Why? Maybe it was remembering her truck accident with Hattie, how important it had seemed that the right person found them. She'd been so relieved she'd almost cried when Trent pulled up. He'd helped them both out of the car, wiped Hattie's head with some stuff from a kit in his cruiser. He'd swore at them, sure. They were dumbasses. But he wasn't going to report them, get them in trouble. At the time, Cassie had thought it was because he was cool.

What had he said to Hattie though? *This would be the last thing you and your mom need, huh?*

Cassie could guess now that had to do with Mark. Maybe too with the rumor that his company was pulling out, wasn't going to mine anyway, what they'd found not worth what they'd thought. What were they going to do with the house he'd built—those glass windows, the stocked lake? A place like that wasn't worth much because no one else could afford to buy it—a problem shared by some of the big houses on Big Eagle Lake. Someday Mark's house would become a place like Old Ferdy's, crumpled back to dust.

The light from the headlamp she wore bounced from rock to tree; it actually made Cassie's vision worse, rendered everything outside its small orb darker. She pulled the headlamp off.

They just now were beginning to hear others behind them, though it seemed to Cassie they were not on the same trail but some other, snaking in a different direction. She was sure that when they'd set out she'd selected the path that best matched the direction of the sound. Why were the rest of them going the wrong way? Then again, she was the newcomer here, had never been on these paths. She slowed.

"They're going the wrong way." Jess spoke over the thrum of the ATV. "They remember last year. They caught some man in Jim's deer stand."

Now Cassie understood. You could drink a man's booze all

weekend, burn his specially purchased kiln-dried firewood, but you didn't climb his stand.

They came to a pond and dismounted. Cassie was glad to be rid of the noise—though just as suddenly the sounds of the forest at dusk filled her ears. Creaking, rustling, small scurrying. An odd distant tapping.

"The sound came from this way."

"It was. I was taking aim." Jess said this with such surety Cassie had to think about it for a moment to understand. At the moment of the shot, Jess had been aiming her bow, eyeing the straw targets, all of her senses on, like a superpower. Again Cassie felt the allure of archery as a hobby.

They began to circle the pond on foot. Now Cassie could see in the falling dark, through the trees. A low hum came into her ears. Her mother believed that trees talked to one another, communicated by fungal networks, electrical impulse, even sound frequencies created by slowly moving their roots.

She breathed in moss and mold, rust, a decaying animal body. In the pond, Cassie could see the individual outlines of blades of grass waving against the rippling water. A nearby maple trunk bore the scratch marks of a bear.

Jess saw something and pointed. The two of them rustled and crunched. Cassie wondered if the trees could hear themselves think over the din she and Jess were making.

What she hadn't considered was whether the trespasser would be dangerous. When they came upon the person who had shot the bear, who was standing over it, she leveled her gun at them.

She wore clothing that could have been any human's, thick pants, boots, a solid coat. The woman had her eyes on Jess's bow and Jess put her hands in the air. Cassie did too.

Most bear hunters Cassie knew of tracked with dogs. She looked around, her eyes and ears still tuned as if to a new channel, but nothing came from the underbrush. Only a spilled bag of mushrooms lay at the woman's feet. Cassie had never stood with her hands in the air. The posture was strangely relieving. She wasn't in charge anymore. There was nothing more for her to do. It was like when the truck finished rolling and stopped in the ditch. She'd been left with a sore wrist—aching, on fire, *sprained*, she'd think later when she didn't want to pick up her cello bow for a week, and then when that week became never again.

"Are you okay?" Cassie asked the woman with the gun. These were the first words her dad spoke to people who came in from the water or out from the woods after some incident that had spooked them. His question reminded them that they *were* okay—they would not otherwise be motoring back to the dock or appearing from the line of birch south of the trail. It invited them to feel that relief.

The woman nodded. Cassie wondered if she were as old as her mother, and then if she'd made that connection because this woman also seemed so alone. She'd been trying to remove a leg from the shot animal with a hunting knife—slow going, Cassie thought. Also, that her father said bear meat wasn't tasty. People of the world only ate it for two reasons: for spiritual practice or because they were hungry.

"There are going to be some men coming," Cassie said. "Soon."

"You need to get out of here," Jess said.

The woman didn't lower her gun but looked down at the bear.

"Maybe you'll be able to drag it with our ATV," Cassie said. Talking about the bear seemed to afford Cassie the ability to smell it all the more—its blood and fur. She could smell the woman too.

Had something changed forever in Cassie's nose?

"Didn't know I was on anyone's property." The woman finally lowered the gun. She was moving and thinking slowly, like a person who was cold or a person who was hungry.

"Everything is somebody's property," Jess said, lowering her arms. Then she looked at Cassie, motioned to her to get the ATV. "I think we can get that thing on there."

"Fifty pounds of *head*," the woman said.

Cassie heard their whole conversation as she walked, as she started the ignition. Instead of anyone coming she heard insects scratching leaves, pine needles dropping, denting the ground, giant mammals—raccoons, possums, muskrats rumbling through the undergrowth.

They did it with a rope from the ATV's kit slung over a branch, Cassie and Jess hanging with their combined weight to haul the bulk of the bear the three feet off the ground (its paws dragging, its blood seeping) while the woman butted the ATV underneath. She'd still be half-dragging it if she managed to get it out of here.

When she was gone the girls stood, rubbing their rope-burned palms.

Now they'd helped steal an ATV—given away what didn't belong to them. But who did it belong to? Their mystery host.

"Last year they shot at the person they found, the poacher. At his back as he ran."

"Did they kill him?"

"I don't know," Jess said. "*They* don't know."

"Guess we're walking out," Jess said after Cassie didn't respond. The moonlight caught the gold of her necklace, thin against her collarbone, glinting.

Mark's cabin loomed ahead through the trees, light spilling from the many sprawling rooms and porches and decks of the first floor, and from the few lighted windows of the second, including one in which a figure slipped away from a window. *Julia.*

Julia hadn't told Cassie about Mark's fight with Hattie over the stolen money, that he'd confronted and accused her at some point in the days before she'd killed herself. She'd wanted Cassie to feel guilty for her own reasons, for the things she'd done.

Similarly, Cassie wondered if Julia knew what the real Saturday night fun was around here—riding out to scare people who were hunting for subsistence, living in the woods. Harassing and even beating "poachers" had been a sport in the heyday of the Sylvania wilderness, Bud claimed, and Cassie realized something about this place had reminded her of the old growth forest preserve—the reason it had been preserved for so long was for use by a small group of rich men as their own private hunting land.

"You okay?" Antonio walked out to meet them, Cassie's father's famous question for lost or frightened guests on his lips. No one else seemed to notice their re-emergence from the trees, their dirty clothing possibly par for the course if they'd been out muddin'. Others had been back from their unsuccessful hunt for a while.

"I'm just tired," Cassie said. Had Antonio been out with the men on the ATVs?

The flames of the fire in the iron-girded pit on the deck leapt toward the star-pocked sky. People sat around it in lawn chairs, the weekend continuing.

"Do you need to get out of here?" Antonio said. He had keys. He was leaving.

Cassie remembered how he'd reached for her bike, wheeled it away in response to the smallest signal from Mark.

No thanks, she told him.

She only wanted to see Julia. She didn't even want Jess anymore. Jess had been here before—she knew what happened last year with the other poacher and still she'd come back. Eaten the food and drunk the drink.

Cassie made her way into the house where a different light—whiter, softer—fell from the high chandeliers like a kind of rain. Women in the kitchen picked at a snack plate. Avoiding them, hiding her stained hands and hoping to find a change of clothes, Cassie went for the staircase, taking them two at a time. In Julia's room, she slid to the floor and allowed her vision to tunnel.

Julia emerged from the bathroom, a towel around her head, steam billowing.

"I have to tell you something about Hattie." The last time Cassie's vision had gone like this had been after she flipped her truck, Hattie in it.

Julia knelt, naked under the fluffy robe and towel—or so Cassie would presume—though the effect of the thick robe on Julia was that she seemed more covered than usual. She still wore her make-up. How did Julia shower with her make-up on?

"Hattie and I were in a car accident. Two weeks before she died. I flipped the truck. We rolled completely over and landed in a ditch. I thought she was dead, but she'd just hit her head. Maybe for those last two weeks she was walking around with, like, a brain injury. Maybe that happened, and then when she got in the fight with Mark she really wasn't thinking straight."

More and more it seemed to Cassie that what had happened to Hattie was *everything*—too many things adding together. Maybe that was what went wrong with most of what went wrong in the world, with all the things on the verge of collapse.

Even for those other kids who'd killed themselves last year, their bodies burning across the news, across everyone's social media feeds, there must have been many things until finally there was one last thing, landing as softly as a dropped feather.

Though Hattie had gassed herself in her mining executive stepfather's gas guzzler, no one had wondered if her suicide were environmental protest. No one who knew her would think for a minute she'd cared about rocks or trees, sticks or dirt. And yet the two things were connected—Hattie and the messed up planet; everything that withered for lack of human kindness, was slowly poisoned, so casually, by carelessness—or by outright cruelty and greed.

Julia petted her arm. "You look like you need a soak." She put her soft, clean hands on Cassie's boots and pulled. They were muddy, this pair she'd borrowed from the gear room. She'd probably just tracked that mud through the cabin, which meant anyone downstairs would be able to track *her*, these people who tracked other humans like animals.

Julia led her into the bathroom where the mirror had fogged over and steam rose in visible curtains from the giant tub in the corner, filled to the brim and bubbling.

Julia helped her out of her coat, began gathering her hair, tying it with a tie from her own robe pocket. Cassie yanked her t-shirt over her head, pushed down her shorts. The water was hot, but she was naked, so she lowered herself quickly. Julia sat on the ledge behind her, brushing a tendril of Cassie's hair from her face. It distracted her from the water's temperature, the biting of the water at each square millimeter of skin surface. Sweat broke out on her forehead. She pulled up her arms, but having nowhere to rest them, she plunged them back in.

"And the beers you were drinking the night you went in the ditch might have caused that accident," Julia said. "And if Two Bit hadn't given you those drinks..." Julia picked up Cassie's line of thinking, the chain of things that might have led to what Hattie had done, though her voice was soothing, forgiving.

Two Bit was her name for Trent—Two Barrell's friend, like the two of them were the same. Julia had shown up at one of their parties once, though Hattie had forced her to leave in an embarrassing scene in the driveway. Reportedly the argument was over Trent— Two Bit—the mother and daughter arguing their claims. Trashy. (Like *trash*, what Hattie had written on her forehead.) Though now Cassie didn't believe the story of their cat fight. Julia might joke about doing the school rent-a-cops, but Two Bit wasn't in her league. Who else would be if she broke up with Mark? There was no one in the world like Julia.

Julia cupped some of the water and let it dribble over Cassie's scalp. If it was possible in boiling water, Cassie shivered.

"Let's get this hair wet," Julia murmured, rising. Then, with her hands on Cassie's shoulders, she pushed down on Cassie's head, submerging her. Cassie's feet slid from under her.

Cassie's face stung from the hot water. But to speak was to lose a chance for a breath before she was plunged down again. Julia had climbed in with her, the robe floating around them. Now she had Cassie's hair wound within in her fists and pushed her down again.

Cassie wanted to scream, to thrash, but what kicked in was what she'd learned from horsing around in the lake half her life with visiting guests' children. When someone dunks you, you slip deeper, you pull them after you—though the problem here was that the tub wasn't the lake; it was too shallow. Cassie tried to get her arms around Julia. Scrunched near the bottom of the tub, her knees near her face, she could only hope she had Julia's head under too. The robe swirled.

Then Cassie was up, gasping and clawing. She jumped from the tub and began pulling on clothes.

Julia's face was a mask of sorrow. Her robe slipped open, and Cassie could see her naked body—most of which she'd seen at other times: her razor-shaped pubic hair, the tattoo on her hip, the deep droop of her breasts.

Cassie's breath came in ragged gasps. She pulled on her boots, the lights above the sink flickering, dying meteors at the edge of her vision.

She looked past Julia to the steamed-over window behind her. No one would have seen anything. She alone would have to remember this to know it had been real, like how she'd have to remember Hattie, who she'd been outside of whatever had caused her death. Like she'd have to remember the woman in the woods, gathering mushrooms, taking a bear, preparing for winter.

CHAPTER 13

CASSIE CAUGHT ANTONIO in time to tell him she did want a ride. She needed to leave the cabin where the party around the bonfire was progressing now toward fireworks—something to light the world's sky in red, white, and blue despite the wildfires to the north. But she wondered at her own judgment when she saw his car, a little electric thing like a golf cart. Not even moonlight glanced from its plastic bumper.

She climbed in, folding her legs to fit, her hair still wet.

What happened? Antonio asked.

Cassie explained Julia had tried to drown her. She wished Cassie were the one who was dead.

Antonio's car didn't make a sound as it buzzed from the house. (Cassie imagined its buzzing, its unwieldly motion like a bee's.) They followed the long length of the private road as it crossed back and forth over its private stream.

Cassie told Antonio about the woman they'd found, the gunshot bear, that they'd helped her get away with her catch.

"I wasn't here last year," Antonio said. "I only heard about what happened last year when we were riding out there."

Cassie realized he had been leaving too.

"That man last year—they don't *know* if they hit him?"

"I wouldn't have come if I'd known," Antonio said. "I swear. I just started working for Mark this summer."

Cassie shook her head. She'd asked far too few questions of Julia about where they were going.

They reached the end of the road, teeing with the equally dark and deserted county highway. There wasn't a stop sign but Antonio stopped. Cassie was familiar with this part—the option of directions. This time, rather than be led, she was going to choose.

As they drew closer to a city and a signal, she was able to find Miranda on flash. Miranda had posted only a few hours ago, a first post since June. She was back in Milwaukee.

Antonio hadn't questioned her until Stevens Point winked by. When was she going to name an exit? When Cassie told him how far she wanted to go, she offered to drive too, and Antonio surprised her by pulling over, handing her the keys. In turn Cassie filled him in on Miranda—a girl who had run away home.

She had never been as far south as Milwaukee—the one part she didn't tell Antonio.

His car was not difficult to drive. Trees passed along the side of the road just as they did in the north, though with more roadside margin, which seemed an amazing innovation: if a deer ran out you'd see it coming. As they neared cities, Cassie's phone, and then Antonio's car, began to chirp with various incoming signals—radio, cell, wifi—all their little lights lit, in service.

Cassie found Miranda's father's name in an article about the kids going missing and then his address in another online listing that matched the suburb of his real estate website.

Growing up she hadn't thought much about where their guests were from, what their houses or schools looked like. She understood they didn't have lakes in their front yards and that wherever they lived the sky didn't darken so thoroughly. (Generally guests were terrified of the darkness around Eagle's Nest, escorting each other back to cabins in groups if they were a flashlight short, even sleeping with lights on.) Cassie wasn't prepared, though, for the bright of the city—its streetlights and lit-up signs. She kept checking the digital clock on Antonio's dash—nowhere near to sunrise. She hardly needed the headlights.

As they came further into the city, passing high rises and concrete parks, rusted cars and even cardboard tents clustered at exit ramps, Cassie understood something more: the guests that came to Eagle's Nest, humble as it was with its nubby bedspreads and battered kitchenette appliances, didn't represent "people from the city." They made up one small set. Outside her window, people waited for buses or idled at red lights with their windows up, ignoring the others holding out their hands for change.

Then there was Marius and Miranda's subdivision, one of the high-walled gated ones, the interconnected maze of which made up the suburbs west of the city. A hewn piece of stone at the entrance announced its name with the solemnity of a gravestone. Cassie rolled her eyes and then saw the closed gate. High iron spikes jutted from the top of the fence, and the little guardhouse was darkened. She turned off the car, tears forming at the corners of her eyes. They'd come so far, but she should have come hours ago.

Antonio, who'd been sleeping, sat up.

"You don't have her number?"

Cassie shook her head. Antonio unfolded his legs from the passenger seat and walked around to look at the gate. There was a little black box on the wall, a place to swipe a card, and he inspected this. Then he waved his hands above his head, jiggled his hips and kicked his legs—making motion—and the gate opened. He shrugged, not having known that would work but not surprised when it did. Cassie felt stunned. What she didn't know about cities could fill a container ship, apparently.

"Well that keeps the riff-raff out," Cassie said.

"You'd better go before it closes," Antonio said.

It was darker inside. High above, they might have caught glimpse of a white speck of a star or passing satellite. None of the houses were lit. Each after the next sat motionless, a powered-down toy.

"What happened here?" Antonio pulled out his phone to answer himself.

Cassie took in the humped hills of dirt in place of landscaping, the lack of trees. The street seemed new and clean—wide with white-painted culverts and storm drains. The houses set back from the road had the look of empties, though there were one or two, here and there, with last names on mailboxes, with sprigs of flowers on front doors or in the boxes under front windows. *Fake* flowers, Cassie amended, noting the types in contrast to the season. She didn't see bird feeders or birds, any places for animals.

Antonio snorted.

"What?"

The entire subdivision had been built on marsh, he said. There had been years of droughts, of a lowered water table, so it had been easy to sell the first houses. Then a super snowy late spring had hit, with a rapid melt.

"Doesn't look flooded now," Cassie said. Ahead of them she saw one bright light winking.

Antonio was looking around at the new culverts and drains. He shook his head.

He assessed wetlands, Antonio said. It was what he'd been doing for Mark.

Miranda and Marius's house, unlike Mark and Julia's, had been built to look larger, its rooftop high with decorative cornices. It was fronted by a brick porch with columns—and a sign that this was a model home of the subdivision.

Three a.m. made an awkward hour for ringing the bell. From the front step, Cassie sent a flash to Miranda. A few minutes later the entire house began to turn on, room after room blinking with light as someone descended to the front door.

"We didn't want to wake your dad," Cassie said when the girl opened the door.

Miranda stood within a wash of light and shrugged. Her dad was visiting his other place in Phoenix, she said.

The three of them crowded awkwardly into the front room, which Cassie might have called a living room if it weren't empty of furniture or other signs of life. The wall-to-wall beige carpet smelled new, perhaps the reason the tables, chairs, and sofas had been moved out. A staircase with a banister twisted upstairs. Their voices echoed against the empty walls.

"It makes for a good practice room," Miranda said. The giant square on the floor, its high ceiling, did look like a place for gymnastics. A glance into the next room revealed it, too, was empty.

"When did you get home?"

"This afternoon."

Miranda didn't say how she made it home, but Cassie remembered her climbing into the van of the men with the kangaroos.

Miranda led them into a second living room, this one off the kitchen, where two spaces in the cabinetry held the places for a refrigerator and stove like a mouth with missing teeth. In the second living room sat the only objects they'd yet seen in the house: a Pack 'n Play and a few suitcases, and a brightly colored, plastic play steering wheel and console.

"Nadia picked me up from the bus station," Miranda said. "She and the baby stay here sometimes, but they had to go back to her apartment tonight."

Cassie only barely remembered *Nadia* had been the name of the redheaded woman with the baby who, with her husband or partner Fred, had come in search of Miranda and Marius on Labor Day weekend and chased Kate across the lake, though they had to leave without having found any of them. It had never occurred to Cassie that Miranda and Marius knew these pursuers; that the woman, in fact, was the kind of person Miranda would have called in a jam. They'd been so desperate to find the kids that they'd gone out in a boat on a strange lake at night looking for them. The whole time Cassie's mother had them hidden in the woods.

Antonio had been standing behind Cassie most of this time, catching occasional glances from Miranda. "Is there a place I can crash?" he said. "I'll let you two talk."

Miranda led them to the stairway, passing another opened door that led down to a basement. Cassie saw Antonio give a sniff to the dark hole of it.

Upstairs were air mattresses, suitcases opened on floors, and bathrooms without shower curtains but with toothbrushes on the counter. Miranda led them both to one room. She'd misunderstood that it was only Antonio who wanted to sleep, or maybe she'd paid attention to some other sign of exhaustion in Cassie. Or *she* didn't want to talk—though she wasn't asking them to leave either.

"You guys can have this room." There was one large air mattress on the floor, a tidily rolled sleeping bag at its feet.

Miranda had also assumed they were together.

Cassie supposed she was tired. It settled all around her—driving through the woods on the ATV with Jess, the thick smell of the blood of the bear as they'd hauled it, the chlorine of the hot tub where Julia tried to hold her under, and Antonio who flopped to the mattress, already falling asleep but having left half for her, the option hers to share the air mattress or not, as if that was just how easy it was. You crawled in next to a person or you didn't.

In the morning, Miranda appeared again in the doorway.

"Pancakes?"

"Um, sure?" Cassie came to slowly, groggily. Miranda said she'd meet her downstairs. Antonio rolled back over and to sleep, declining with a half-wave.

Cassie hadn't joined him on the mattress but had curled with the sleeping bag a few feet away on the thick carpet.

She used the bathroom, and then, alone, took a moment to peek through the crack of another opened bedroom door. Light fell from a window half-shaded by a blanket tacked to the frame. Another mattress lay on the floor alongside more boxes of things: toys and clothes and ski poles and what might have been scuba gear. Marius's things. It was the only room Cassie had seen yet with anything hung on the walls. On one poster a man dangled from a high cliff by one hand. *Achieve*, it said. The other featured lines of similar text crossed out: *Quitter talk*. On the floor by the mattress sat a framed photo of a woman with her arms around Marius. Cassie picked it up to get a look at the boy and his mother.

Miranda sat on the bottom of the stairs putting her shoes on. They were going out for breakfast.

"There's no stove here," Miranda said. "And I don't know how to make pancakes, do you?"

So what was the story with Antonio, Miranda asked.

Cassie didn't know—she hardly knew him at all. They'd slept in the same room. Did she know him now? She hadn't known Julia. Hadn't known Hattie.

"Well he's cute," said Miranda.

They slid into their booth at the pancake house. The room was larger than most places Cassie was used to being, filled with more people and people whose names she didn't know. It made her think again of where she had lived her whole life, its small box.

"You don't want to join your mom in Canada?" She asked Miranda.

Miranda poured syrup the way Marius did, making loops. Most of her life Cassie had wanted to know what it would be like to have a sibling, though she'd observed enough families to know some were people with nothing in common other than they'd lived with each other through their formative years, bickering and bristling, growing like twisting branches around each other's personalities. Still, a sibling would have given her someone else with whom to discuss her parents, to understand how she had become herself.

"I don't want to go to Canada—no," Miranda said. "I told that to Kate all summer, but would she listen?"

"But Marius wants to go, doesn't he?" Cassie asked, remembering the picture.

"He wants to see Mom," Miranda said. "He thinks Mom wants to see him."

"Anyway," said Miranda. "My whole career is here."

When they returned, Antonio was on the phone. He had a new smell this morning, but it wasn't terrible. Cassie thought she probably smelled of BO and pancakes.

"Do you have water?" he asked Miranda.

Miranda went to the pantry in the kitchen, opening it with ceremony to reveal a case of plastic bottles.

"You don't drink the water here do you?" Antonio said, nodding in the direction of the kitchen, the sink.

Miranda shook her head.

"Good," he said. "Don't."

And later, he didn't want to leave without Miranda.

"Didn't we come to get her?"

"She doesn't want to leave," Cassie said. She had asked Miranda again, to be sure. But also, she'd slipped upstairs for a glance at Miranda's room. Like Marius's, a blanket hung over a window, darkening everything, so at first the hulking pointed shapes that took up almost the entirety of the floor space appeared as a forest of dark stalagmites, some as high as Cassie's waist. She'd opened the door further to see they were trophies, dozens and dozens of them. It only took a little light to make them gleam.

Still, Antonio said, he worried they should convince Miranda to leave. She shouldn't live in that house, he said. Someone had put in new carpet, but you couldn't cover over mold. It was like what they'd done with the new culverts in the streets—too little too late, and only a sign there was a reason they would be needed again.

But Cassie's mind was made up. She left her information with Miranda, an open offer to come back for her anytime, but she wasn't going to wheedle with anyone who'd decided something for herself. Girls not much older than her made bigger decisions about their own lives all the time.

He wanted to show her something, then, Antonio said, as long as they were here.

They needed to charge his car and he knew a place downtown. That they weren't *in* the city yet came as surprise to Cassie. They drove another hour, for a constant blur out her window of businesses and intersections, convenience stores and street signs—and more cardboard tents, flapping tarps, and junked vehicles.

But compared to the night before, Cassie couldn't believe how few people she saw. "Is it always like this?"

"Like what?" Antonio said.

The people were indoors, of course, inside their buildings or their cars, traveling quickly to get from the one to the other.

In the center of the city, they pulled into a charging station and an attendant came out to meet them. It would take a while, Antonio said. In the meantime, she should see something. He set off, crossing the street at a quick pace on his long legs.

Cassie still wore the jeans and t-shirt she'd put on to go to school and the tennis shoes she'd worn at the Lake Superior beach and in the woods on the ATV. She felt dirty and hot and though she was tall too had to work to keep up with Antonio. When they rounded another corner, and then powered down three more blocks, the air shifted, and Cassie felt a breeze on her arms. A lake breeze.

There lay Lake Michigan—just beyond the rim of the noise and the traffic, behind a row of buildings she hadn't been able to see around. Cassie couldn't believe she'd been this close and hadn't been able to sense the lake—though maybe Michigan had its own smell and presence, like Superior did, that she simply didn't yet know but would. A walkway crossed over another busy avenue ahead of them, and Cassie saw the hint of a grassy park along the lake's edge. White birds circled.

Over the bridge and the thronging traffic, Antonio was hurrying again. How far were they going? *The beach*, Antonio said, and Cassie began to picture the scene on a hot day like this, the stretch of sand and umbrellas. Resort-goers never failed to comment on how peaceful it was at Eagle's Nest, how there were *just no people around.* Now Cassie would see what they meant, what they were comparing it to.

The lake itself, and then the beach, lay broad and empty, the water ruffled in the distance by a strong soundless wind.

"Where is everyone?" she asked Antonio. They'd come to stand on top of an iron-girded wall at the edge of the green park. If she looked behind her Cassie saw skyscrapers, a busy boulevard, a city teeming with people on a hot day. Below lay a muddy black expanse contoured by the debris of a changing tide. You'd have to trudge another two hundred yards to get to the water.

"How do we get down?"

"We don't," Antonio looked at her as if startled. "You don't want to go down there."

Cassie had seen muddier, dirtier beaches and shrugged.

He indicated something further to their left, a long concrete pier that led from the shore. Upon closer inspection, Cassie saw it wasn't a pier but an enormous pipe.

She wrinkled her nose. "Is it a treatment plant?"

"No," Antonio said. "That's for intake." He knew how many millions of gallons a day.

"Is that where Miranda's water comes from?"

"That's where she *wishes* it was from."

Though they'd been hot in the city, where they'd parked their car a few blocks back, the wind from the lake brought out goose pimples on Cassie's skin. The wind on the high wall rocked her. She'd survive if she fell from here—the muck looked soft. But how many miles would she have to walk, and in which direction, to climb out? There was no access; there was no beach.

Antonio shifted, the heat of his body for a moment drawing closer to hers. If they were together, if they were a couple, this might have been a moment they touched, put their arms around each other for comfort.

You couldn't see any of the water moving into the pipe but now that she knew what was happening Cassie thought she could hear it, all the water being sucked like through a straw, the draw of pipe like a giant sea creature's lungs; the lake that lay so still, so motionless, was in fact under quiet siege.

"What could be more Wisconsin than beer, brats, and Classic Rock?"

The radio station to which Antonio had tuned was nauseating to Cassie by the time they neared Eagle's Nest. Was this the way guests making that drive from Milwaukee felt when they arrived? Cassie felt sick with the motion of trees out of the car window, the bumping of the cracked, potholed county highways.

"This it?" Antonio slowed as they approached the low row of fencing that marked the turn-off from the county trunk. Her mother had hung a flag for guests, a sunny yellow one with a beach umbrella image on it, but it *was* hard to see, Cassie thought—thinking of things guests had said throughout the years. It was hard to see something so much smaller than what you'd been expecting.

No one came to greet them as they pulled into Eagle's Nest. Cassie was struck by the thought that everyone might have gone—that her parents were *still* gone since she'd left with Julia. Maybe Eagle's Nest would revert to the wild the way it had been when her parents bought it, a legend Cassie had heard repeated her entire life.

It turned out, though, that there were quite a few people in Maples cabin. They were having a meeting in the Great Room— the screened porch nominally designated as a communal space for board games and puzzles on rainy days.

So much for being closed for the season. Usually locked, the door between Maples' kitchen and the Great Room hung open today. Cassie and Antonio entered through the kitchen and a woman on crutches and wearing a t-shirt that looked similar to one Cassie's mother owned came through.

"Gwen," she said, re-introducing herself as she poured coffee into a mug she pulled from the cabinet. "We met a few weeks ago."

She was the one with the little girl, now playing with the Scrabble tiles under the table in the Great Room in a way Cassie had never been allowed to play with any of the board game pieces, spreading them under everyone's feet.

Marius was here too—though not, Cassie noticed, Kate. She took note of other absences: her father. And Christina, who had told her about Miranda.

"Did you bring Miranda?" Marius said.

"No," Cassie said.

Did it matter if she explained that she'd gone all the way to Milwaukee? That she'd tried?

"She's home," Cassie said. "And safe."

"If she got home," Marius said, shaking his head, "they'll know right where to find me."

Preparations began in earnest, as if the thing Marius said had been the thing everyone was already thinking—though it couldn't have been, Cassie thought, or why would they have been lounging about with coffee the way they were? Cassie's mom hauled gear from the kitchen closet: rain boots, a cooler, her emergency aid kit. She paused to shake Antonio's hand, unsurprised by another stranger.

None of the items her mother was packing were things anyone could need for a three, possibly four, hour drive to the Soo, a quick trip over the bridge to deliver Marius to his mother. Or was someone driving him all the way to Toronto? Honestly, what was most frustrating about the last weeks, every day since Kate had arrived, was that no one had taken the boy to his mother *yet*. If that was the plan, why wasn't it happening? What had Kate been waiting for?

Now the plan was that Cassie's mother was going to take him.

"Mom?" Cassie found her mother in her room—Cassie's room. "Where is Kate?"

Kate had been arrested, her mother said. Taken in. No one was sure when she'd be released, what the charges were—or if in fact the charges were related to her grandchildren. She'd gone to Satuit, had been asking around at a bus station when someone recognized her and remembered the story of the missing children. Bud had seen all of this on the news. Otherwise none of them would have known what happened.

Marius was still here, hidden by her mother. Cassie could hear him helping to gather the gear. What if the police came here? The real police this time, not Nadia and Fred, employees of their father sent to retrieve his children.

While she talked, her mother was attempting to rip the lining out of Cassie's cello case. What she was thinking came to Cassie with a flash of horror.

"Are you kidding?"

"We can make air holes."

"You'd have to close the latches to make it look real. Are you going to ask Marius to scrunch in there and close the latches on him?"

That Cassie was the only one who could see the flaw in this plan was mind-blowing. What if there was traffic and they had to wait for hours on the bridge over the locks? What if her mom was asked to get out of her vehicle, led away somewhere? What if she were in an accident, some fender bender where someone knocked into her, and she had to be taken to the hospital and Marius was left behind trapped in a case? What if the car and the case somehow went over the wall of the bridge, plummeting to the locks below?

Cassie had been through a checkpoint herself, though Trent Lapham hadn't even asked for her ID. She remembered the sign, though, about dogs. And an actual border crossing might be different than Trent Lapham's lawn-chair-outfitted stop.

"Why do you care about this, Mom? Why does it have to be you?" Cassie asked.

"I think Kate wanted me to do this from the start. She's had convictions—you saw online. She'd have to travel even more discretely, if she could get across at all."

"Why do you care, though?"

"Why don't *you* care?" Her mother asked.

And Cassie regretted the question, that it had betrayed something so babyish in her. Was it the summer of following cars that had somehow worked its way into how she needed something to lead her, like she couldn't decide for herself what was right?

Then Nadia showed up, with her baby.

Cassie remembered the Pack 'n Play and the baby toys at Miranda's house, the bright spot in the empty living room, and that Miranda had said she'd called Nadia for a ride from the bus station. Now Nadia had come here on Cassie and Antonio's heels.

Nadia parked in the gravel lot and, with her baby on her hip, came around the side of Maples so that Antonio met her first, which wasn't helpful since he didn't know who she was or that she was connected to Marius and Miranda and had been part of a high-speed chase by canoe—if such a thing could have been explained. Antonio was picking remnant squash from Bud's garden, on his hands and knees with a basket nearby. He'd asked Bud what he could do to help; others seemed to have jobs leading toward the creation of a group meal.

Nadia asked for Allie, jiggling baby Ferdy. Antonio brought her into the house and then upstairs, where he'd heard Allie and Cassie talking over the cello case.

When Antonio and Nadia appeared in the doorframe, though, they found Allie alone in the room, as if she'd been talking to herself.

Cassie watched all of this from inside her closet, from behind the line of hang-up clothes. She watched Antonio inspect her white dresser with its green and blue painted knobs, the model of the San Francisco bridge she and Bud had built, her computer and modem, her big bed in the alcove with the green comforter. When they'd heard footsteps on the stairs, her mother had pushed her to the floor inside her closet and Cassie—giving in for once—had agreed to be pushed.

Allie greeted Nadia with one of her best resort-hostess hellos. She reached for the baby. All the while Antonio's eyes were roving: from Cassie's penguin pillow and her bulletin board with pictures of the orchestra girls to her opened cello case on the floor. He found Cassie's eyes in the back of her closet. She imagined she looked to him like a raccoon, misplaced from her nocturnal world, and blinking.

Antonio didn't move, didn't give her away, but he stared back quizzically. Covered by her mother's voice—the chatter that anyone who knew Allie would know to be false—Cassie backed through the eaves-length passageway at the back of her closet that led to the back of her parents' closet. It had been years since she'd squeezed through, and she remembered the terror of doing so when she was very small, when she'd first discovered the long tunnel that was both so fascinating and so scary. Her mother had used to make her practice crawling through it because it was important not to be afraid of things; to do things even when you were afraid.

Now she was old enough, big enough, that she might have become stuck, but she made it.

Cassie went through her parents' room backwards, from closet to the door, not looking over her shoulder to the window, to the lazy, glinting lake. She made her way downstairs, fully practiced now in leaving.

CHAPTER 14

THE MORNING LONG ago when the towers fell, Allie took to water—slicing, kicking, her vision a blur of blue. At the country club outside of Chicago, alone in the outdoor pool, she'd flipped for one turn after the next, breathless, until someone tapped her on the shoulder. *Hadn't she seen the news?*

The day hurricane Monique tore into Miami, Allie went into labor with her daughter. Early on reporters nicknamed it "the she-wolf." For days the storm that the radar showed to have a distinctive jaw shape had been gathering in the Caribbean, and Allie had paced the interior of Hemlocks, passing in front of the window's box fan, moving in and out of the radio's volume range. She ate handfuls of wild berries, her fingertips purpling, her gut wrenching. Was it time to go to the hospital? Bud asked. Each time she shook her head. And in the end, just like the she-wolf birthing her cubs—each smaller storm sent spinning, snarling, snapping up and down the coasts—Allie's baby was born at home.

Because she wasn't in the hospital, she didn't have to see any of it on the television: the people who could get to the airports, and those who couldn't; the highways that seemed from the traffic cameras to be moving themselves, though these were the cars inching

261

along—the cars and busses and scooters and riding lawn mowers, anything on which anyone could flee. She didn't have to learn about the travel rules and quotas, the decisions about who could enter where and who couldn't, who would be directed to the camps.

And she didn't have to think about what was happening to people even farther south, those who met with the other cubs of that same storm.

Alone in a cabin in Vilas County, Allie held her new baby in her arms. During labor, and briefly after, she lost the ability to hear. Not the lake, the loons, even what she and Bud had grown used to as the constant shivering and moaning of the trees. On the floor around her spread the scene of her crime—bloodied water and towels, the chair she'd grasped, the kitchen knife. It would take years for Bud to forgive her for what she'd risked (maybe he never did), the stack of library books he'd read just in case notwithstanding.

Then baby Cassie screamed, a wild red-faced thing, her nails already her own tiny claws.

Allie suspected what her daughter had done—that she'd left to take Marius over the Soo—before she came downstairs and saw the empty spot under the maple tree. Along with her daughter's truck, the bag *she'd* packed was missing. Now that was like Cassie.

Allie was glad her daughter had taken the bag. She'd pushed her into the closet at the sound of Nadia's voice the same way she'd once ordered her into a bathtub during a tornado, dragging a mattress on top. *Mommy! I can't see under here.* The same way she'd chosen Vilas County for her daughter all those years ago to begin with.

In the kitchen, Nadia had no idea what had happened—that anything had changed. She announced she had a headache after her long drive from Milwaukee.

Allie knew that Nadia had seen Miranda in the city. What had Miranda told her about them? She would hold the woman at arm's length until she knew.

Nadia handed baby Ferdy over to Allie and tipped her head back to take an aspirin. Allie felt sleepy herself with the baby's small weight on her shoulder. His little wisps of reddish hair floated, lighter than the breeze that wafted in through the screen door, and on it the first real touch of fall cool.

Allie shivered. Nadia pulled an envelope from her pocket.

"Miranda wanted me to give this to you."

Inside Allie found cash. Repayment for Miranda's bus ticket, Nadia explained, for which she'd stolen from the kitchen drawer at Eagle's Nest. Allie hadn't even realized the money, the actual paper bills—Kate's originally—were gone.

Now Nadia attempted to smooth the bills Allie had set on the table. "I'd have paid you online," she said, apologizing for their condition. "But then Terry would have seen it—that's their father." She was his secretary, Nadia explained, and accountant, and maid, and personal trainer, and babysitter—she attempted to laugh.

"He didn't send you here?"

"No. Not like last time," Nadia said.

Nadia explained that, just after picking Miranda up from the bus station, she'd had to drive their father to the airport in Chicago. She had been sent by him the last time because he didn't think the kids would have gone willingly with the private detective he'd hired—the man she'd been with, Fred. She'd known the kids so long they were like her children. When Miranda had called her from the bus stop, Nadia had sobbed that she hadn't called her earlier; she'd have come to pick her up. She'd offered that the girl could stay in her apartment too, but Miranda wanted to go home to her own house. Miranda had also told Nadia that Marius was still with Kate, and that Kate had been planning—as their father had suspected—to bring the children to their mother.

The baby was fussing so Allie stood, moving him to her other hip and rocking. "So you're here to bring Marius home?"

No, said Nadia. After driving him to the airport she'd quit. She wanted to go with Marius to Canada and bring her baby. That was what they did up here, right? Help people get back and forth?

Allie shook her head.

"She is his mother," Nadia said, standing and reaching for baby Ferdy, still fussing. "Even if she doesn't always act like it."

Why did she want to go? Allie asked.

There was nothing in Milwaukee, Nadia said, blinking like Allie had asked too obvious of a thing. She needed a new job, some other kind of work and there was none. She was tired of the traffic and the water shortages. She didn't want to raise her baby near his father. What were the reasons everyone was leaving anywhere? Hardly anyone had only one.

And who was Allie to judge.

Because she had just packed a similar bag—gone through a similar mental checklist—it wasn't hard to get ready to leave again. Allie found a different bag in the closet and loaded it with the rest of the energy bars and water bottles.

"We're going now?" Nadia asked. "You can take us just like this?" In the kitchen, she shifted the baby back and forth. "I mean, how does this work?"

Allie had no idea. It had come to seem to her, though, that the thing to do was to try it. More so, she was thinking they could catch up with Cassie and Marius and figure out something together.

Or just catch up with them. That would be enough. She lugged Cassie's cello case down the stairs, bumping it along just as Cassie always did.

They loaded their few things into Nadia's car, a mid-sized sedan, blue.

Last Allie went to the garage where Bud had been working this whole time. He'd returned from a trip to Satuit with multiple different brands of anti-freeze and was experimenting today with mixing it with his home-brewed biodiesel—the problem with which, all along, was its too-high freezing temperature. The fuel was useless in winter. Was all this necessary to mess with today? Allie had asked earlier. Their daughter was missing. In the garage Allie found Bud still standing over their deep freezer, the same one in which they kept meat, lowering in gallon-bag wrapped plastic jars of the toxic, stinking fuel.

"You have a wrench?" Allie asked.

It seemed useless to try explaining anything to him anymore.

He nodded to the pegboard wall.

"I need something to pry a license plate off." Allie had thought as far ahead as that. Nadia's car was a better choice than her own, which drew attention, but there was a chance that the children's father, if he suspected his former assistant had plans of her own to continue the chase after his son, could call in a report on her car. Allie wondered about Nadia's baby's unnamed father too—if he might be the same as Miranda and Marius's.

"Try that one." Jars of sludge in his hands, Bud pointed with his chin at what Allie saw to be the perfect tool for her job.

"Hey, if Kate gets released, if she comes back here, will you tell her where we've gone?"

"Where *are* you going?" Bud laughed but not kindly. He

laughed as if he were bored, or tired—deeply tired—of anything Allie might say.

"The Soo," Allie said.

"That bridge today isn't what you think it is," Bud said. "It won't be easy to cross."

Allie tipped her head. She remembered Phil and Frieda, the guests who'd been at their bonfire over Labor Day weekend who traversed the Soo bridge on bicycles twice a year as tourists.

If they got that far, they'd find out what the visas cost. Or the fine for pretending not to know you needed them.

She only wished she had a number for Cassie—that Cassie still had her old phone. Marius had said she had a new one, and Allie, in attempt to reach her the other day, had blasted the orchestra girls' flash pages with messages for Cassie to call her. She never had.

* * *

Cassie and Marius crossed into Michigan via another backroads route Cassie had once discovered while following someone. Part of it was a private drive, though whose she didn't know. It joined highway 2 somewhere between Iron River and Crystal Falls. Cassie planned to spend as little time as possible on 2, with its new checkpoints. Someone could recognize Marius from the Amber Alert or the news, the way Sam had done.

She thought of the trees that grew on boundary lines, state and international borders, their trunks bisected by invisible planes that didn't bother them. The branches and roots of millions of trees grew over and under and through all kinds of lines: county and town, intercontinental, public and private land.

On 2, fewer trees grew near the side of the road. Cassie tried to think what day it was—a Sunday, she finally figured—which made for some explanation of how few cars shared the road. The summer season had also passed, draining the upper peninsula of its summer population. She and Marius came upon one small town—more quickly than Cassie could skirt it—but found even the speed limit signs didn't ask them to slow. A bank marquee seemed to be the only thing working.

"Didn't the time change?" Marius asked.

Up to that point, he had ridden quietly, willing passenger, not insisting that he be allowed to choose the turns or even the radio station. He'd eaten three of the granola bars. Cassie wondered if her mother had put any money in the bag.

"Some of the towns this close to Wisconsin keep our time."

"That's odd." Marius sneered, the first time Cassie had heard him be so judgmental. She figured he was scared.

"Are you going to like Toronto?"

"I guess. We'll probably head back to the States at some point."

"Well, wait until after winter," said Cassie. "Stay south for the warmer weather."

"Huh?" said Marius.

"Toronto *is* south," said Cassie. "More south than we were in Wild Fire, more south than we are right now."

Marius laughed. "I didn't know that," he said. "That's hilarious. Go south to Canada."

Cassie turned on the radio. She spun the knob, once fast and then a second time slowly.

She wondered what her mother would do when she discovered she'd gone, that she'd taken Marius. Would she send someone to follow her?

She thought of Antonio briefly before discarding the idea. He wouldn't come after her. He didn't know enough of what was going on at Eagle's Nest, nor enough yet of Cassie. She had been glad to have him with her in Milwaukee, and that he'd driven her all the way home. But once they were back at Eagle's Nest, once she'd been drawn, again, into her parents' orbit, Cassie understood it would be a long time before she'd want to be with Antonio—dating him or doing anything with him, if that had been a budding option. She'd need some new way to understand what that was, what it was supposed to look like.

Her mother might try to send her father after her. Cassie squinted, trying to picture if Bud would do that—summon what it would require to believe Allie's interpretation of events. Her parents didn't even name the world in the same ways anymore. Briefly, Cassie tried to imagine her parents together following in one of their vehicles—and equally discarded that idea. You didn't have to be a relationship expert, just have eyes in your head, to see what had been happening to them for years, though so slowly and with only Cassie as witness, and only out of the corner of her eye.

Like how over a hundred years a forest could shift. Three feet, four feet, ten.

Only faded billboards, most with surely out-of-date prices and phone numbers, dotted the empty stretch of 41. Fields to the sides of the roads ran abruptly into walls of forest. Some may have been farmed once, but none here brimmed with food the way her father's garden did at home.

They passed through a town where a set of stoplights at the center had been wrapped up in garbage bags. Here the bank branch marquee gaped, an open mouth. Leaving town, which happened quickly enough, they passed fields of blueberry bushes. In row after tangled row, the unpicked berries bulged from the branches like a black-blue blot, more like an infestation of the bushes than its fruit.

Cassie came to a complete stop on the middle of the empty highway.

"What?" Marius looked up angrily.

In her headlights a moving sea of brown deer milled on the open road. She nudged forward on the gas attempting to part them, but they did not run, showed no hurry. She thunked the doors locked, and Marius laughed. "What are you locking the doors for?" But then the side eyeball of a deer loomed large in a window, glaring in at them. *Drunk*, Cassie thought, thinking of the fermenting berries. The deer closed in behind them, were in front of them still as they proceeded, until finally, like something expelled, they slipped from the back of their pack.

Cassie knew she should text her mother, at least give her Hattie's phone number. But today she wanted to do the right thing first and then be able to tell her afterward that she had.

* * *

Allie and Nadia gained an hour to the time zone shift, Nadia's clock, connected to satellite, ticking over. Allie had forgotten about satellites and wondered if there were some way they could or should disconnect the system. At least Cassie's truck wasn't hooked up to anything—this was suddenly an advantage of the ancient Fjord. The radio in that truck hardly worked.

Thinking of the radio made Allie reach for the knob in Nadia's car. What was the station Cassie and her father had been talking about one night a few weeks ago? One that broadcast from a college up here somewhere, and that Cassie had been listening to? Allie had tried to tune in one day at home. What kind of music did her daughter like these days?

Hey sports fans. It came on like it had been waiting for her. A college girl's voice prattled on.

"Allie?" Nadia leaned between the seats. She'd climbed in the back to feed the baby, removing him from his car seat against what would have been Allie's objections if she weren't trying to catch up to her own child, worried about losing any more time.

"Can you pull over so I can pee?"

Allie rumbled onto the gravel shoulder and rolled down her window. To still herself, to calm her tapping on the wheel, she forced herself to take in the trees as she waited, their half-naked shocks and red and yellow wigs askew as if after some hell of a party. There were so many more kinds of trees in the Northwoods than evergreen, though Allie only remembered that in fall when the deciduous stepped into the spotlight, transforming the green of summer with the triumph of someone lighting a match, tossing it into a barrel of gasoline.

She'd been wrong the other day to think this annual event wasn't reason enough to christen a town. *Wild Fire.*

Nadia clamored back into the front passenger seat. Allie put the car in gear and pulled onto the highway even as Nadia twisted around, cooing at the baby, and then, turning back, her eyes locked on something ahead.

"What's that?"

They were on highway 2 heading east, the land fairly open around them, but from a small rise on the otherwise flat road they caught sight of a line of cars in front of them, all stopped.

Nadia double-checked her seatbelt, looked back to see that

she'd re-belted the baby. Red and blue lights blinked at the head of the line.

Allie's heart jumped to her throat. Was Cassie—with Marius—stuck somewhere in that line ahead? And what were they checking for? Gwen had warned about something like this: new stops, random check points. It came to Allie that if her daughter's story about the Amber Alerts were true (and why had Allie never believed that? Checked it out herself?) that Cassie may have already, technically, crossed a border with a missing child. A felony, Allie thought. And Cassie was now eighteen.

Allie pulled over. For a second, in case she might vomit.

"What are you doing?"

"We're turning around." Allie wanted to get back to the small hill they'd come down, see if from there—if she stood on top of the car—she could see if Cassie's truck waited anywhere in the line. It was not too late to try to trade places with her. She could duck along the length of the stopped cars. She could crawl.

"You can't do that—that just draws their attention."

Allie pulled back onto the road but with a U-turn, heading back the direction they'd come. "You'll say you dropped your hat where you got out to pee."

"I don't have a hat."

"Your purse, then."

But from the rise, standing on top of the car as she'd planned, Allie didn't see anything that looked like Cassie's truck. It was possible she'd gotten through. It was possible if her daughter had taken a different back road that she'd come out ahead of the check point.

She climbed back in to proceed forward.

When it was their turn, when they were signaled by the two guards to pull over, they were asked about why they'd circled. Nadia said the thing about peeing, her purse.

"And why'd you stand on the car?"

"I was trying to see what was going on up here." The voice that came out of her now—to her surprise—wasn't her mother's but some version of her slightly exaggerated Northwoodser accent, the one she used to poke fun at their neighbors at bonfires.

"You from around here."

"Oh no," said Allie. "Wisconsin." Though they'd traveled less than forty miles, it was the distinction she knew anyone from here would make.

He walked around the front of the car to look at her license plate. It would read Wisconsin, Allie thought, heart pounding, though wouldn't match the registration for this car.

"Pinch the baby," she said to Nadia.

"What?" Nadia whispered, but she reached from her seat to do so. Baby Ferdy, generally so quiet and good, began to wail. Nadia turned around as best she could with the seatbelt on, fussing.

The guard came back to ask for Allie's ID but stepped away from the screaming baby to read it.

"And where are you headed?"

Allie couldn't think of a single place in the U.P. she might be going with a woman she didn't know, with a baby that was not her own.

"Bruce Crossing," she finally said, naming Gwen's town. Gwen said travel was being permitted as residents gathered possessions, tied up loose ends.

The officer nodded, still leaning away from the screaming baby. She'd said something that made sense enough, and he waved them on.

"Well that wasn't so terrible," Nadia said, exhaling a few

moments after they'd pulled away. "If they just want to see an ID and know where you're going." She shrugged.

Allie looked at her, boring holes.

Baby Ferdy was howling.

Allie checked her phone, but she'd received nothing from Cassie. Mentally, she flung a message forward: *Stop somewhere! Wait for us.*

Allie didn't know what she feared more—that her daughter would be stopped, or that she'd get through and be gone.

After an hour or so, Nadia began humming.

The song took shape in Allie's mind. It was a tune she knew, one with words sung in a high male voice, from an era in which people regularly sang with that amount of earnestness. Was this the one about the fair? The list of herbs from that song came to her: *parsley, sage, rosemary, and thyme.* It wasn't that song, though, but a different one.

Finally, Allie understood Nadia was humming along with the tune on the radio, an orchestral version of it. She turned it up.

Nadia laughed. "Wait—is the song a signal?"

"What do you mean?"

"'Bridge over Troubled Water'" is playing. You just turned on the radio as we've been approaching the bridge. Is it some kind of signal? What does it mean? That we can cross today or that we shouldn't?"

Allie remembered that Nadia thought Allie knew what she was doing, that she was connected to some group of people who regularly helped others cross borders.

For the lark of it, she ran through the song lyrics in her mind. What if there was a signal? What was the line after *See how they shine?*

She had to shake her head. "Honestly, I don't know. I don't think it means anything." It was true, though, that her daughter was newly interested in this station, and that Christina—last spring on the Madison trip—had talked about it in the car. And Christina had been helping people to cross the border, Kate said.

They were coming into the half of Sault Ste. Marie that lay on the Michigan side. So much had changed since Allie had last been here—mainly that there *was* such an established city on this side.

They came through a roundabout, and then a second, Allie figuring out how to navigate each one while she was on it.

That ends that set. Stay tuned for when we get back to that. And now for… said the voice on the radio.

The next music made for a jarring change, fast and loud, of a different era.

They were in traffic, passing buildings, empty lots, gas stations. Allie didn't know if they were on a road that funneled to the bridge or not but allowed herself to be sucked along.

Finally, they came to a place they could see it. The traffic that waited to cross the International border at Sault Ste. Marie, the Soo, sat stalled bumper to bumper. Bud was right—it was nothing like she remembered. Allie couldn't even see how one got into the line that was waiting to go over, or got out of it if they were in it now.

A helicopter looped overhead.

* * *

From where Cassie and Marius sat, the Soo was a zoo.

It was hard to fathom where the people had come from, given the barren expanse of the Michigan peninsula over which Cassie and Marius had traveled.

Cassie had experienced her first traffic circle—what-do-you-call-it. She'd been spun around once, aimed back the way from which she'd come. Now she and Marius waited in a small, black-topped lot next to a hut-like store, a coffee shop, which appeared to be closed. From here they could see the enormous bridge, its span over the short but seemingly impossible distance to Canada. The cars backed along it sat without moving, and beneath, giant freighters—like the kind Cassie had seen pass near Ashland—crossed slowly, regally, like the parade balloons that bounced along between buildings in big parades, like the Thanksgiving one her father said they'd used to be able to have in downtown Manhattan.

Overhead, like directionless geese, tiny black dots circled. Cassie knew what those were—not birds. She whistled long and low. She looked over to Marius, whose face had fallen, his shoulders. He was looking at Cassie in bewilderment.

What had Kate thought she could do? How had she thought it was possible to get across?

That was why Kate had never tried to come. Why she'd only half-heartedly tried to set up Cassie's mom so she'd try to do it.

"Do you really want to go?" Cassie asked Marius.

He was crying. He said he didn't know if he'd ever see his mom again. He'd seen a video on her YouTube channel where she said she missed him, told all her subscribers that she'd been trying to get him back.

"Don't worry," Cassie said. They weren't giving up. They would try a different way than the bridge.

Cassie asked Marius to read her the name again slowly. He had the Gazetteer in his lap as she drove. He'd read name after name.

"Ojibwe Bay?"

"That one," said Cassie. "How much further?"

Marius flipped to another page in the book of maps, used the tip of his thumb to measure. "Twenty miles?"

As they abandoned Sault Ste. Marie and its traffic, they re-entered the forests Michigan. The trees felt like a relief, something familiar.

They worked their way along county roads and then a lakeshore road that led to Ojibwe Bay. At Mark's friend's cabin, Jess, the archer, had said that the private road to the summer place her parents had bought, after their stay at Eagle's Nest, had been a lot like the drive into Cassie's, a maple-shrouded lane. They were passing now beneath red-dipped boughs like through a tunnel of fire.

She knew they'd stumbled upon vacation properties by the size of the homes. In glimpses through the trees their giant garage doors winked by like lidded eyes. Cassie knew what other things to watch for: the absence of patio furniture on otherwise beautiful porches, driveways too steep for anyone to have intended them for winter use, annuals in pots.

They passed a blue house with white shutters (decorative), and then three log homes. Cassie decided there might be application here for the skill she'd developed this summer, following cars. She'd relax, see which driveway pulled her.

If anyone were home she planned to pretend to be selling newspaper subscriptions, a thing someone had once navigated their long county road and then long driveway for the supposed purpose of doing. Newspapers must be hard up these days, her father had said after they'd left. Her mother maintained the solicitors were thieves looking to see if anyone were home.

Cassie told Marius to stay in the truck as she climbed out, scanning for dogs. She suspected that anyone who lived in a house like this one she'd picked at random—one that loomed over the three big log homes that had preceded it—would have tame enough pets, pets that got enough to eat. A bright blue sky backed its façade. Behind this house, and much lower, lay Superior.

No one was home. Cassie became certain as she stepped onto a thick Welcome mat and stared into the darkened windows of the door. Were anyone home they would have opened the upstairs windows on a day like today for its rare gentle breeze. They'd have opened the front door to gape in shock at the ugly truck pulled into their driveway.

She knocked and waited. She tried the door. Then she picked up the Welcome mat, flipping it over. She picked up the nearby pot of annuals, the soil dried out. Behind it she found the fake Fleet Farm rock with the compartment inside. Here was the key.

It wasn't Jess's house—but some family like Jess's.

Cassie moved through the house spotting signs of its seasonal use—the board games and movies tucked away in clean cabinets, the otherwise lack of clutter or perishable groceries. Marius poked at couch cushions and decorative pillows, each springing back from his finger. Cassie stopped at the picture window that looked down over the glistening blue of Superior.

She knew from the Gazetteer they were at the edge of a big bay, but still the water in front of her appeared as an inland ocean. The lake was larger than the plumes of wind that descended to tickle its surface, visible where they pocked and patterned the thin skin of the deep lake, striped and shadowed in blues and greens. A strip of land, the shoreline, curved northward to her left, but it was not possible to see any land across from where she stood looking north-east, nor exactly where the water met the sky. Perhaps out on the lake in the middle they were one substance. Cassie had been right that this house would have this view, would front this bay; and that, from the edge of its grass backyard, a stairway would lead down to a stone pier and a boat. It was one like those her father was forever ogling in the new watercraft dealership in Wild Fire: white and silver-railed, with twin engines and even its own dinghy, a double-decker made for a real lake.

"Are we going to stay here now?" Marius had turned back to the living room, the empty kitchen with its bar stools and long dining table, the curtains held back by sashes, like in a movie.

He sounded exhausted. He'd been kidnapped from his own school in June, let out after the last day not for a ride home from his grandma but for a longer ride north—for which he hadn't had a chance to pack anything he loved, anything of his own. He'd been god-knows-where for weeks and then camped at Eagle's Nest as if on some endless vacation. He'd forgotten entirely about going back to the city to live with his father and now all he wanted was the thing Kate had been telling him was the end goal all along—that he would see his mother again.

"No," said Cassie. "We're looking for a set of keys. They'll have a floatie attached to them."

Marius' face lit with wonder, with hope. He did know, he'd told Cassie, how to contact his mother. He could use the comments feature on her video channel. He could tell her they were coming.

That was the only way? Cassie paused, for a moment second-guessing the entire plan.

Then they found the keys on a peg in the laundry room. There too were a pair of thick windbreakers and a set of maps. One map was for a tract of wilderness in Canada, a conservation area. She didn't like the thought of aiming straight for bear country, but

Cassie packed this map too, in case. They found more clothing in the half-emptied drawers of the bedrooms—socks, sweaters. In the garage they found a back-up container of gas, large but they could lug it together across the lawn and down the steep stairs, out along the stone pier.

There was the problem of her truck. It would be easy to deduce who had stolen the boat. Maybe that meant she'd have to stay in Canada. What else had she planned for her future anyway? What else was she going to do?

"Cassie," said Marius. "You think your phone will work in Canada?"

She thought so. She didn't know what a border had to do with a cell signal. The lake, maybe, would black them out for a while—all that distance with no towers, and Superior with its own weather system.

Just in case, she would text her mother before they left.

* * *

The text appeared on Allie's phone under the name Hattie.

Allie knew immediately that it was her daughter—and also what she should have known all along, allowed herself to see: Hattie had been her daughter's friend. Why had it been easier to believe the other, terrible thing? Easier than to look straight on at her daughter's pain and grief, to live day by day with it, side by side with her own.

Now Allie and Nadia (and baby Ferdy) were following the directions Cassie had, finally, supplied. Ojibwe Bay? Her daughter hadn't been able to say exactly how far down the road of giant summer homes they'd be, but if they saw three log homes in a row they'd next see her truck. Of course she thought Allie was back at Eagle's Nest, hours away. Cassie didn't know how quickly her mother would catch up.

"Are we here?" Nadia asked when Allie pulled into a driveway, came to a stop behind the familiar bumper of her daughter's truck with its dangling parking pass and (she could see this now too) its clearly dented side passenger door. When had *that* happened? Allie heard in Nadia's voice that she'd started to doubt if Allie knew what she was doing. She hadn't understood why they'd left the Soo, why they hadn't joined the line of cars making their ant's trail over the bridge, that there wasn't a mysterious message, a secret underground signal in the college girl's voice on the radio station.

Allie had been listening to the station all afternoon. *My dudes,* the voice went on now, *it is the season for fall boots. Now there are two ways of looking at the conundrum of the fall boot, do I want it to fit under or over the cuff of my jeans? Here was my dilemma, just the other day in our local thrifty thrift...* The DJ was joking and light, both satirizing and indulgent in plain old-fashioned girl talk. It was endearing. Any girl listening could imagine herself part of something larger, an audience of girls throughout the North-woods, each alone in her truck, like the DJ herself alone in her station booth in Houghton.

That was the sum of the message, Allie had come to believe. There was no secret meaning, no message about passage over the bridge, but simply this offer of fleeting connection.

Nadia strapped the baby into the sling, gathered the diaper bag. They followed a path of landscaping rocks, imported stone with pale-pink flecks. Ahead, Allie saw the vast blue-gray-nothing of the sky and lake—more sky than lake—which meant they were up quite a way from shore. Stunted, uneven shrubbery bore the mark of the violence of the wind off the lake, its direction down from the north.

Superior glinted as sharp as an ocean, as wide and deep. In the distance, a white boat drew Allie's eye, a small white cruiser out a few hundred yards. The thin line of its churned wake formed a hairline fracture in the lake's placid surface, a line that pointed directly back to the rock pier in front of them.

"Hey!" Nadia began yelling.

Allie rushed across the yard, down the steep steps, and out onto the pier. Metal cleats indicated where a boat that size could have been tied.

Nadia caught up, the baby bouncing. "Text her," she said.

Allie remembered the phone. *Come back. We're here*, she thumbed. She even tried *Nadia wanted to go with you*.

But Cassie must have known what her mother would have done if she did turn back. She'd have leapt on her shoulders; she'd have thrown the keys in the water.

"Are they going to be okay?" Nadia asked, dumbfounded. And in this Allie heard again that Nadia loved Marius. That time Nadia and Fred had come for him and his sister, and Allie had hid them in the woods, how terrified Nadia must have been, believing they were about to disappear with Kate into a national forest. Nadia wrapped her arms around Baby Ferdy now, whispered in his ear.

The phone in Allie's hand trilled. Cassie had texted back. Allie and Nadia huddled over the message.

Drive my truck home pls.

A hard little laugh caught in Allie's throat. Never so keenly had she felt the truth of what it was to be a mother. After the initial labor ended. After the baby had grown from infant size, its body no longer needing your body, and all the interest of biology, the continuation of the species, shifted from you.

"We should get out of here, I guess," Nadia said.

That was true, Allie realized. And true too that she should take Cassie's truck. It might not be that everyone in this row of houses had left for the season, that no one stood behind any of the darkened windows watching the white boat leave—so exposed for its long trek across the open water.

Cassie would have to travel miles before she fully disappeared.

CHAPTER 15

LATELY, IN THE week since Cassie had gone, Bud had been remembering when he first met Allie.

She'd been lying on her side in the library stacks in Bud's first library, outside Chicago, in the borderlands between adult fiction and non. She wore black running shoes, yoga pants, a gray hoodie. Only the bell of her hip gave her away as a woman, and then only her fingernails, when she reached for her hoodie, that she wasn't homeless. When she spoke he understood she was from one of the suburbs, one with a word like *brook* or *deer* in it.

"Yes?"

"We have a no sleeping policy." He hadn't been planning to say anything, certainly not to enforce the policy no one ever enforced. (That they didn't discuss this non-enforcement, that the homeless sleepers were allowed by the librarians to rest their heads on the tables, was either a sign of their collective morality—or, he thought some days, deficiency of morality: how could they go day after day without commenting? Without action? They lived their lives alongside these sleeping people as if they did not exist—neither the homeless nor the librarians.)

"Good thing I don't sleep."

He saw that was true, her eyes. "I don't like the policy myself."

"Well then, we're both champs, now aren't we?" She made a move as if to stand, pulling herself up on her elbows. It was weird to stand over her, so he sank into a nearby wingback, leather upholstered, donated. He'd never before sat in this chair and immediately he felt tired. Good God maybe it was something about their chairs and not the homeless. They came here looking for jobs, for higher knowledge, for some art or poetry, but were foiled by the soporific sofas of the reading room, the lulling quiet of the stacks.

She'd angled her book before he could see the cover. She got to her feet, stuffing a sweatshirt she'd been using as a pillow into her backpack.

He didn't know, had no inkling, that he'd ever have reason to remember this moment differently. He was meeting the person, the only person ever for Bud, to whom he'd be married. The person with whom he'd create from scratch a whole other person, Cassie, who was out there now in the world living her own adult life without her parents, having begun, and just like that.

Nor had he known that he'd come to see homelessness differently.

It had been so warm that people were still calling Eagle's Nest to inquire about availability. Perhaps the fliers outside of Kent and Kendra's place were working, or these were B.J.'s referrals, though most of them did not arrive with kayaks or appropriate gear for trekking. People wandered in on foot at the end of their backpacking trips, some as if they'd been out all summer, as if it had been that long since they'd had a bed or a shower. Bud couldn't say he was bothered by it—not like the callers-in on the regional talk radio shows who demanded the police do something about the trespassers. The campers included people of all ages, even families with children who must have been homeschoolers like they'd been.

The backpackers, the transients, had their own culture, as any subculture would. Some appeared on the steps of Maples to ask if they could do a chore in exchange for their stay or a meal. (Already there was enough firewood to last until March.) Others, though, would let themselves into a cabin, leave their imprint on a mattress over which they hadn't put down any sheets. At first Bud thought they should lock the cabins. What was their liability here? Not to mention their livelihood. Allie insisted on leaving the cabins open, leaving sleeping bags and cleaning supplies. Some of those who crashed without paying did clean up after themselves before they left.

Sometimes the backpackers who wandered into Eagle's Nest stayed for only an hour or two, sitting on the dock or the beach, spreading out freeze-dried snacks for their meals on the lawn. One day Bud found that what drew some of them to Eagle's Nest was the lawn—the open space of it.

A man with a curling beard explained it. He'd settled himself into the middle of grass Bud had mowed as if helping himself to a patch of public park. He'd stretched on his elbows, tilted his head toward the weak white light of the late September sky.

"It's like coming up from underground."

"I guess it must get close in the woods," Bud said. Soon it would be cold too. He didn't say this. He figured it was the reason so many of them did seem to be coming out of the woods now. They were finishing up their expeditions, their forays. If it were the case that they didn't have homes to return to, that these were people who were choosing now to live out of doors, out of cities, or who were in transit, then they'd need to be pushing south now. The North-woods were no place for extended winter camping—no matter how experienced, no matter what gear. Winter storms were as volatile as they'd ever been, as every other season's storms were becoming.

"It is tight in the woods," the man agreed. "But it's hard to know if it's the trees or your own head. Most of us are tick-bit, you know."

"Huh," said Bud, taking that in. Now he understood something he hadn't yet. Of course he'd been bit by ticks—Allie, Cassie—practically everyone he knew had pulled at least one tick from somewhere on their skin. It was all the deer these days but also the mice—another reason it was good to have old Bridget the Eagle around. But people who lived indoors could change their clothing. They had showers, lights for checking over their bodies. If they missed a tick, if a red bloom developed, doctors in Eagle River or Minocqua would see them. But unchecked ticks brought a malaise, one that made a home inside you, was with you and of you, and became the filter through which you perceived reality.

Tick-bit, you might not know if the world around you, what you perceived, was true.

He went to Tiki's every day. Today, as usual, Christina slid him a beer. Bud wondered how long his wife and daughter could have lived together in the space of an RV and one shared bedroom behind a bar, shared a workspace and job.

Christina had something to report. Antonio had left.

Bud had liked Antonio. He'd always promised himself he wouldn't be a prude about his daughter's sex life, that he wouldn't attempt to exert ownership over her body or her choices. Antonio had hung around for a few days. He'd said he was between jobs, that he'd left his former employer, was looking for a new way to live. (Bud had smiled at the earnestness; perhaps young Antonio should go on a backpacking trip.)

"You know where to?" Bud asked Christina.

"Not back to Wausau. Said he was headed west."

"I liked him," Bud said.

"You like too many people," Christina said, but she topped off his beer. This was their way with each other, ribbing.

What Bud still regretted was that he hadn't yet convinced Christina to apply to the university in Minneapolis, or to move there and take some classes at the community college at least. He'd given too much deference to her supposed judgment when she'd decided not to try for winter term at Stanford. He should have—like a good pseudo-parent would have—nagged her.

If Shara returned to Wyoming, would Christina go with? That would take her halfway to California.

Christina shrugged.

Bud did wonder about Marius. He could hardly believe the story Allie had come back with about the boy and Cassie, what they'd done. Cassie had stopped answering the phone she apparently now had—which might have confirmed she was on the lake, or simply meant she was down the road in Eagle River, either out of signal reach or choosing to be, and as effectively out of touch.

He didn't completely mind the idea of Cassie on the lake driving one of those big boats. He'd taught her the northern stars, and how to use a signal flare if she needed it. She was capable on her own. Anything the girl could touch she could learn: the throttle of the outboard or the oil stick from the Ford, she knew sheep sorrel and lamb's quarter, food you could find if you knew how to look. Then there were things she could just put her hands near and learn—a keyboard, a circuit breaker.

Kate had something to say about Cassie's skills. She'd been released from questioning (*what nincompoops* was her report). She showed up at Eagle's Nest again a day or so after Allie returned with Cassie's truck. Kate had a way of weaseling out of anything that was hard, Bud thought. She'd left Hemlocks a mess, the fridge full of half-used groceries, the kids' clothing spilling from drawers.

"Don't be mad at me," Kate said. She invited him to the end of the dock and handed over a small joint as a peace offering. Inhaling, Bud recognized it as his own, or as Jeff's, from the patch in the woods Jeff had started and Bud had taken over gardening. Things were getting confused in the sharing economy. At the bar, he didn't use cash for beer either but let Shara or Christina add a tally to the slip that hung on the back wall. Every so often, when he brought over a new batch of his home brew—biodiesel for Shara's RV— a chunk of the tick marks were cancelled.

Ticks were money these days. Ticks and ticks and Tiki's.

"I can tell you news," Kate said.

"Okay," he said. "Tell me news."

"There's rumor of a border patrol sweep coming through here. Folks are getting tired of seeing *people* on their game cameras."

Bud waved his hand. Tell him something more interesting. Big Eagle Lakers who sat around watching footage from their perimeter cameras, the bait they left for bears or salt licks for deer, had too much time on their hands for jawing, like everyone in the bar at Tiki's who liked to imagine they lived in an interesting enough place for the border patrol to bother with. Didn't anyone remember how far the border lay north of here?

"Okay," Kate said, "Here's other news. The high school is not re-opening."

Bud winced. This had been what people feared. Each day the banner crawling the top of Satuit High School's webpage read the same: closed until future notice. Allie had heard some parents were sending their kids as far south as Antigo. Bud didn't know what it signaled for this part of the Northwoods if the last high school closed. It was like when they'd shut down his library. There's the internet, legislators down south said—legislators who'd never tried to load a web page up here.

Kate hadn't meant this to be bad news, though. She'd meant it to mean something like *at least Cassie's not missing school.*

Maybe any day soon his daughter would return. But then what would she do? Work in a bar like Tiki's? Or at Eagle's Nest, which was about the same thing. Bud didn't know why he'd never fully pictured the end game of raising a child here. He'd accused Allie of burying her head in the sand, but he had too.

When Cassie returned they'd have to figure out how to launch her again, this time for real, and in a direction with force and momentum: in a direction that would be good for her.

"Your girl?" Kate said, and she took a drag, held it. "Don't you worry about her. She's got the skills for the new economy."

Bud knew what Kate meant—what she thought she meant—but he didn't feel the same about it as she did. He didn't think it was funny to imagine Cassie with a career as a *coyote*, someone who helped guide people crossing borders to where they needed to go, or whatever it was Kate said was the version for the northern border. A wolf? No. Not a wolf.

A *monarch.* That was the term Kate had used. Now there was a creature that could travel.

On one of their first dates, back in their city life, that momentous summer, Allie had invited him to a party.

Bud had picked her up on his Yamaha at the place she was living at the time, her Aunt Bea's in that suburb with *deer* or *brook* in it. (Incidentally, the Yamaha wasn't a moped; it just wasn't a Harley, a distinction that actually confused people—grown adults—in Wisconsin.) The house sported three stories, pillars, the works. There was a giant water fountain, but no water ran in it. It wasn't Allie's house, and she gave it this look over her shoulder as she crossed the circular drive toward him. A shudder.

If Bud had worried about the monstrous house, that backward look told him everything he needed to know. She didn't belong there. Maybe, he'd hoped, she belonged with him. Allie accepted the helmet and climbed on the back of the motorcycle like she'd been expecting no other form of transportation, even when she'd put on that flimsy yellow skirt, selected those shoes.

Bud had dated lots of women. He'd emerged from his awkward teens and twenties (during which he'd read a lot of sci-fi) to discover his skill of being able to talk to anyone translated well, finally, to dating adult women. When he'd met Allie, though, he'd just ended the longest relationship of his life, and it had felt like the failure of his life too. That interpretation had translated, and maybe too quickly, into seeing Allie as the new forever. Forever was a modern romantic construct, a destructive one.

Allie—Allison, she was on the verge of changing her name—wanted to stop to pick flowers for the party. She'd explained to him already what it was: rooftop kegger with some "kids" with whom she worked at a downtown museum. He hardly knew Allie but suspected she had no idea what kind of party this would be, had no experience with which to imagine it. Then she directed him to pull over to the side of the highway where she gathered various ditch flowers and held them in her arms, losing many as they wound down into the city. She said she didn't know any of the flowers' names and that she'd never done that before—pulled over on the side of the highway to gather some up—but she'd always wanted to.

At that time, instead of flowers, she knew the names of the skyscrapers that shot dizzying distances from the street where they parked; she knew who owned them and in some cases who the architects had been. Her arm and chest and neck were red and blotchy from where she'd held the weeds, but she was beaming as they rode a freight elevator in a dirty building up to a rooftop.

She brought him to the bar and then let him be. She knew everyone else and flitted away. If it had been a game Bud would have been annoyed. He'd been on enough dates to know the pretending parts were the boring parts. But that wasn't the case, he saw. She was just legitimately enjoying herself on this rooftop, in the sun, where she was older and overdressed and too actively showing her happiness to be there—and unaware of it all. Each time she came back to him, she had something to say. It was better by far than the two of them standing around, shoulder to shoulder, draining conversation topics one by one.

"My aunt thought you were a Mormon."

"You didn't tell her I was coming to pick you up?"

"It was the moped."

"Oh yes. Well, my moped *is* Mormon."

And Bud himself was fine in groups of strangers. He enjoyed them—even a crowd like this, full of expensive humanities degree holders who'd managed to complete their programs without becoming any more human. The more he noticed how they looked at Allie, with wry amusement, with some disgust, the more he liked her. She had no idea that everyone was sizing up the cost of her skirt and shoes, that in this crowd she was losing because they'd cost *too* much. (Though the folks in the crowd did know the prices, the brands.)

Every once in a while, a gust of wind came along and blew at the yellow skirt, once to reveal a backside covered in a giant pair of blue underwear, cellulite-pocked thighs. She wasn't a twenty-something.

"I'm not who you think I am," she said another time she came over. He wondered if she'd had a lot to drink, but he'd been making small talk near the bar and hadn't seen her there. Later he'd learn she rarely drank.

She told him she was going through a divorce. She said she was sorry she didn't tell him earlier. She wasn't sure at what point in a conversation one worked that in. She'd been married for ten years.

"Guess I'll have to ask your aunt out instead," Bud said.

"I'll warn you," Allie said. "She's a clinger. One date and she'll want to get hitched."

Then she said, "Seriously, I should also tell you I don't have any money. I'm living at my aunt's because it's a thing for her to hold over my mother's head." This was not at all true of her aunt, he'd later find out. She loved her niece. (Though it was somewhat true of her mother's jealous suspicions of Allie's aunt, the older sister who'd inherited the childhood home.) It was true that there was far less money than the house suggested. When Aunt Bea died, most of it went in meticulously plotted chunks to causes related to animals. She believed the world would be better if there were fewer people in it.

"If you've been divorced recently there's got to be some money." He was taking a chance here, playing lightly with her story. "A house you sold, all his guitars you hocked. An engagement ring to pawn."

He was trying to let her know what his world was, one with words like *hocked* and *pawned*.

"I left him and didn't ask for anything," Allie said. "I said, why stay in this life when there are mopeds out there I've never ridden?"

Later they went for a walk on Navy Pier. The yellow skirt blew all around. It had seemed like hope.

Shara, these days, was easier to talk to.

In the room behind the bar, daylight filtering through the purple cloth curtains, Bud slid his hands over her naked arms, along her side. They were in bed, under a pink patched quilt. A silver mobile of stars that Christina had made from tiny cut pieces of aluminum reflected the light, made a twirling pattern of pin pricks on the ceiling.

Shara's long nails were painted red, white, and blue. Bud pulled one of her hands from where she'd tucked it between his thighs and turned it over to admire the paint job.

"You didn't become a Patriots fan did you?"

"As if." Shara's mouth was beautiful—full with red lips. She was round and soft, and not only her hips and breasts and butt, but her stomach and thighs, her upper arms. Every surface of hers curved, convex or concave, half spheres like half-moons of varying sizes. She lay on her back with one arm flung over her head and Bud eyed the infinitely traceable valley system of her armpit, of her breast and nipple.

Bud had sent her away the last time, with Jeff, who had more to offer. He'd thought if Shara were gone he'd be able to forget her. That if he could just focus on Allie—if they could focus on each other—they'd find each other again. He'd thought that was what he was supposed to do.

"The red, white, and blue are for our country," Shara said.

"What?" Bud tried not to laugh, caught himself at only a smile, *this* the most innocent assertion ever to escape Shara's mouth. But Shara did have a thing for the Fourth of July, putting up a big flag at the end of the dock and studding the back yard where she and Christina sat in their lawn chairs with a dozen tiny ones, the little wooden dowels flapping their colors their many cheering subjects.

She'd liked that Bud, while she was gone, had delivered the packages of supplies she sent back to Christina to sell, even if he hadn't known what the boxes contained or that they were from her. The camping gear and food and water and other supplies now made up as much of Tiki's sales as the beer or Friday night fish fry, and all of it was profited by Shara and Christina. Presumably, she'd have to travel somewhere again to refill the RV with the fishing line and freeze-dried meals, the tiny fuel canisters and flashlight batteries.

Bud's eyes traveled the room to the line of Stoli boxes that separated the view of the bed from the door to the bar. The supplies had run down precipitously in the last week. Shara had asked him for extra fuel, though he'd warned her it didn't store well through cold.

That meant she was leaving again before winter.

"You should come with us," she said when he asked.

He allowed the *us* to confuse him. Did she mean Jeff? To live with her and Jeff? (And what if she did? So what?)

Then he realized she meant Christina. She was taking her this time.

"Are you driving Christina to Palo Alto?"

"You know how much farther California is than Wyoming?" Shara said. "Shall I draw a picture?" She began sketching an America on his chest, Wyoming his left nipple.

"Kids go to college," Bud said. "It's a thing—it's okay."

"I think they used to," Shara said.

Here was a belief she had in common with Allie, but Bud disagreed with both women. Bud couldn't imagine a future where knowledge wouldn't be needed. Wouldn't be valued.

Bud found her Wyoming, her Pennsylvania. Oklahoma, Texas, its gulf shore, where the gulls dove in and out of the surf, cawing.

Christina burst into the room from the bar. They could see the top of her hair over the wall of boxes.

"Yeah?" said Shara, her voice low, like coming up from sleep.

"Time to go," Christina said. "They're coming."

Shara kept the keys for the RV on a carabiner attached to a belt loop of her jeans. Christina had grabbed the cash drawer and the handgun they kept under the bar. The three of them left through the side door of the little apartment and Bud followed them into the RV.

He didn't think about why he did that. Maybe he'd only planned to kiss Shara goodbye, like when she'd left the last time—that time he'd backed down the RV steps, waving as she left.

This time Christina indicated the seat he could take and Bud took it, strapping himself in.

"You have an ID on you?" Shara asked.

He nodded, patting his pocket. It was all he had with him.

Shara checked her mirrors, and—to the sound of snapping twigs and bent-to-breaking branches—they pulled from Tiki's, angling up the pitted drive. As they turned, Bud saw a small boat nearing the landing, someone else crossing to the beach in a ducking run.

"*Who's* coming?" Bud asked Christina.

But she only waved her hand. "Whatever you want to call them these days. Every once in a while they think it's a good idea to freak everyone out."

As if going through a carwash, they broke through slapping leaves, their windshield scrubbed by the pale green undersides of aspen, the heavy brush strokes of pine. They weren't to the highway yet, and time remained to ask Shara to stop. He could walk home through these same trees and find Allie at one of her various projects. These days she was back to work in Pines. She'd yanked the toilet and sink from the bathroom, had some new scheme in mind. But what could it be other than a bathroom? Bud couldn't follow the vision anymore. He was, frankly, exhausted by it.

And night after night since Cassie left, he went to bed alone. Allie rotated where she slept—in whatever cabin she'd been working in that day, or in their daughter's empty room. Every day they waited for a sound of a car in the parking lot or the hum of a motor on the shore. Maybe she'd return by sky. Once Bud thought he'd heard a helicopter.

"You sure you want to come honey?" Shara asked.

Bud almost answered in a shout. *Yes.* Since the RV had first lurched forward he understood he'd been waiting for this moment, waiting to leave, for months. He hardly cared where they were going. West would do.

Then he saw Shara had been asking Christina this question, her eyes to her daughter's in the rearview mirror.

"Yeah." Christina nodded. "I'm ready this time."

CHAPTER 16

ALLIE STEPPED ONTO the porch of Pines for a breath of cool air. With her emerged a cloud of dust from the thick-tiled bathroom where she'd pulled the fixtures, sink and toilet. She'd been working today for hours. She had a plan for this space.

Skyward, it was a day for news of the air. A flock of geese swept along on a current of its own creation, so many birds it was almost alarming. If they rested here they'd cover the lake; there'd be nowhere to land but on top of each other. At the same time, it was a relief they were finally passing, late as it was for them to do so.

Allie stepped back into Pines, ready for more work.

She didn't see any signs of disorder until she flipped the light back in her own cabin, Maples, later that night, exhausted and sore.

Almost as quickly she backed from the kitchen, whipping to survey the lawn behind her. The lake lay still. A thin layer of red leaves coated the top of the beached raft and dock sections hauled in by Gary and Bud just the other day.

In the kitchen someone had toppled chairs, ransacked cupboards, spilled a bag of flour, and pulled contents from the refrigerator, leaving its door to swing. A jar of ham salad had been sent rolling but hadn't been opened. A block of still-packaged cheese rested mid-floor. Whomever had been here had left the food.

The only things missing were the laptop and, in the check-in room with the official front desk, the big book into which people signed their names, if for years it had been more novelty item than working register.

She reached for the tool she'd found in the rubble of Pines a month ago—the one with the still-mysterious function if twice now she'd considered it as a weapon. But it didn't even sound as if Bud were home, and that was a relief too, Allie supposed.

She set out to make a reconnaissance of the other cabins. A kind of tornado had been through, one choosey in its path. Red Oaks had been entered, though there hadn't been much to take or spill, only the TV overturned. In the cabins where the last few guests had been, quietly, staying—Gary's, and Gwen and Mayella's—Allie found trace elements: a toothbrush, a shirt, one of Gary's books. An oven door had been ripped from its hinges, but Mayella's stuffed turtle was gone. This meant to Allie that the little girl and Gwen had left of their own volition, that they'd had at least a few minutes to pack.

It wasn't clear that anyone would return. She counted the canoes. One was missing. (Gwen and Mayella, she hoped.) Gary's jet ski no longer bobbed at the end of the eastern dock where he'd been tethering it. She supposed she could walk over to Tiki's, find out what had happened there.

But Hemlocks came to her first. She had a sense that Bud was gone, but if he were still anywhere at Eagle's Nest, it could be Hemlocks, a good place to hide, the cabin where they had first lived together.

But there the only signs of occupancy were those left by

Kate—some of her clothes, thickened noodles in an uncovered pot, a good lantern that must have been too heavy.

The cabin had not otherwise been ransacked, overturned, touched. You had to know Hemlocks existed to find it. Allie decided to spend the night there, and then the next.

She dreamed.

She dreamed that she was giving Cassie and then Christina a bath. They were babies to her in the dream—but their bodies were their grown sizes, Cassie's limbs too large for the tub, Christina's hair a matted nest. Someone had drawn on them with marker: *garbage, trash.* The words littered the lengths of their bodies like in that one horrible video in which they had crossed Hattie's forehead. Allie scrubbed the letters from the girls, gently, in circular motions.

She dreamed that Gary was exhuming the corpses of the old graveyard across the lake at Old Ferdy's, that after he'd brought up the coffins, he dug further. In the dream he called it an archeology project. He hoped to read the timeline of the glaciers. Then he let Allie look into the hole and it wasn't that deep at all, hardly any deeper than Bud dug to plant potatoes. That was only as far as you had to dig to return to the time before humans.

And she dreamed about Bud. That they were together at a party on a rooftop that he'd wanted to leave but she didn't. That was the whole dream—a dream of a regular night out where one of a couple has grown tired before the other. It's a small thing; everything will be fine in the morning. In a week or a year neither will remember who was tired and who wanted to stay. But whatever they decide this night will leave at least one of them unhappy. Compromise, ultimately, isn't always possible.

Allie was wearing a yellow skirt in that dream, similar to one she'd used to own, and had hated.

She even dreamed Miranda and Marius's father, Terry, showed up looking for them. In that dream he appeared through the woods, stepping along the path over the downed trees in a full suit. She invited him into Hemlocks cabin, asked if he wanted a cup of coffee.

The children's father, in this dream, took a seat on the flowered couch, sinking into the thin layer of cushion barely covering the broken springs.

Were he a wolf, a forest creature, he'd have been able to tell with his nose that his children had been here. But he was just a man.

"These are beautiful cabins you have," he said, accepting his coffee.

"Thank you."

"You did well this season, I bet. A lot of tourists."

Allie nodded. "We even extended the season."

"It's been warm enough," he said.

"Sure."

Then he said that what they had in common was their children, and my how children grow up fast. Then they take their place in the world.

In the dream, and when she woke, Allie smiled at that.

For some children, the world worked itself around to fit them. Some of those children then changed the world.

Allie walked down to the beach. She had her funny tool in her hand, tapping it against the other palm. She hadn't seen anyone in days. She'd thought about driving to the grocery store, but there was so much food here. Bud's garden—bigger than ever—overflowed with ripe things that needed to be eaten. Not to mention the food he'd already preserved, stashed in cupboards and stuffed in the deep freezer. He'd prepared to leave her.

Though she hadn't seen anyone for so long, she was not alarmed to hear the high drone of a jet ski making its way across the lake. It came from the direction of Kate's hidden trailer.

It was Gary.

He pulled onto shore like Kate and the kids had arrived in their canoes. He didn't seem surprised to see her, though he looked twice at the implement in her hand.

"Oh," he said. "What a cool old ice chipper!"

Allie was amazed. Of course she could see the function now, how the prongs could be used to chip a large block of ice, to create smaller chunks to pack around food or even add to drinks. She'd been right so long ago when she'd known it was a tool with an everyday use, just one that had fallen out of fashion, out of necessity. What was truly funny, though, was how her tool fit with her new project in Pines. After not knowing what to do with the wreckage she'd created, she'd realized she could convert the old bathroom with its thick, tiled walls and floor drain into an icehouse. She bet she could keep it cool enough to use as an extra freezer, one that wouldn't need to draw energy from the grid.

She was taking Eagle's Nest offline.

She was eager to show her project to Gary. After not talking to anyone for days the words kept spilling. It was just the kind of thing he was interested in too, so they spent awhile discussing the problem of the door of the icehouse, what Allie might use for the best seal.

Finally, though, he said that he'd been sent with a message.

From Kate? Allie guessed.

From Christina, Gary said. And Cassie, he suspected.

The message could be shown from his phone. They walked to Maples' lawn for the best cell signal. Allie had dismantled Cassie's wifi, which Gary agreed was a good idea. You didn't know who was listening, reading, monitoring your use.

The video he wanted to show her had been seen already by millions of viewers via a popular social media channel.

"Marius's mom's?" Allie asked.

He thought so, Gary said. Christina had seen it and sent it to him. She'd said Cassie had contacted her and asked if she could make sure her mother saw it.

Allie felt that for a minute—the hurt of it. Cassie had been in contact with Christina, but not with her. Allie had been leaving her voicemails but didn't know if Cassie knew how to listen to them on Hattie's phone. She kept leaving the messages anyway. She wanted Cassie to know that she was still here, that all of the cabins would still be here, unlocked and free anytime she needed.

"Let's see it."

The video was short. It opened onto a woodsy scene near a lake on a day like the last days they'd been having here: late summer, the sun bright against the water, the tree line along the shore lit up in its first seasonal gold.

The camera panned the lake slowly, first capturing geese (some of the same she'd seen today?), then a heron—it was like a video a tourist might have taken—and then the shot came to rest on an old paddleboat, half-bogged in the sand as if it had been beached there years ago. On the beach nearby, similarly half-buried in lake-lapped sand, lay a boy's hand and then his body. A few feet away spread the tousled hair of a woman. *Cassie.* A piece of seaweed had been draped artfully over one of her legs. The bodies did not move.

Allie began to laugh. Gary stared at her, uncomfortable and not sure what to believe.

"They're playing," Allie said. "It's that scene from Labor Day weekend, where the kids were pretending to be shipwrecked." The seaweed over her daughter's leg was the perfect touch, as was Marius's elaborately twisted posture, the waves lapping over one of his heels.

Plus, that they were both in the frame meant someone else was filming, that someone was there to help them. Marius's mother? Allie felt a flash of hope. That guess felt right. Miranda too would be able to read this message they'd sent, know it meant her brother was safe.

She'd have to get in touch with Nadia, make sure she would understand, if somehow she'd seen it. Nadia was still trying to get out of the country. She had followed up on a different, if more treacherous lead, through the wild fires of the boundary waters.

Allie invited Gary to a beer at Tiki's. She imagined they still had some there. He'd give her a ride, Gary said, if she wanted to try his jet ski. He'd been meaning to ask her about the interesting totem over at Tiki's anyway, the one with the lion's body and eagle head. What did she know of its origin? Who had made it?

Lion's body? She'd never seen the lion in it before. She'd thought it was just a woman. "Let's see if we can rustle up a beer," Allie said.

Tiki's had been left unlocked. Its front door swung easily. Its cupboards and refrigerator doors hung askew, but no food or supplies remained. Gary righted a downed stool and pulled it to the bar and Allie laughed at him. The doorway to the back room had been left open, and through it, from an open door on the other side, Allie felt a thin, cold breeze. Like winter. Fresh.

One very sticky spill coated the bar top where she put her elbows. Two bees hovered nearby. Could they be related to her old hive? Logical or not, Allie always wondered. It was five or six years ago now when she'd come out to check her boxes and found all her bees departed—everyone save the queen.

Another smell wafted, an animal one, and with it she heard a rustling like of newspaper. Allie stood from her stool and peered over the bar top to see the animal, a large one, sleeping below in a nest of dried leaves. Her heart leapt at the kangaroo—that it was safe and living here.

At the same time the screen door swung open again, and a man in a hat entered. He stood against the falling light so it wasn't easy to see his face. There was just the uniform. A DNR agent? A ranger? Allie craned through the window to see one of the shiny new cruisers that had been appearing here and there in the county.

The officer spoke, and Allie heard the high, unfinished voice of B.J. Spring, the local boy her husband knew, the one with the side business of ferrying kayakers.

"Mrs. Krane?" He was surprised to see her too.

"Hi B.J.," Allie said, noting how it made the boy frown. What had Bud always said about him? *That he'd wind up in law enforcement.* From Bud that wasn't a compliment. Allie thought B.J. looked grown up in the uniform though. He rested his hands on his belt, so long on his thin waist that the loose end wrapped around his back.

"Your husband around?"

"Not that I know," Allie said, more to cover the rustle of the animal behind the bar. It had started to move again. They'd woken it.

"Well, guess I can tell you," B.J. said. "Then you can tell these girls, if they come back." He looked around the bar, nodding at the mess. "We're just coming around to let all of you know, all you business owners, that we've cleaned up most of the problem. You should feel confident about reopening your businesses next season. The Northwoods are open for business." He repeated the final slogan, one of the Chamber's, Allie thought.

"Will do," said Allie, which was something she never said.

As soon as B.J. left, the animal began thumping. Gary jumped from the stool. Allie reached down, and the kangaroo raised its head to meet her palm. It looked at Allie quizzically, almost accusingly. How dare she disturb it? And who was that man—who did he think he was?

Come see, Allie gestured to Gary. It's okay. You'll love this. He wasn't going to believe it, this new inexplicable mammal come to live among them now.

ACKNOWLEDGMENTS

WRITING AND FINALLY publishing a novel over a period of years requires the work, patience, kindness, and encouragement of more people than one lone author.

There are so many who have influenced me in my life, and you are in this book too.

I wish to thank Diane Goettel, Angela Leroux-Lindsey, and the team at Black Lawrence Press. Black Lawrence Press, you put out beautiful books with engaging, important, and relevant themes. I am honored for life to see this work among your titles. Thank you Caitlin Hamilton Summie, Rick Summie, and Libby Jordan for helping me get out the news of *News of the Air*.

This book wouldn't have happened without the support of my colleagues in the University of Wisconsin Colleges English Department and at the UW Colleges Marathon County campus. I am grateful for writing grants from the UWMC Foundation and Distinguished Faculty Society. I am similarly grateful for my colleagues in the University of Wisconsin–Stevens Point English Department, including Ross Tangedal for copyediting the manuscript. Thank you to Shake Rag Alley and Write On, Door County and Jerod Santek for writing residencies. Thank you, too, to my fellow committee members of the Central Wisconsin Book Festival for doing the work of celebrating Wisconsin writers and for connecting writers from all over with readers.

So much of my life as a writer and my love for writing goes back to my abiding, lifelong friendships with my fellow students in the New Mexico State University MFA program. Those years in the high desert, in darkened bars and under the cool shadow of the Organ Mountains, are part of me forever, and when I write I relive that time and hear all of your voices. Thank you to my teachers: Kevin McIlvoy, Robert Boswell, Antonya Nelson, Connie Voisine, Kathleene K. West, and Chris Bachelder; and at Marquette University: C.J. Hribal, Angela Sorby, and Paula Gillespie. And before that Dee Paulson and Gretchen Montee. And many others.

At different times different readers have shaped this manuscript. I am grateful to *Midwestern Gothic*, which published a short story where I played with my early ideas for this novel. Heather Herrman first suggested that story become a novel. Daneen Bergland, Travis Brown, and Lauren Genovesi provided important early reads. Other readers—Yvonne and Keith Stukenberg, Susan Reetz, Julie Bunczak, Casey Gray, Alice Mills, Jennifer Stiles, Jeff Leigh—gave key feedback. Katie Kalish and Emma Whitman took photos for me, and Aaron Steffen, Paul Whitaker, and Brett Barker answered my questions about things like wildfire smoke or tree sap (pitch!) or woodpeckers—though all mistakes and fanciful misrepresentations are my own. Thank you for the website, Brian Kalish, and for being fantastic writing residency housemates, Maryclaire Torinus and Andrea Lochen, and for your clutch advice and encouragement about publication Joe Scapellato, Shena McAuliffe, and Ann Knol.

Thank you for rooting for my writing Sarah Rudolph, Rose Stukenberg Bennett, and Susan Gilson, and for always being in my corner Karli Webster, Holly Hassel, and Dana, Gina, Jenny, and Kate.

This book wouldn't exist without my family, the Houses, Hands, Gilsons, and the Browns. Thank you to Pierre, Kay, Susan, and Nancy, companions on a trip to the Northwoods that lit its spark. Thank you Presque Isle Resort, and Pine Hill Resort where I did some revising later. I am lucky for grandmothers and other family and extended family who taught me to find joy in the natural world—and to feel responsibility for it. Thank you Senarighis, Eckbergs, and the whole cottage crew with whom I grew up leaping from docks and flipping canoes.

Thank you to my father, a teller of fantastic stories, and to my mother, who read to me every night, and who, when I wanted to study writing, helped me drive 1,500 miles away. (I came back.)

Finally, thank you to my son, Julian, who loves the creatures of this world and sees himself as one of them, and to my husband, Travis Brown, who could be thanked in every section above. For every atom belonging to me as good belongs to you.

© Emma Whitman

JILL STUKENBERG grew up in Sturgeon Bay, Wisconsin, and is a graduate of the MFA program at New Mexico State University. *News of the Air*, winner of the Big Moose prize from Black Lawrence Press, is her first novel. She is an Associate Professor of English at the University of Wisconsin-Stevens Point and lives in Wausau with poet Travis Brown and their child.